THE POINT

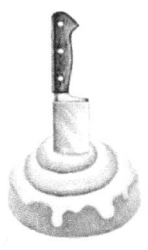

ALINE STRONG

The Point

Copyright © 2017 by Aline Strong

HP BOOKS

Richmond Hill ON L4S 1B7 Canada

For information, contact: aline.strong@gmail.com

Library and Archives Cataloguing in Publication

Strong, Aline, 1947-, author

The point: a novel/Aline Strong.

Issues in print and electronic formats.

ISBN978-0-9920399-4-3 (paperback); ISBN 978-0-9920399-5-0 (epub)

To my husband,

Davis Strong

CONTENTS

HERE I SIT A-SEWING

Here I sit a-sewing

In my little housie

Nobody comes to see me

Except my little mousie

So, rise Sally, rise

And shut up your eyes,

And point to the east

And point to the west

And point to the very one

Who you love best.

Children's nursery rhyme

DECEMBER 22   4 AM

The ingredients for the last breakfast are ready. I spread the melted butter, toasted pecans, and extra large chocolate chips on the puff pastry. I cut it, creating small swirls of tan and brown dough, and sprinkle toasted coconut. I nestle each bun into my mother's dark, old muffin tin, seasoned with years of baking, which accounts for my present figure. When I'm finished, I wipe my hands on my apron for the last time.

A crackle on the baby monitor startles me. It's in Sally's room because at three, she occasionally suffers from nightmares. She says something comes to hurt her and no one's there to protect her. She has no Daddy at the moment.

A woman's voice leaks out of the monitor: "It's your turn."

"Oooh, babe," a man groans.

The woman's voice snaps, "Get out of bed and feed that baby!" There's a loud thump, like a body being pushed onto the floor.

Picking up baby monitor signals in the ether is unnerving. The first time I experienced it, I heard a cops and robbers TV show. At least, I hope it was a TV show, what with the gunshots. Another

1

time it was a romantic interlude that a stranger—that'd be me—should not have heard.

Unfortunately, my model is out-of-date. I should buy a better one, and I will if the B&B ever makes a profit, and if Dale ever pays child support. Meaning, it'll be a while.

I slip the tray of buns into the hot oven, and within seconds the smells of warm yeast, melting chocolate, caramelizing sugar and cinnamon fill the air. I'll wait to eat one. I will wait at least until my guests have two each, no, at least one each.

These may be the last guests I ever have at Riverwood B&B. We are located off the beaten track in the Village of Forest River, an hour north of Toronto. "A little North, a little Nicer," that's the Village slogan.

I'll miss the smiling faces at the breakfast table. They're a vast improvement over the morose faces I lived with as a kid with my mother and father, or the angry face of Dale, my husband, who is presently in an affair with another woman.

I'll also miss the naïve questions my American guests ask. They think Canada is England.

"Where's the best fish and chip restaurant?" There are none. "Do you have any pubs in town?" Yes, but they're terrible. "Do you serve spotted dick at breakfast?" Not only do I not serve that, but the question alone makes me blush.

The better-informed European tourists ask after poutine, which is French Canadian, so wrong province. Fiddleheads come from New Brunswick, sorry, and crab cakes are best in Newfoundland.

But one and all know to talk about hockey. Unfortunately, no, I can't get them tickets to the game tonight. I explain they're sold out for every game in spite of the fact the Leafs haven't won a Stanley cup since 1967.

I tell them I don't root for the Leafs; I root for the Los Angeles Kings, who actually win games. This goes over very well with the Americans who like to win at everything.

The baby monitor crackles again. There's a gasping noise then an ear-splitting scream. I freeze. An hysterical woman's voice cuts the air.

"What you do? You suffocate him? You bad! I tell."

There are thudding noises, like people running. What on earth's going on?

Then a different woman's voice snarls, "If you don't shut up, you're next. Come back here!"

"No, stops push me!"

"You deserve this!"

Then I hear a strangled cry, a door slam, silence.

I press my hand to my heart.

Suddenly, a man's voice rings out. "What did you do?"

The woman's voice is inaudible. She's too far from the monitor now. "You killed them? You maniac!"

Kill? They killed someone? I slump onto a kitchen bar stool.

He roars, "Keep this a secret? To keep my secret? I'll kill you!"

There are running footsteps. Then all is quiet.

4

DECEMBER 22   6 AM

I slip down the bar stool and sink onto the cold floor tiles. Sweat's dripping down my forehead, and my heart's hammering. My heart is damaged from childhood scarlet fever, but my doctor thinks heart attacks are unlikely.

Surely I've misunderstood. It had to be a TV show. Except, it didn't sound like any TV show I've ever heard. I tug my phone from my tight jean's pocket. I have to call, report, get help.

But I can't punch 911. I can't call the police. I know I should call the police; that's what a normal person would do. A normal person would call and say, "Police, I think I heard a murder, or two." But I can't. The police are my enemy.

I hear a loud thump in the hallway. My heart ricochets in my chest again. But it's only Andy Nash. He crashes open the kitchen door and hollers, "How's the cow, Sira?"

There he stands, all 6 feet of him, broad-shouldered, broad-hipped without an ounce of fat. He's dressed in loose jeans and a red flannel shirt. Nora, his petite wife, scrambles to his side, adjusting her soft pink vest over a blouse stenciled with fairies. With her small chin and bright green eyes, she looks like the Tinker Bell fairy. She says something to Andy but in an English so fast I can't catch a word.

My job for the next while is to pretend all is normal. Isn't all normal, except…? I smile over-brightly and speak in a high-pitched camp counselor voice.

"Okay! Well then everybody, let's go into the dining room for a yummy gourmet breakfast. And what's on the menu today? Well, we have French vanilla coffee, white fruit salad of starfruit, white grapes and mangosteins. And in a minute, hot cinnamon buns! Mmmm."

I bundle them into the dining room where Nora giggles, turns to her husband, and launches into one of those high-speed utterly incomprehensible Newfoundland speeches.

I back into the kitchen to snatch the cinnamon buns from the oven. They are sizzling and syrupy. With still trembling hands, I lift a gooey bun from the tray and tear off a hot strip, downing it without caution. The sugary dough slips into my parched throat and drowns my frightened brain. That's better. That's what I needed. Sugar, my drug of choice.

Andy calls from the dining room. "Sira, we were t'rilled wit' downtown Torono. Never seen so miny restaurans of ivery nationality. Loik Asian and African and Indian. How do ya manage to eat it all? We can't wait to get back to Brinch to lose some of this weight." He laughs.

I call back, "Losing weight? It's my life's work."

I struggle to leave the remaining buns on the plate and rush to the table. There's an intake of breath as they smell the warm cinnamon, sugar, and chocolate aromas.

I leave them reaching for glory, and hurry back into the kitchen. My hands still tremble as I slice two thick wedges of homemade bread for their French toast. Delayed shock's setting in. I dip each piece of bread into a mixture of egg and cream, not milk. Only the best for my guests. Sumptuous breakfasts are what my B&B's known for.

As I dribble two large drops of hazelnut liqueur into the egg mixture, my hands start trembling more. I pour a little liqueur into a

6

glass and down it. The heat of the liquid hits my stomach, mixing nicely with the resident cinnamon bun mash. I could go on like this for hours, but there's breakfast to be cooked.

I set the bread in the electric frying pan and the smell of browning butter and hazelnut liqueur's a balm to my brain. I pour and drain another glass of liqueur then screw the top back on the bottle.

Andy calls out, "Did ya know, Sira, oi hiv ancestors who came to Newfoundland in 1767?"

"No, tell me more," I call back. I pull out the ancient egg poacher, which clatters on the black marble countertop. Because the decorator said it was all the rage at the time, Dale had to have it. That was Dale.

The noise when we put something on it rattles everyone's nerves, but the kids' rooms are upstairs at the far end of the house. Anyway, they've learned to sleep through early morning B&B noises.

Nora chimes in, "Me family settled in Newfoundlind then, too. D'at's woi we loves it so."

I knock three shots of Tabasco into the lemon and egg Hollandaise sauce, and then set a homemade English muffin on pretty flowered plates.

"We loves Brinch more d'in inywhere in the world, and we've trivelled, hiven't we, Andy? Been to Germiny, which oi loves, and Frince, even Disneyland. Bot for us, nowhere's as lovely as Brinch."

I call back a response while plating the Eggs Benedict. "But Branch is so small, isn't it? I mean, don't you feel root-bound?"

I top the English muffin with pea meal bacon and a firm white, runny-yolk poached egg, a slug of the Hollandaise sauce on top and a dusting of cayenne pepper.

"Yis," says Andy, "Bot, we're Brinchites first, Newfoundlinders second, and uh, roit, third, proud Canidians."

He stops to ogle the food as I come through the door. Who wouldn't? Hot fudge sauce, French toast, and Eggs Benedict.

My own mouth's tingling, but I watch as they lean in to pick their choice, getting my delight from their radiant faces.

While they eat, I talk, mostly to distract myself from the food and from the memory of those voices on the baby monitor.

"Surely it's a little stifling in Branch? I mean, you've known everyone and they've known you all your lives."

"Roit," says Andy, cutting into the soft yolk of his egg as a dollop of Hollandaise sauce slips down into it. "We've known everyone our entire loives." He smiles with his soft brown eyes.

Nora interrupts. "We wouldn't lives inywhere else, even t'oh we both hiv degrees from university."

The Nashes arrived yesterday morning, but this is the first chance I've had to talk to them in detail. The kids dominated their attention, especially Andy's. They're on the needy side for father substitutes.

"I was a Library Science major." I don't tell them I didn't get an MLS because I couldn't afford to stay in school that long. But I imagine an undergraduate education's as high as they went, too. "What did you study in university?"

"Andy studied Geogriphy, has a Master's, and I hiv an MSW." Well, that puts me in my place. "And d'oh I don't work in Brinch for me job, I come home to Brinch. And d'at's what comfort is."

Nora, wrinkling her nose in pleasure, lifts a sticky waffle off the plate and ladles on the hot fudge sauce. I know I have to wait until they've each taken one. I look at Andy. He looks at me. I look at the waffle plate. He gets it.

Once his is taken, I snatch one and douse it with hot fudge. I sink my teeth into the waffle. That crisp outside and soft fudge in the wells make me shiver and tingle. I know this is a sexual substitute, I know that. But hey, better than the nothing. And soon my worries about those voices on the baby monitor slip away as I sink into a deep, satisfying sugar high. When Dale first met me, he insisted I looked like Marilyn Monroe. Nowadays, she's considered 40 pounds overweight.

I pour myself a mug of the hazelnut coffee, add cream but no sugar. I have to cut back somewhere. They're looking at me. Is it my turn to talk? The sugar has my brain in a fog already. What were we talking about?

"Canida," says Nora, as if I'd asked out loud. Did I?

"Okay, so you claim to be Branchites first, then Newfoundlanders, leaving Canadian a distant third. I feel rejected."

Now why did I say that? These people are paying guests. They can feel however they like about whatever they like. When I'm in the sugar, I say inappropriate things, like an alcoholic.

Andy swallows. "Oi loves me country, whatever it's called."

Nora steers the conversation to safer shores. "Did you know, Sira, when we visited Ireland, 'd'ey tought we were Irish, but couldn't tell from which part." She grins. "When me ancestors came to Canida from Ireland, the fishing villages were so far apart, and d'ey only saw jist supply boats once a year. So, d'ey kept talking d'way d'ey'd been taught. Now, 300 years later, d'eir descendants speaks a version of ancient Irish." She laughs.

"I could listen to your accents all day."

"Sira, if me and Andy gets going, oi bets you won't recognize it as English."

Having experienced this already, I've no desire to take that bet.

"Oh, Andy." Nora giggles, pointing to the twig of mistletoe I hung above the table. "Will yous looks at d'at?"

Andy bounds up in one leap, grabs her and kisses her with gusto. Nora wraps her small arms around his bulging neck, her straight blonde hair shaking with the effort.

I hold my breath. I haven't had a romantic kiss in more than two years and even then, I never experienced such a kiss.

Andy sighs. "D'at was a marvelous good breakfast, Sira. Now, how do we pays?"

I stand up so fast I knock over my chair. I'm drunk with sugar, yes, but not blind to cash. Until I get a job, theirs is all the money I have for Christmas.

They join me in the dark front hall as I take out the green metal cash box from the oak hall table. The table's worth $60. I checked on eBay. I know what I can get for every piece of furniture I have. It's not enough to keep us afloat. It's going to take another two or three years for the B&B to be fully profitable, and I've no more savings. I need a job to support my little family since Dale refuses.

When Dale was forced to give me a paltry alimony amount as a onetime payout, I used it to renovate the house into a B&B. I'd always wanted to run a B&B, but when we were together, he wouldn't hear of it.

"I'm not having strangers roaming around in my house."

"Tons of other people do it," I said, "and there's been no trouble."

"Trouble's just around the corner," he countered.

It was something to consider, I suppose. So I said, "I'll put in a partition to enclose the staircase leading to our quarters."

His face bloomed red. "You're not going into business and compete with me!" And he stormed out of the house.

In these last two years, he has sent exactly one child support payment. As a result, my checking account is at zero. On the other hand, we have a great asset in this house cum business. Asset rich, cash poor, just like the big boys.

So why do I want him to move back in? Is the illusion of being a happy family again so much more important than my having a happy relationship? Yes, it is. I'll take that.

Andy throws his arm around my shoulders. "Sira, you hiv an open invitation to visits us in Brinch, anytime…."

Nora interrupts. "Bot, oi wouldn't recommends winter."

"Or Spring," Andy adds. "Bot, July sometimes has good days."

I nod, amused. "Newfoundlanders love to talk about their bad weather."

"And d' worse it is, d' more we loves to talk about it." Andy grins.

Nora winks. "Shows we're tough."

They leave and I'm left alone with the memory of those voices on the baby monitor. My hands begin to tremble again. I am not tough.

3

DECEMBER 22   8 AM

Why don't I call the police, for heaven's sake? I shake my head. I can't. The police have made my skin crawl.

"Raid! This is a raid! Stop what you're doing and come out, Mr. Forsyth!"

That day, six-year old me was in my bedroom enjoying my Grade 1 reader about Dick and Jane and Spot. Dick and Jane were playing with Spot who wouldn't give up the red ball. How would it end?

The shouting in the front of the house startled me. I dropped my book on my bed, my heart pounding, and tiptoed into the hall. I saw two huge, black-uniformed officers looming over my pale father.

"Where are your betting slips, Mr. Forsyth?"

I knew. I sneaked back down the hall into the den where Dad kept all these bits of paper. So, these were betting slips and bad, apparently. I grabbed them up, crept to the bathroom, and flushed them down the toilet. A few scraps fell from my shaking hands, scattering on the pink floor mat, but I scooped them up and flushed

11

them all away. Brave Sara had saved her father from the big bad police.

I snuck back to the kitchen. The cops had Dad in handcuffs and one was pushing him out of the front door while the other snooped around the house. I saw the neighbours gaping at us from the sidewalk. Ronnie Judd, and her slack-jawed mother, her mean, skinny father, and her three thieving brothers were thrilled by the turn of events. It was usually their house that attracted police attention.

My mother was sobbing. She grabbed her purse, turned to me, and pointed at the kitchen table.

"Eat that for dinner."

The police officer growled, "We'll be back tomorrow. Do not touch anything."

She ran out the door and he followed her. I slammed it shut in the Judd's gargoyle faces. I could spell gargoyle if I wanted. I won the spelling bee this year.

The house was quiet but my heart was still beating fast, too fast. I'd had Scarlet Fever the year before and my heart wasn't back to full strength. I was six years old, home alone, and my father'd been taken away by policemen.

What my mother had suggested I eat for dinner was a freshly baked chocolate cake. I looked at the chocolate cake and it looked at me. Only one of us survived that night, and it wasn't the chocolate cake. I got a stomach ache, of course, but from that moment on, food became my best friend, always there when I needed it.

Even though the cops combed through the house again the next day, they couldn't find any evidence of gambling. I had done a good job. Dad came home.

They couldn't figure out where he was getting the money to cover his illegal bets, but I knew. I heard my parents' constant fighting.

"Seymour, your clients believe you've sent in their insurance premiums. They think they're covered by SunnyCare for their homes, their cars, or their life insurance. What if someone makes a claim? The company won't pay."

"You're such a worry wart, Lorna. I've got a bet this game. If the number spread comes out right, it'll be steaks tonight, sweetheart. No one's going to make a claim before Monday. And I'll have a bundle of cash by then. I'll send in their premiums a bit late, that's all. Now be quiet. I can't hear the TV."

"At least stop taking bets for other people. It's illegal to be a bookie, you know that. "

But he never listened. His eyes were always glued to the TV, feverish and overly bright. The police raided us regularly after the first time, getting meaner and rougher. The thought of them still tightens my throat.

I imagine what will happen if I do call the cops to tell them I overheard a murder. A squad of cop cars will come zooming down our street, sirens blaring, waking the whole neighbourhood.

My two children will rush down the stairs in their pajamas, bleary-eyed from disturbed sleep. They'll sit on the stairway frozen with fear, as I had, watching a parent interrogated by big, black-uniformed men. The memory alone's enough to start my heart ricocheting in my chest.

Maybe I misunderstood what I heard on the baby monitor. What if it was just a play rehearsal? The local acting troupe uses the Forest Village Golf and Country Club for plays, and it's only four blocks away.

My sane brain intervenes. Why would a Golf and Country Club have a baby monitor? I'm grasping at straws. I rub my temple, a headache beginning. Ronnie taught me a calming technique she learned at the Beau Vista You Spa.

"You have to sit up straight, keep your chin level, close your eyes and look between your eyebrows. Then breathe in Calm, and breathe out Stress. Sometimes you fall asleep but you're not supposed to."

Ronnie Judd and I grew up together. Now she's married to Marshall Stohl, an important village lawyer. He's tight with money and affection, but they have a house far nicer than the one she grew up in. She settled.

I can't call the police, but I can call Ronnie. She'll tell me how to proceed without involving cops. She's phobic about them, too, due to her own childhood with her slimy brothers.

I punch in her phone number. She doesn't pick up. That's not like her. If she sees it's me, she always picks up. I call again, letting the phone ring longer.

Finally, a chirpy voice answers, "Beau Vista You Spa."

I look at my phone, puzzled. Ronnie's in New Mexico at this luxurious spa, but I dialed her private cell number.

"May I speak to Ronnie Stohl?"

"One moment, please." I wait. I wonder if she's shopping. She does that to excess sometimes. She even buys me gifts. Doesn't everyone love black velvet paintings of big-eyed children? And like the angel friend that she is, she buys the kids toys, good toys.

Dale never sends toys. The last time the kids asked him for one, he emailed me.

Medusa, your little manipulation won't work. You force our kids to write me for money? I thought your B&B was a big success. Didn't I tell you I wouldn't put a nickel into it because it would fail? You probably eat all the profits, hahaha.

When Ronnie read that message she exclaimed, "How can you let him call you that?"

"Call me what?"

"Medusa! Snakes for hair?" She shuddered.

"It's his pet name for my hair, which he loves."

"That insult is not love."

I lodged my only defense. "But he smiles when he says it."

We laughed at that until it hurt.

The spa operator comes back on the line. "I'm ringing her room, but there's no answer. She must be having a treatment. Would you like to leave a message?"

This is strange. "No, I'll try again later."

Missing people make me nervous. Seven years ago when I hadn't heard from my parents for a couple of days, I drove to their house. It was on fire. Both died. No one ever found out who set it, but I figure it was one of Dad's disgruntled gambling creditors. The police closed the case after a year.

There was no fire insurance, of course. My dad wasn't insured for anything. Our premium money, like that of his clients, went to his gambling addiction.

The sale of the lot their house had paid for their funerals, but nothing more. There was only one asset I inherited, a secret my mother kept from my father and me.

It was a large diamond and pearl ring owned by my grandmother, inherited by my mother, and now by me. The insurance evaluation attached said it was a flawless two-carat diamond with seed pearls, appraised five years before at $25,000. In my mother's handwriting was a note: "Grandma's engagement ring."

My mother had kept it hidden in a safety deposit box for all those years, and there was no question why. Dad's fever knew no bounds. He'd have pawned that ring in a second to gamble, and that would have been that. She also hid it from me because I would have spilled the beans. I loved my father. When he was flush, he hugged me and bought me lovely presents.

That Dad never served jail time was a miracle, or a tragedy, depending on how you looked at it. Maybe if he'd gone to jail once, he'd have stopped.

I begged him to quit once, but he said, "I can't. The sounds of the casino, the feel of the chips in my hand, the excitement of a win at the race course is exhilarating. Of course, it's less fun than it used to be, I don't know why. But I've lost so much, I have to score just one big one, then I'll stop."

When he saw the tears in my eyes, he cradled my hands in his large, warm ones.

"Sara, sweetheart, I'll tell you what. I won't bet on election outcomes anymore. How's that?"

His winnings never covered the insurance claims he had to pay out as if he were SunnyCare. That way his clients never guessed he hadn't sent in their insurance policies and kept paying their monthly premiums, which he gambled away.

We went without new clothes, occasionally food, even medication if he was having a long streak of bad luck. He expressed sincere regret about this, but never stopped. The pleasure he got was worth the pain. Of course, he got the pleasure; we got the pain.

I thank my lucky stars to this day I didn't inherit my father's gambling gene. Unfortunately, I did inherit my mother's coping mechanism, bingeing on food to push down feelings.

I dip the last waffle into the congealing fudge sauce and don't stop until both are gone. Then, with sticky fingers I text Ronnie again.

Where the heck are you? I need to talk to you. I think I heard a murder.

That should get a response.

DECEMBER 22   9 AM

Ronnie always leaves her phone in her room when she goes to Beau Vista You Spa to avoid calls from Nurse Kim Park, who doesn't approve of Ronnie's eating.

"You fat. Too much too much. I take away," Kim always says, and snatches dishes off the table before Ronnie can take a second helping.

Kim Park lives with the Stohls, on call to Marshall 24-hours a day. She's a tiny, bob-haired Korean who's fiercely protective of Marshall because he's doing pro bono work to get her two teenage children into Canada.

Her English may be ESL, but she gets her point across. She lectures Marshall, too.

"Be patience. Things improvement soon. Maybe tomorrow."

I like her. She cooks Marshall kimchi-laced Korean dishes, which is the only food he enjoys now. Sometimes I drop over for dinner. Who doesn't like Korean pancakes studded with shrimp, pork, and green onion?

Though things haven't improved for Marshall because of his illness, they have for Ronnie. Once he no longer controlled their finances, she burned through their credit cards till they smoked. That's how she's at Beau Vista You, the famous beauty spa of movie stars and wives of rich, sick men.

I check my emails again for a message from her. There it is but from the Spa's computer.

You won't believe what happened! When I read your text about a murder, I dropped my phone into the toilet!!! The spa got it out, but no-no-no, it'll never touch my shell-like ear again! I'll buy a new one when I get home. They're forwarding my calls to the reception desk if you need me.

Oh, and Sarie, the desserts here are to die for, but so low cal, I can eat all I want and still lose weight! I'm down almost a pound. Bet I'm beating you! I'm not sleeping well, though. I'm so tired I feel like a slump on a log.

Vintage Ronnie. She regularly makes verbal gaffs, like the fictional Mrs. Malaprop, who said, "It was the *pineapple* of my experience" instead of the pinnacle.

Marshall was fuming when he told me Ronnie's latest misspeaks, which had publically humiliated him for the last time.

"I was at the Three Coins Cafe for lunch with my newest, biggest client, Stanley Ansell, the rich owner of three Chicken Chalet franchises. Hirsch Reynolds, my accountant, was there along with Jules Stringer, my old friend from law school, now a Toronto District Attorney.

"Ansell was on his usual soapbox, trying to get us all to buy a Chicken Chalet franchise from him. He pressed us, 'Gentlemen, for the millionth time, what're you waiting for?'

"Stringer leaned forward aggressively in his best district attorney manner. 'Ansell, you made a million bucks because you got in on the ground floor. Will you admit there's far more competition in fast food now?'

"Reynolds joined in the attack. 'We've crunched the numbers on franchising. With the right company, and at least two stores, you might make money. But Chicken Chalet franchises costs a hundred thousand to start.'

"'That's chump change.'

"'Not if you haven't got it, Ansell,' Stringer said. There was a knowing silence. Lawyering hasn't been good to most of us lately, which was why a big client like Stanley Ansell was so important to me.

"Reynolds wouldn't let up. 'Ansell, what do you do with the feathers?'

"He boomed, 'We sell them for pillows! Unlike your businesses, there isn't an ounce of waste. Invest! Get rich!'

"I wasn't going to risk my precious money on any project with him, but I didn't want to alienate him, either. I clapped him on the shoulder. 'Leave Ansell alone, you losers. Feathers are how he affords my exorbitant fees.' Then I changed the subject quickly. 'Hey where's our lunch?'

"I craned my neck and saw our waitress, Margie, leaning on the lunch counter, her big rump swaying back and forth commiserating with Hank Samuels, the thin dairy farmer whose wife died last spring. I waved a little so as not to bring on her usual tirade: 'I'm not anyone's servant, Mister.'

"Margie spun around but not to acknowledge me. She snapped on the radio. It was time for the popular local confession show, 'Wish You Could Say It Out Loud?'"

As I listened to Marshall's story, I said, "I've never heard it. Who has that kind of time to waste?"

"Well, you're missing something, Sara," Marshall replied with a chuckle. "It used to be the funniest part of the week for me. Ernie Poole, the brash, humiliating radio host uses our villagers as witless victims to entertain the secret, salacious side of the rest of us.

"Uncle Ernie, as he calls himself, poses a prying, outrageous question on the air, then people, mostly women, call in to reveal their secret thoughts and actions. Why they do it, I've no idea. Most of the time, they only give their first initial, but sometimes you recognize the voice.

"And after that, anyone who heard it in town walks around with downcast eyes to avoid any member of that family. It's social suicide. But, some people are either that stupid, or that desperate to get things off their chest.

"So naturally when the show came on, every face in the café turned to look at the radio as if it were a TV. Ernie's voice, now low and confidential, whispered, 'Today's question: Who's having an extra marital affair?'

"I scanned the crowd in the café. Did I notice a few red faces?

"Poole crooned to his first caller: 'Wish You Could Say It Out Loud? Tell Uncle Ernie your first initial, sweetheart.'

"I wasn't interested. I was trying to gauge the right moment to mention this year's retainer to Stanley Ansell. I needed to squirrel away the money in my Swiss account before Ronnie found out about it."

"Excuse me?" I interrupted Marshall again. "You hide money from your wife?"

"Come on. You know she's a shopaholic. I have to protect our future."

"Maybe she wouldn't be such a shopaholic if you gave her an adequate house allowance. She calls you Marshall the Miser."

"I am not!

I pursed my lips.

"Listen, do you want to hear the rest of this story or not?"

"Keep talking, miser."

He glared at me but he wanted to tell me the whole thing.

"The woman on the radio said, 'I'm R.S. and I have a perfect life except for one thing.'

"I froze. The guys at the table didn't recognize the voice, but I did. It was Ronnie, my wife on a radio show whose subject was extra marital affairs.

"I felt a cough in my throat. It'd been annoying me for a few weeks, never getting better. I suppressed it. I had to hear what she was going to say.

"Ansell hissed, 'Her perfect life doesn't seem to include her husband if she's having an affair.' My friends grinned.

"R.S. continued, 'I had to have an affair because my husband can't give me a child. He took tests, and he's, uh, impotent.'

"It was vintage Ronnie. She said impotent but she meant infertile. And yes, we found out I'm infertile, mumps as a kid. But I'm definitely not impotent.

"Everyone at our table sat still, eyes assiduously avoiding mine. They'd recognized Ronnie's style. And they knew I knew.

"'Tell me more, sweetheart,' Poole urged, probably afraid she'd hang up after dropping her load.

"'I had to take up with another man, a milkman...' soft guffaws from the tables around us, 'because I know milkmen have the manliness to give me a child because they drink milk,' her voice spun on, 'which is good for the manly man.'

"We were all glued to our spots while the café erupted in raucous guffaws. Thank God the cough I'd been suppressing rose full force. I hacked so hard I couldn't catch my breath. My companions competed with each other to pound me on the back.

"I shook them off, stumbled out of the restaurant, and coughed all the way to my car, a red Veloster, the impotent man's substitution?

"I collapsed in the driver's seat, my chest heaving, trying to get a full breath. What was this, pneumonia or something? I'd call Dr. Subrisco for an overdue physical tomorrow. But before that, I was going home to kill Ronnie!

"I revved my engine to race home but I saw the gas gauge was grazing E. More Ronnie. That woman wouldn't put gas in if she had a million dollars. I pulled into our regular gas station. Tony, the attendant, ambled over. I gave him a thumbs up, our shorthand for a fill, but he knocked on my window. I opened it.

"'Hey, Mr. Stohl, had your milk today? It's good for the manly man,' he snickered. I stiffened. Was he making sly fun of me? Tony knew Ronnie. Or would Tony have said that to anyone who drove up just then.

"What if everywhere I went in the village someone mentioned drinking milk and laughed. Everyone would be mentioning it for weeks, no doubt about that. I'd never know if they were enjoying a village joke, or making me the village joke.

"My wife was having an affair. That was hard enough to take. My wife was having an affair and announced it on the radio? That was bad, but even worse, my wife was having an affair because I was impotent? How could I conduct business with my male clients and colleagues after that? And it wasn't even true, but try to have that conversation.

"I'd worked so hard to build a reputation in this village. I was a respected lawyer, but now, I was a laughing stock. Even if I left her, divorced her to rags, I was going to have to move away, sell my practice, my lovely home, and lose my whole life. She destroyed my life, so I was going to destroy hers.

"My cough came on so strong at that moment, Tony hailed a cab and I went to the emergency room where they discovered tuberculosis.

"If I still want to kill Ronnie or even leave her, I'm too sick to do either now."

My husband left me for a thinner woman. It's my fault because I'm overweight. He seldom connects with his kids. That's his fault because he spends all his time with his new girlfriend, Chloe-the-Very-Thin. And he refuses to pay child support on any flimsy pretext which is his lawyer's fault, Marshall Stohl.

Before the separation, Marshall was a friend of mine. I didn't ask him to represent me in the divorce because he contracted tuberculosis from an immigrant client and coughs all the time, spits up of blood, shakes with chills, and weighs about two ounces. But Dale had no such compunctions. And Marshall agreed to be his lawyer.

"Sara, I need the money," he croaked when I forced myself to confront him. "I have bills. And Ronnie." Then he coughed that horrible cough and I let it go.

Marshall's a good divorce lawyer, too, nasty. In our two year separation, Dale has sent one child support check. The first time he came to see the kids after he left, I was wearing a new pair of jeans and he accused me of spending the kids' money on myself.

"That's why Dale refuses to pay child support, Sara."

"So what am I supposed to do for money for the kids?"

Marshall coughed then caught his breath. "I shouldn't be telling you this, but you're a friend." I glowered but he ignored it. "Dale doesn't intend to pay child support. He wants to keep his money for himself and…his new friend."

"But you know he can't do that, so why do you let him think he can?"

Marshall panted to get his next breath. "He has instructed me to delay until you give up."

Left to me, I'd have given up long ago, but my own lawyer, Louise Dejardins, will have none of that. She's kept Marshall busy with dunning letters, court judgments, even orders for court appearances, though he always gets excused for health reasons. Thus far, I've received no more money from Dale.

I grope on the top of my fridge for the cookie tin. It's full of homemade 7-layer bars: graham cracker crust, sweet evaporated milk, coconut, chocolate, butterscotch and peanut butter chips.

I settle on my wide soft sofa and look out at my backyard and at the wind rustling the last oak leaves on the stand of trees along the narrow Rouge River. It runs from the moraine in the North down to Lake Ontario. Miles and miles. And I eat one cookie after another. Ronnie's at that expensive spa losing weight and I'm not.

I sit bolt upright. Why haven't I reached Ronnie? Why hasn't she called? What if she came home early to buy a new phone and Marshall managed to make good on his threat and kill her? Was the gasping I heard on the baby monitor Marshall strangling Ronnie?

I'm hallucinating. Marshall lives in his bed, works from his bed, and eats in his bed. He's more likely to be a murder victim than a murderer. Anyway, it was a woman's voice that did the deeds. The man's voice was shocked, furious.

I sink back into the couch and look out the window again. The wind's whipping the snow around into little eddies. Cold air sneaks through the leaks in the caulking. I've no money to fix it. I never knew all the details of my finances when I was with Dale, but I know them now, to the penny, too few pennies. And pennies aren't even legal tender anymore.

My mind drifts with the snow until another thought occurs to me. Why doesn't Ronnie buy a new phone where she is? There are enough stores in the area. And who has a credit card? Something's off here.

I hear soft giggling in another room. The children are up. I creep along the hall and peek into the kitchen. Stevie and Sally are perched on their knees at the breakfast bar, a carton of milk high in Stevie's small hands. In Sally's even smaller hands is a box of marshmallow and chocolate S'Mores cereal. That box had been secretly on the top shelf of the pantry for my binges. Not so secret.

I growl. "Stevie." He whirls around. "Red River's your cereal."

He turns his back on me. He has such high cheekbones I can see him smiling from behind. "That's for you, Mommy."

"Red Riverrrr."

He shakes his head No. "I want S'Mores. Red River's ...healthy!" he spits. Is he going to follow in my fluffy footsteps? I tug the crushed cereal box out of Sally's hands before she can pour more. He and Sally are slim, and they're going to stay that way.

"Go play until breakfast's ready."

They giggle off their stools and settle on the floor near me. While I make up a batch of Red River at the stove, Sally exercises her small motor skills by picking up the mini-marshmallows, which have skittered into the corners.

How do they get that sweet tooth so early in life? They take the fruit-juice sweetened treats I allow them which are half as sweet as sugar-laden food. Yet they crave the oversweet. Did they get these taste buds from birth, or are they imitating my secret eating life? If so, I'll change how I eat. I'll stop baking; I'll throw out every single sweet thing in the house. Right now.

I yank open the pantry doors. The first thing I see is a large bag of white sugar. Down with sugar. It thumps onto the counter.

Sally looks up from the floor. "Where Mr. Andy? Horsey today."

I shake my head. "The Nashes had to go home."

"No! Play horsey!" She drops on all fours and starts to rear up like a horse then crawls under a barstool.

Stevie appears. "Mommy, are we going to nursery school today?"

My neighbor, Cheryl Andersen, is a former ECE teacher and we have a reciprocal babysitting arrangement. When things get too chaotic, we bundle up our kids and take them across the street for respite. The balance's in her favour these days with my kids over there at least two to one. But her family still has a husband and a daddy, so she lets it slide.

"Hurry up and finish eating your breakfast, then we'll go."

Today the kids will be staying there late to give me a chance to enact my plan for our future survival. I have to beg my old boss, Edward Osler, for a job.

Edward Davis Osler, the principal of St. Ives Private School, is also the only son of Lawrence and grandson of the powerful Senator Davis Osler. In the late 1800s, the Osler family made a fortune in lumber and have untold acres of undeveloped land, or used to. Rumour has it they've been selling off slowly, no one knows why.

But their name's still synonymous with wealth and power in Ontario, especially in politics. The New Conservative Party's home to Senator Davis Osler. His son, Lawrence Davis Osler, Edward's father, is campaigning to be the Conservative candidate for Hinton Township, which includes the village of Forest.

Wealth and prestige aside, before I met and married Dale, I had a romantic interest in Edward. I forced myself out of it though because he's married.

His wife's reputed to be gorgeous, but camera phobic. She never attended any school functions when I worked there but their names are reported at ballet galas, gallery openings, and Granite Club parties. They are the golden couple.

I hope I can arrange a meeting with Edward this evening and ask for a job.

I clap my hands. "Okay, let's go to Cheryl's. Everybody get dressed."

Stevie jumps off his seat, gives me a tight hug around my knees, and races up the stairs. Red River cereal issues forgotten. Never a grudge. Sally takes cautious steps up the steep stairs, looking back, waiting for my praise.

"Good job, my Sally," I say.

She answers with the ritual response, "Good job, my Mommy."

I stuff my kids into their old winter coats, too short and too tight for their growing bodies. I'm afraid and ashamed.

When Cheryl unbolts her clean white front door, the scent of gingerbread wafts warm from the tray of reindeer cookies she holds in her slim hands.

She and her two girls, both dressed in expensive Oshkosh outfits, are making Christmas cookies. Far from looking frazzled, her green eyes sparkle like a jolly skinny Mrs. Claus. At least her face's blotchy with heat from the oven.

Stevie and Sally dump their coats in the foyer and struggle out of their boots, Sally with a little help from Cheryl. Then they dart into the kitchen to join the screaming girls. In a short time, I hear the faint chanting of a nursery rhyme.

"Ring around the rosies,

Pocket full of posies,

Ashes, ashes,

We all fall down."

Cheryl, in her most animated ECE voice, says, "Did you know that nursery rhyme has a double meaning? It's not just a children's song, you know. Did you know? "

To Cheryl's delight, she has now put me in the humble role of student to her teacher. She's insecure because I have a university degree and she has a two-year certificate.

"It's a dirge from the days of the black plague. One of the symptoms was a rash around the mouth, like a rosey ring. They put posies in the dead person's pocket to hide the smell of decay since the bodies weren't picked up any time soon. Then they were burned, see? Ashes, ashes? Of course," she goes on in her high-pitched voice, "some people say it isn't ashes ashes at all, but achoo, achoo because another of the symptoms was sneezing. Then they all fell down because they died!" she ends with a flourish.

"A children's rhyme about death?"

She smiles broadly. I wonder if this might be an opening to confide in Cheryl about what I heard on the baby monitor. I need to run this by someone and Ronnie's still a no-show.

"Care for a cookie, Sara?"

I take one. I eat less when watched.

I stare at Cheryl, and she dimples up at me. I think if I told her about a real life murder, her sweet face would crumble to ashes ashes.

I'd love to be Cheryl. Cheryl has a husband who works, brings home money, helps with the kids, and loves them all. A dark funk starts to drip inside me. I grab another cookie.

On the outer edge of my hearing, there's a change in the tune from the children. Sally's quavering voice sings, "Rise, Sally, rise…"

Cheryl takes a breath, about to tell me a new meaning to that nursery rhyme when I shove her aside and the platter of cookies drops from her hands. All those beautiful cookies, breaking on the white tile floor.

Sally's voice trebles out again, "Point to the one, point to the one…"

It's the only line she knows from "Here I sit a-sewing." She sings it pointing at me as 'the one that you love best.' But if I'm not in the picture, it only means one thing: she needs my love because she's scared.

I race to the kitchen, but they're not there. Where are they? I check the backyard. Not there. I turn for the basement stairs when Sally's voice gets shrill.

"Rise, Sally, rise!"

I storm down the basement stairs one step ahead of Cheryl. A sobbing Megan, Cheryl's youngest, is rocking back and forth on the carpet, her knee bent oddly.

Stevie looks up white-faced and wide-eyed. "She was walking along the back of the couch, Mommy, and she slipped."

Sally runs over to me and grabs my knees. "Fall down!" she cries. "On four legs!"

Stevie translates, as usual, for his little sister. "Megan fell on her hands and knees, but one knee made a bad sound, Mommy."

In short order, Cheryl has Megan off the floor and up in her arms.

"Ow," yelps Megan. Her knee clicks and falls straight.

She looks down in amazement. "Mommy made it better." She licks tears off her lip. "I get down now."

Cheryl and I exchange worried glances. I say, "Try to walk for us, Megan, but slowly."

Megan slips down and hops away on the once-sore leg.

Cheryl recovers instantly and chirps, "Crisis averted. Everyone back into the kitchen to finish our baking."

Three of the kids pound up the stairs with Megan leading the charge, but Sally stays fearfully close to me, her face still tear streaked. She's a sensitive child. Sometimes I think she feels people's pain more than they do.

I pull her up into my arms and she snuggles. How can I leave her here now? I'll have to cancel my plan to meet with Edward, that is, my job interview.

When will I be able to set it up again? I'm stuck between my children and money for my children. My children need me to get a job, but Sally needs me here to comfort her. If I leave, I'll feel like a wicked mother. If I stay, I'll feel like a stupid mother.

Cheryl calls down in a singsong voice, "Sally, I've a Rudolph cookie up here for you."

Sally gives my neck a soft kiss, then squirms down. Children are more resilient than mothers. Sally heads for the kitchen, me for the foyer.

There's Cheryl holding another platter of fresh gingerbread cookies. Isn't she perfect? I snatch a cookie and wolf it down, letting crumbs fall to the freshly swept floor. Cheryl's smile tightens. My hand shoots out and snatches another one before I can stop myself.

30

6

I trudge home stuffing gingerbread cookie into my mouth, but not tasting it. It's time to call Edward.

Edward has been a friend of mine from way back when I was a librarian for SunnyCare Insurance, the largest Canadian insurance company in the country. He was a lawyer in the corporate department, which proved lucky for me.

In a fit of creativity, I had drawn a comic book cartoon of the President of SunnyCare and the Board of Directors playing volleyball on a beach, batting around our new product line. I thought it added a human touch and humour to our stuffy corporate image, so I submitted it to the Bulletin, the corporate newspaper, and they loved it and published it.

Mr. Demarkis, President of SunnyCare had a different opinion. He ordered me into his large, bare office, the thin hair on his head vibrating with suppressed rage.

"The Board of Directors must never be made objects of ridicule. You're terminated."

Tears welled in my eyes. "It was a bit of fun, sir."

"No excuses. See Human Resources."

This was a disaster. I sent part of my paycheck home to help the parents buy groceries when Dad was "under the weather," as my mother called it, aka on a losing streak. It could take me months to find another position if I didn't have a good reference. A Liberal Arts undergraduate degree with a major in Library Science didn't carry much weight in the job market.

On my way to Human Resources, wringing my hands, I bumped into Edward Osler, literally. We tumbled together into a wall. I blushed to my curly blonde roots.

Edward Osler is a Justin Trudeau look-alike from his intense blue eyes, curly brown hair, cleft chin, straight white teeth and perpetually tanned skin. All the women on the staff were after him even though he was married.

I started to cry. Not only was I without a job, but I was also a clumsy fool.

"Whoa, you look like you need a friend."

He took me by the arm to the staff cafeteria where he charmed me into revealing my troubles, including my parents' situation.

He listened, nodded, shook his head in sympathy, and told me not to worry. He strode off somewhere, and I slunk to Human Resources, miserable. What was I going to tell my mother when she didn't receive a check?

When I got to the Staff Coordinator, Denise, she urged me into her office, excitedly.

"Edward Osler saved your job!"

I shook my head. "What are you talking about? I barely know the man?"

"He's so gorgeous." She giggled. I waited for more. She sat up straight, and cleared her throat, reasserting her professionalism.

"Edward told Mr. Demarkis it was his fault you submitted the cartoon because he okayed it, legally." Denise leaned forward conspiratorially, "Demarkis knows all about the Osler family, all that power, so, he rescinded your termination. He's giving you one more chance. Edward Osler's your hero!"

I didn't know what to say. Edward Osler took on the CEO of SunnyCare for me? I began bringing him homemade goodies, like seven layer cookies, lemon shortbread, and even chocolate pecan cinnamon rolls.

Finally, he begged to stop to save his waistline. He had nothing to worry about in that way. Though he was married, I began having romantic fantasies about him. I mean, how many real life heroes come along?

So when he was appointed to the Board of Directors at St. Ives Collegiate, his old alma mater, the most prestigious private school in Ontario, he asked me to follow him there and be the school librarian. Of course, I said yes.

Once I was working there, he backed me up time and again. When I first arrived as the new librarian, I was shocked at the state of St. Ives' book collection. There were electronics everywhere you turned, but partially empty bookshelves with a collection woefully out of date.

All modern libraries were keeping paper as a format for learning. I proposed the school library increase its book collection as opposed to its computers for a two-year period. But, the head of the Parent Council, Joseph Irondale, was a tyrannical know-it-all.

As soon as he heard of my plan, he stormed into the library and roared, "High tech's the only thing we upgrade at St. Ives. Books are a thing of the past, a waste of parents' money. If that's your intention, St. Ives has different intentions for you! "

I reported this interaction to Edward and we spent days researching the scholastic and financial benefit of books. He suggested we back up our research with examples from U.S. Ivy League universities, Irondale's Holy Grail.

After that, the library not only got new books, but I also got a raise. And, with all modesty, I must report I won the Ontario Library Association President's Award for Exceptional Achievement.

Yet there was constant resistance from Irondale. When I began to upgrade the periodicals and foreign newspapers, he blew out fire.

"It's a waste of parent money to buy foreign language newspapers!"

Edward turned the International Language Head onto him. Marie Claude pouted at him, pinched his cheeks, and called him

Cherie. Irondale's florid face went pink with pleasure, and I got no more interference.

I hope Edward can solve my most pressing problem and get me a job at St. Ives, a part time job. They seldom hire part-timers. They expect full time commitment in their hallowed halls. I can't commit.

I reach over and pull out a Snickers bar from the drawer of the closest end table and bite off a chunk. Soon my happily distracted mind wonders if Edward could solve my other little problem, the one that starts, "No one but me knows there's a murderer on the loose in Forest."

Rising through my fear is an even more disturbing idea. I don't know who got killed.

7

I have to think clearly, and since there's caffeine in chocolate the more I eat, the faster my brain will work. This is my new mantra: Chocolate is food for the brain.

Unfortunately, this mantra and others like it have caused me trouble in the past. I once went on the Atkins Diet. *"Eat all the bacon you want and be thin as a breadstick!"* I ate all the bacon I wanted, got constant heartburn, and gained back all the weight plus a few more pounds when I stopped.

When I went on the Paleo diet, that is, no grains, no legumes, no flour, no sugar, no-no, I felt like a food freak. According to Ronnie, I was. When I returned to normal food, what weight I lost came back on with the typical extra pounds.

Finally, I tried Dr. Lou's clinic. Protein and happy shots of Vitamin B worked for a year. I lost 30 pounds, but when the happy shots stopped, it took far less time than a year to regain it all, plus.

While I didn't try jaw wiring or stomach stapling, Ronnie did. She had her stomach stapled. She lost 80 pounds in three months and gained back 60 by eating a bit more each day, stretching her stomach little by little. To the thrift shop went the new clothes, and to the graveyard went her dreams of getting slim the fast and easy way.

Now we're both on the Think Thin diet. "If I were a thin woman, how would I eat? If I were a thin woman, which food item would I choose?" This time, it's going to work. This time it will be different. It's going to be permanent this time.

My brain is distracted. Sugar does that now and then. All the time. What did I need to do? Oh yes, before I can become model thin, solve multiple murders and save the village of Forest, I have to call Edward Osler and beg for a job.

I find the number for St. Ives and ask to speak to Edward Osler. The new secretary doesn't know me. What if Edward doesn't know me anymore? How humiliating that will be.

A stern male voice barks, "How many years has it been since you called me, Sara?"

I break into a smile. He remembers who I am. "Edward, I can't count that high."

He laughs. "I don't require librarians to do math. How can I help you, my dearest Sara?" Dearest? I can't think of what to say next. "Sara? Are you okay?" He sounds concerned.

"Couldn't be better." Now, why did I say that?

"I'll pick you up at 8 p.m.," he says, "for dinner and a confidential chat."

I'm that obvious? Of course I am. It's my first call in three years. I stammer, "I'll be ready to eat when you get here."

There's a soft chuckle. "Sounds wonderful." And he hangs up.

I disconnect the call, furious with myself. Sexual innuendo? I'm a single mother of two little kids. I can't be interested in that stuff.

But I also feel queasy. Something more bothers me. Something I don't want to contemplate. I must be tired, stressed, hallucinating or something because the man's voice I just heard on the phone sounds strikingly similar to the man's voice I heard on the baby monitor.

8

E dward Osler involved in a murder? Impossible. My ears were playing tricks on me. I was tired this morning because it was so early. Also, people can sound like other people over radio waves. Edward was just on my mind because I need the job.

I'm distracted because I realize for the first time in three years, I'm going out to dinner with a man, a handsome man. I gurgle like little Sally. It just comes out.

The last dinner I attended was the one Dale's company hosted for Toronto realtors. He mingled in the room and left me sitting at a table with strangers.

As I was the wife, they smiled once then ignored me. I knew nothing about a new marketing technique called Guaranteed Listing where the secret was to mirror the potential client's every move. Subliminally, it implied they were on the same wavelength. Grasping at straws they were.

At the end of the evening, Dale came back to our table and gave me a great though brief kiss, which I enjoyed. He was always a good kisser. Lust was one reason I married him.

He was short, but built like a prime rib roast. He had powerful arms, thick legs, and a chest so hairy it foamed when he lathered in the shower. And a beautiful mouth. Though little beautiful ever came out of it.

After the luscious kiss, in front of all his staff, he slapped my behind, grinned, and said, "That's how you tell if a watermelon's ripe."

This is a business dinner, but it's been so long since I've been out with a man, it also feels like an occasion. I grope to the back of my closet where I remember my black silk suit. Black hides weight. Nearby's the cranberry silk top. It's a little low cut for a business dinner, but not for a date. It also might just distract Edward should my hair frizz up.

I catch my reflection in the wall mirror. I should have looked sooner. My curly hair's springing all over from the damp weather. I run to the bathroom where I keep my arsenal of hair tamers, thick mousse, extreme flat iron, and wide-toothed comb. I set everything on high and straighten every strand.

The effect is stunning, if I do say so myself. Swaying down my back is a long smooth wave of white blonde. If I don't walk outside for too long tonight, it might last the whole evening.

I slip on the suit and blouse. I put on my black high-heeled boots, my ruby earrings from the rich Dale days, and view the whole effect in the mirror. I look like a dark chocolate torte with raspberry coulis.

9

It's getting dark, nearly bedtime for Stevie and Sally. I hope Cheryl will honour their 8pm lights out. She often plies them with permissions I never grant to win them over. She's the indulgent mother to my good-for-you mother.

They love her for it, but I resent her. She gets to be a good guy while I'm left with tired, cranky children. Maybe sometime I should let them sleep over; let her deal with their hyper sugar-induced behavior in the morning.

I'll be out so late with Edward, maybe they should sleep over tonight. I pick up the phone, and then I put it down fast. Is it healthy for my children to sleep away from home at such a young age? They'll be going to university soon. Will I regret them being away from me now?

Stevie going to university? By then, he'll be tall but not fat. I see him with a tennis racket over his shoulder and a black and white v-neck sweater tied jauntily around his neck, like in the old '40s movies. He's grabbing up his textbooks, from his law class, no, no, biology, human biology, because of course, he wants to be a doctor. And not just any doctor. He wants to be a pediatrician.

It's all a breeze for him because he's so clever. But before he races out the door, he comes to hunt for me. He gives me a quick hug and the arm of his sweater flops on my head. It smells of Old Spice. He brushes it off my face, but not before I can blink away the tears. Men wear Old Spice. Where did my Stevie go?

I switch to Sally, younger by two years, my little girl. What will Sally be like? She'll be laughing as usual, her blonde curls so like her Mommy's shining in the morning light. Her eyes are as green as rain-soaked leaves. She's wearing a soft lilac sweater, and a navy pencil skirt. She has a perfect figure. And she's smiling the soft smile she's had since childhood.

She's going to meet her fiancé. They met in engineering class. Sally's in the top 10 percent of her year, and so is he. His family's a little small. Only a dad and an aunt, but he's a generous man who dotes on Sally. Sally getting married?

Fantasies aside, it would be better for the kids to stay over at Cheryl's. I punch in her number.

"Cheryl?"

"Yes!" she snaps.

"What's all that noise in the background?"

"No! Megan, don't pour the milk on the floor! I mean, we pour it into cups, dear."

I think better of letting the kids sleep over. It's too much for everyone.

"Cheryl, something's come up. Is there any way the kids can stay a little later at your house tonight?"

Cheryl shouts into the phone, "How late? "

"I'm not sure. But before midnight."

"Oh, well, I guess so. Megan! No! I mean…" She disconnects. That child would drive anyone nuts.

The perfect Mom has an imperfect child while I'm an imperfect Mom with perfect children. I can't help it. I smile.

10

DECEMBER 22   8 PM

Iₜ's almost 8 pm. Shouldn't Edward should be here by now? And as if I'm in a fairy tale, the doorbell chimes. I prance to the front door, head high, large boobs preceding me.

There stands Edward wearing a brown leather jacket, ivory turtleneck, brown slacks, and brown leather boots. He looks like a chocolate cream.

He crinkles his blue eyes, lingering over me, and says, "You look so …hip."

I step aside to allow him to enter. He smiles, dimples deepening. Do women still swoon? I pull myself up short. I promised myself I'd listen to his voice. I need to concentrate.

"I've made reservations for a quiet dinner at the McMichael Art Gallery. Thought we'd look around at the art afterwards. But with you looking so cool, I'm changing things." He presses a number on his speed dial, murmurs a few words, and clicks off. "We're going to downtown Toronto to the hottest new resto in town, Scatter! Where all the patrons are young and beautiful."

"Beautiful?"

He grins.

I can't help it. I gurgle like Sally.

"All set?" He takes my arm. The warmth of his body electrifies me. Has it been that long since someone over three feet tall touched me?

The cold air's a shock, as always. I shiver in my silk coat, which looks good but has no warmth. Rather like Dale.

Edward says, "My car's over there," and points to a white Ferrari sports car camouflaged in the snow.

"Edward, you own this?" He's Chairman of St. Ives Board of Directors, but how much can that pay? We're talking luxury vehicle here, $260,000 to $460,000 depending on paint colour among other things. I know because Dale lusted after the exact car but in red. Male mid-life crisis. But even as a CEO of a successful real estate firm, he couldn't afford it.

He settled for a mistress. Lower down payment but higher maintenance costs. Not such a clever realtor after all.

Edward mumbles, "It was a present." He opens my door, waits for me to settle myself on the cold leather seat. My perfume, Mandarin Orange, permeates the chill interior. He slides in on the driver's side. His aftershave drifts towards me, cinnamon and cloves. Between the two of us, we'd make a delicious cake.

Edward pulls out of my driveway quickly and smoothly, the powerful engine making a racket I could do without. He adjusts his shoulders in his leather jacket. It makes a squeaking sound against the tan leather seat. Why is this sexy? I pull myself up short. Was that his voice I heard on the baby monitor early this morning? I have to concentrate on his voice.

He clears his throat. "Sara, name one of your favorite things."

Do I now think his voice has the same timber, the same resonance as the man's on the baby monitor? It's so hard to tell. People's voices don't sound the same in person as they do over radio waves.

"Sara?"

"Oh, that's easy— kids."

"Bingo!" he roars. My body jerks and I bump my head on the side window.

"You always were tightly wound. You okay?"

I rub my head. My nerves are shot. "I'm fine." He glances over at me, so I smile brightly. "Fine, really. So, you love kids, too?"

He nods his head. "That's an understatement. Did you know I ran an inner city school for five years?"

I'm dumbfounded. "You were a teacher? But you're a lawyer. Isn't that why you're on the Board?"

"I got a teacher certificate before I became a lawyer. And I loved it. Sara, have you ever had something you loved, really loved?"

"You mean other than my own kids? Because I love my children more than anyone or anything in life. Everything I do's for them now. I gave up being a librarian and am running my B & B so I can be with them when they're young." Whoa, I'm frothing at the mouth.

"Well, let's say that I loved my school for those disadvantaged kids almost as much as you love your children. Did you know my distant uncle was Sir William Osler, the famous medical teacher?" His voice is loud with enthusiasm.

I'm listening hard and that wasn't the voice I heard on the baby monitor. So why did I think it was? I take a shaky breath. Maybe I imagined the whole thing. I mean, a murder, a double murder in Forest Village?

"He was my role model for JFSS, the Jane/Finch Storefront School. He was the first teacher to have medical students spend less time in the classroom, and more time where their knowledge was needed, in the hospital wards.

"So I used the neighbourhood to teach academics." He's smiling, his eyes alive with excitement. "Instead of drilling them on math for hours in front of a whiteboard, I took them to the nearby Canada's Wonderland." He laughs. "You should've seen their faces when they heard about that!" His white teeth are in full view. What a hunk.

"I made them work for those rides. They had to calculate the G-forces of the roller coasters, estimate the angles of the support beams, and record the reactions of the passengers they interviewed at the end of the ride." He bangs the steering wheel with his gloved hand. "Their math test scores skyrocketed!

"So I continued with the practical connection to academics. When I taught them English, I used poetry to get to them, not from old dead white guys. I used music, song lyrics from rappers, rock groups, and street poets. That way, I taught alliteration, rhythm, and metaphor and they didn't know they were learning things." He laughs in delight.

"At the end of the unit, I set up the classroom to look like a coffeehouse from the 60s. I brought in doughnuts and drinks and they read their poetry to each other." His eyes glisten. "You wouldn't believe the personal pain they revealed, the nods of recognition from their peers, hoodlums giving each other knuckle bumps for poetry."

He face is beatific with what has to be called love. But, a muscle tightens in his jaw. "Then I lost my line of credit and so I lost my school."

I wait for more, but he's glaring at the road. The story has taken an unfortunate turn.

"I'm sorry, Edward. Did the bank lose confidence in your experiment?"

He guffaws. "It was my father who didn't think a school for street kids, delinquents as he called them, was dignified enough for our very dignified family. He said a word to the bank manager and end of credit line. Even His Lordship agreed."

"His Lordship? You have British royalty in your family?" My stomach cramps. My family's out of his league big time.

Edward stares straight ahead. "Everyone calls Grandfather 'His Lordship' because he's a sitting member in the House of Lords in Ottawa. Didn't you hear that through the grapevine?"

I look out my side window. I've heard a lot about Edward Osler, his society marriage, his family wealth and power, but I didn't know he had a Senator in the family. So much power, so much money. I feel even smaller.

"Yes, Senator Davis Osler's my grandfather. I went to law school to please my father and His Lordship, and I got this car when I graduated."

"Sounds like it was a bribe."

He flinches. "A car for giving up the only thing that gave zest to my life?" His brown leather gloves squeal on the cold steering wheel. "Would a car replace your children, Sara?"

"But Edward, you're in a school again, on the Board. Why haven't you used your ideas there? "

"He jests at scars that never felt a wound."I'm thrilled. Shakespeare? This guy's something else.

He shrugs. "Don't be too impressed, Sara the Librarian. That's a pretty famous quote."

Large heavy snowflakes are falling now, obscuring the road ahead. Edward has to concentrate on his driving. His large hands grip the steering wheel expertly, the Ferrari making the turns with ease and grace. The silence continues until we're on a better cleared street.

He continues. "I tried to implement my ideas at St. Ives, but the Parent Council scoffed. You know Joseph Irondale."

"Oh, I know him, Edward. He tried to get me fired so many times for suggesting innovations, I lost count. And every time, you stepped in to save me."

I look over at him with renewed gratitude, Edward Osler, my constant hero.

"Well, he got the entire Parent Council up in arms over my suggesting teachers take the kids out of the school to Canada's Wonderland to 'play.' And when I persuaded the English department to allow modern song lyrics into their poetry classes, he threatened to get me removed from the Board of Directors for promoting rap and gangsterism. So dies student enthusiasm."

Maybe it's the street lighting, but when he looks over at me, I think I see a film of tears in his eyes. Here's a man rich beyond my wildest dreams, yet he couldn't get what he wanted most in life.

So, money really can't buy happiness. Or maybe he didn't try hard enough.

THE POINT

11

I lean against the door to be farther away from this rich man and his rich family. In my family, wealth came and went according to a set of rules I never understood.

For my 13th birthday, Dad gave me a beautiful pearl necklace. It was so lovely that when I wore it to school, Ronnie wanted to try it on. Her try-ons were permanent. It would have meant weeks of me asking, begging, and then threatening until I got it back. When I refused, she grabbed me around the neck in an effort to either choke me to death or unclasp the catch, whichever worked first.

"Get your hands off me!" I shouted.

"I just want to see it up close," she whined, dogging me as I ran away. I knew better. She'd grab hold of it then threaten to break it unless I let her keep it. But it couldn't go out of my possession or chance getting damaged. I knew from bitter experience it wasn't going to be around long. Sometimes my father came into a windfall, and that was when I got things. But shortly after, they disappeared, no words ever spoken.

Ronnie wouldn't take no for an answer. She caught the back of my turquoise sweater, whirled me around, and snapped her hands around my neck. She hissed, "Best friends share!" I pinched her hard

48

on the inner arm with my sharp fingernails, kept only for that purpose—defense against the dark Ronnie.

"You witch!" she howled but she dropped her chokehold. She ended up with a nasty welt on her arm, and I got several finger-shaped bruises on my neck. I had to wear a turtleneck sweater for a week to hide them. All the girls thought I was hiding hickies. Because of that, Cynthia Bollinger, the most popular girl at school, became my new best friend.

"Who's the guy?" She giggled. She and her posse followed me around school for the next several days, peppering me with questions to which I made up the most provocative lies I could without being caught. "Oh, he's from out of town. Buffalo." That was a good one for two reasons. First, no one could insist on meeting him. Second, anyone American caused panting. "He goes to university." Yes! An older man. "An only child of a wealthy car magnate." Oh, I had them drooling.

Ronnie refused to talk to me the entire week. But one morning I woke up, and the necklace was gone. I didn't bother to ask. I already knew who'd taken it.

At breakfast, I heard Dad whisper to Mom, "Guido won't come back, dear, he's paid." My mother was trembling. "Dear, believe me, the gun was a toy, a harmless joke."

The day the bruises faded and I stopped wearing turtlenecks, Cynthia et al faded away, too. But Ronnie came back, walking me down the hall to our next class. All forgiven, all forgotten. Equals once again.

Edward clears his throat in the car. "Excuse me. I shouldn't be boring you with my troubles. Enough about me. Let's talk about you. I'll bet your life has been a series of peaches and cream, and summer camps." He smiles warmly at me.

I can't stop my eyes flashing murder. Summer camps? How about paying the rent late month after month, buying bruised fruit from the aluminum trolley at the back of the store, hiding from unshaven debt collectors, like Guido at the door with a gun?

"Rich people have troubles I only wish I had!" I snap. Edward shoots me a look. "If the university hadn't given me a scholarship, I couldn't have gone."

I don't have to tell him why, that there was too much horse racing that year. In fact, my parents didn't even attend my graduation because the day before their car was repossessed right off their driveway. Of course they didn't have cab fare.

The only person who showed up was Ronnie. She wanted to see the dress she designed for me in her Fashion class. She wanted to be a dress designer at the time, but it wasn't going well. She needed someone to wear one of her designs in public, and get a picture of it in order to pass.

The dress was a scarlet red with white and black feathers hanging from the shoulders and the hip. I looked like a bloodied chicken. But I had to be red because Ronnie refused to wear glasses, and wouldn't have been able to pick me out on the podium to take the picture. And, well, it was free.

Out of over 1,000 students, I was the only one the photographers crowded around. No kidding. So Ronnie passed her class in spades.

The only sound in the car is the squeaking of the tires on the snow-packed road. Then Edward picks up the conversation as if we'd been talking all along. "I guess it's a goal of most Canadians to move to Hawaii."

"I'd move to Alaska," I say softly.

"I wasn't expecting that," he says, delighted. Then his face takes on a yearning look. "I've read about Alaska, too. A columnist in the Star moved there, and sent back reports. He made it sound so rugged and natural. And then, one of my favorite poems is by Robert Service. Not the one about "Dangerous Dan McGraw," from elementary school, but the ones about the stars being so hard and clear and sharp in the black sky, and the snow being so big a part of life you talk to it. Skagway, Ketchikan, Anchorage. That's for me." Then, he ducks his head. "Not that I'd fit in up there. Where would I get my suede jackets?" He barks a laugh, but it doesn't sound like laughing. It sounds like it hurts.

"Then why don't you go to Alaska? You can obviously afford it."

He ignores the jab. What am I doing, anyway? The man's taking me out to dinner, possibly going to hire me. Am I that self-destructive?

He swallows hard. "I'm an Osler. That's why." He looks down for a moment at his hands. They're manicured, each healthy nail pink with a hint of clear polish.

"I've seen a painting of Alaska which I've never forgotten at the McMichael Gallery in Kleinberg."

He smiles. "I visit there regularly. Gorgeous inside and out."

I go on. "They have this giant painting at the end of a hall. In the foreground's a man riding on a dog sled. The dogs are off into the picture and pulling him homewards. The mastery of the painting's the lighting. The sky's the pearly gray it gets sometimes in Toronto before a heavy snowfall—do you know what I mean?"

He nods, and picks up my train of thought. "It's a deeper blue than the Toronto skies, and colder-looking."

"That's it. And you can see that the man's heading home and his dogs know they're going home, home being another part of Alaska, and they're happy."

I'm deep into the painting now. "It draws you into it. The dogs pulling him, all of them loving the ride, the bitter weather, and the blue-white stars in the black sky. Even though I hate the cold, I wanted to step out of the gallery central heating and go with them. It stirred something in me like the echo of a wolf howl in the night."

I shake my head. "I wanted to buy that painting. But it's tens of thousands of dollars. And anyway, the painter meant for me to experience Alaska in reality, not in an artificially heated apartment in Riverdale Village. "

His eyes haven't left the road, but he's able to finish my thought. "And the cold edge of that pierces through you, and on very cold nights in Toronto, if you look up in the sky and see the stars, shimmering and blue, the howl of Alaska starts deep inside you."

I close my eyes. He knows. I feel his warm hand close over mine, and we ride in silence.

At last, we turn into the restaurant parking lot. Scatter! blazes in brilliant blue across the night sky. "Should I let you out to wait in the lobby while I park the car? No need for both of us to walk in the cold."

I take a deep breath. What was I so upset about a while ago? Oh yes, his family has money, but who cares? Tonight he's sharing it with me. I hurry through the frosty air into the warm foyer. Indoors, the neon lights blaze purple, creating an atmosphere of cool, hip, young.

There are dozens of small tables on the main floor, and at each sits a well-dressed man with a sexy-looking woman.

There's a second floor. The people up there are looking down with amusement on the people below while several main floor diners crane their necks upwards to watch themselves eat.

I, on the other hand, am looking at the refrigerators, which line the walls of the dining room. The food's visible through the glass doors. And I'm hungry.

Edward appears beside me, bringing with him a gust of night air. His cheeks are ruddy and his eyes an intense blue from the cold. He looks rugged, just like those love comic heroes. My eyes linger over him. What would it be like having him as my lover?

Edward says, "Would you like to be on the top or on the bottom?" My cheeks flame as if he's read my thoughts. He raises his hands in mock horror. "Innocent remark." He grins.

I need to concentrate on my mission. I'm here to get a job job job.

The maitre d' swoops in front of us, bows a greeting, then leads us through the happy throng to a table for two, holding out my chair.

Edward says, "They specialize in martinis here. That's what I order." I'd prefer my usual plain orange juice, but he's my host. I nod. "Okay," he says to the waiter, "A martini for me, and a glass of orange juice for the lady." He winks at me. "I've had enough lunches with you to know that."

The waiter bows from the waist like a faithful servant in a Tolstoy novel, and hurries away.

"How do you like the atmosphere?" Edward smiles.

I gaze around the room. The sparkle of diamonds is everywhere. "I like it. Are all these people the Toronto elite?"

He laughs. "I don't know about them, but I'm not." His white teeth flash.

I feel light-headed. It's his charisma, yes, but also, I'm starving. I sneak a look again into those glass refrigerators. With a curt nod, Edward gets right down to business.

"Tonight they have a prix fixe dinner. The appetizer's cold cucumber soup, the main course's veal piccatta with melted cheese on saffron rice, and for dessert, black raspberry ice. So, let's have the prix fixe dinner."

I bristle. My feminist instincts are second nature what with having dealt with a control freak like Dale.

"Yes please, you order for both of us," I say in my imitation of an airhead.

He laughs. "Then next time we come, you can do the ordering." And he winks.

He gets better every second. I'm about to try my hand at a witty response, when I see he's no longer paying attention to me. He's staring at a table across from us where there's a gorgeous, black-haired woman.

This woman's more than a little noticeable. Her low-cut, silver dress is backless, with a sparkling chain lolling down her back, a la the Roaring 20s. She has sparkling bracelets on both graceful arms, and dangling earrings that have to be diamonds from the over-casual way she wears them. She also has a luxurious black mink coat draped behind her.

Her features are chiseled with an aquiline nose, high cheekbones, languid, half-lidded eyes and a small dimple in her chin. At the moment, she's licking a dusting of icing sugar from her lip with a tiny, pink cat's tongue. She looks a little familiar, but I can't place her.

Edward stands up and marches to her table. The woman notices him approaching, and bends to whisper something to her well-dressed companion, a balding man in his 50s. They both laugh.

Edward leans down and whispers something in her ear. She stares at him, and then shakes her beautiful head no. She lifts a long, slim hand to brush at her nose. Then she pats Edward on the shoulder and croons in a husky voice, "Happy birthday to you."

Edward jerks ramrod straight, nods to her companion, and strides back to our table.

I open my mouth to ask, but he shakes his head. We sit in silence, him staring straight ahead, me surreptitiously peaking in her direction. She's nuzzling the old guy's cheek, while his hand's caressing her thigh.

"Is she a call girl?" Edward glares at me. I blush. Did I say that out loud?

"She's a colleague," he answers, tight-lipped.

I glance back to her table.

"I can't believe you have a colleague who looks like that. Does she work at SunnyCare or St. Ives?"

She definitely looks like someone I know but I don't remember her from either place I worked.

For the next several seconds, Edward makes a herculean effort to calm himself. Finally, he asks, "Where's our waiter? I know how hungry you are." He lifts his hand in the air and in a second, the waiter's there.

Despite this intriguing interlude, I'm ravenous. It's late for dinner.

The waiter sets down two large, brandy snifters full of martini, and a small glass of orange juice. Edward shakes his head. "We didn't order two…"

The waiter smiles. "We always bring two, sir, remember? It saves wear and tear on the waiter's feet." He looks down at his pad. "Ready to order, sir?"

Edward's attention's back at the black beauty's table. I step in. "We'll have two prix fixe dinners. I'm faint with hunger. Can you hurry?"

54

The waiter smiles, as if I'm joking, and scurries away. I'm getting a hunger headache. I down my orange juice quickly, but it doesn't help, so I wrap my fingers around the untouched martini glass, and polish it off as if it were pop. That does it.

Candy is dandy but liquor is quicker. I grin. I feel fine now.

It seems like only seconds later when the waiter reappears holding aloft two bowls of a pale green cucumber soup, which he names before scurrying away again.

Edward brings his attention back to our table. He picks up his martini, downs it, then reaches for the second martini. His eyes sparkle.

"You drank this whole martini? Well, this should get interesting."

I ignore him and lift my spoon to take a sip of the soup. It's smooth and tangy. I even like the pale green colour. Is there a hint of ginger adding heat? Edward hasn't touched his soup. At a nod, the waiter brings two more martinis. None for me this time. I have food.

When the veal dish arrives, Edward and I are laughing and talking to each other like the old friends we are. I dip my fork into the soft, hot cheese topping the veal medallion. The meat's dry.

Edward hasn't noticed. His veal remains untouched.

After drinking a third martini, Edward stops staring at the beautiful woman and focuses his full attention on me. He leans across the table and takes my hand. Suddenly I feel like I'm in an oven. I stop everything, powerless to speak. He leans back. There's an immediate cooling. What on earth was that?

12

I lean my chin into my palm and stare into Edward's handsome face, tipsy from the martini. There's that cleft I always loved.

"Sara?"

I snap out of it. For heaven's sake, I'm on a job interview. He laughs and his eyes crinkle at the corners. He has such beautiful eyes, sometimes aqua like the Mediterranean Ocean, sometimes deep blue like the Pacific Ocean, and sometimes, if he's furious at something, as pale blue as Arctic ice.

I grin sloppily at him. He shakes his head, used to women's silliness around his appearance. "Have you heard this one? Victoria Lamboni says our arch enemy Joseph Irondale's son is a druggie, supplying kids in the school with everything illegal. I've already talked to the principal about him, but Victoria says the kid's getting out of hand. St. Ives may have to bring in the police. Can you imagine Irondale's reaction?"

"We know what it'll be. You'll be out on your ear. Anyway, why's Victoria Lamboni telling you this stuff? You'd better watch your back with her, Edward. She may say you're the source of the rumours to Irondale."

Victoria Lamboni is a short, squat, ambitious 40-something woman who favours black and white suits which she thinks add authority to her short stature, and bright red lipstick. She looks like a barber pole.

"I know how to fight fire with fire." He leans across the table again. That handsome face comes closer and those blue eyes look deeper into mine. The room blazes with light. My face and body glow.

"Like that," he whispers.

Then he leans back in his chair. The air around me cools. For a second time, I'm stunned into silence. If there weren't a table between us, I'd have jumped him.

"Nowadays, I just have to give her shoulder a little squeeze, like this." His large hand reaches across the table and grips my shoulder. I feel a burning through my silk blouse. "And she offers to help me any way she can. I want her to know I can't be manipulated."

His blue eyes veer off in the direction of the woman in black.

"Edward, who is she? What's her name?"

His mouth tenses, but he doesn't answer. That woman's obviously an ex-colleague immune to his shoulder squeezes. With a shake of his head, he comes to himself. "I'm sorry, Sara. I know you need a job."

I'm chagrinned. Do I look that desperate, or shabby? I drop my eyes.

"Don't be embarrassed. Most single mothers need a job, but part-time, so they can be home with their kids in the morning, and after school."

Tears spring to my eyes. He understands. But, can he help me? He leans back against the dark leather of his chair and takes a deep breath.

"Damn the timing, Sara. Joseph Irondale addressed the Board of Directors yesterday, exhorting us to find extra money through fundraising. The Parent Council wants the fees to go down, but we know they have to go up."

I can't stop myself. I reach across the table and clutch his hand. "The children and I are hours away from the food bank, Edward.

Dale refuses to send any more money, and hasn't for two years. He cleaned out our savings account before he hooked up with his...." Do real adults call each other girlfriend and boyfriend?

Edward's warm hand rests on mine. This time all I feel is comfort, reassurance, caring. I'm scared I might grab onto his other hand. It's been so long since I had anyone to lean on.

"I think the Library Head, you remember Paula, is drowning in marking library tests. Yes, I think she might quit if we don't do something. I think Irondale might buy that.

"I'll list you as a teaching aid; no one need know you're a human teaching aid. You can work from home and only come in to school to return papers. It'll pay well enough to buy groceries for your children."

I open my mouth but I'm unable to speak. He's going to tangle with the dreaded Joseph Irondale again on my behalf.

"In the meantime…" He reaches inside his jacket pocket and pulls out his wallet. He extracts several $20 bills. I watch in abject humiliation. He's a colleague, an equal, a friend. I don't want to borrow money from him. Worse, I'm not sure if I'll be able to pay it back.

He lays the money beside my trembling hands. "Groceries for the kids." It's a hundred dollars I truly need. "Drop by the library tomorrow first thing, and I'll have Paula give you a pile of her unmarked tests."

I have no other option. Dale's pretending we don't exist now that he has Chloe-the-Very-Thin. I feel the rejection and the betrayal. What a contrast between Edward and Dale. Why, why, why do I want that man back? Is the perfect family photo worth the price?

"Thank you, Edward. You have no idea."

He waves away the gratitude. "You won't be thanking me when you start to read those tests." He laughs, but his blue eyes darken with compassion. "Now, how about that dessert I know you're craving?"

The second he mentions dessert, I feel better. The waiter swoops in at a nod from Edward and deposits glistening blackberry ices on the table. I'm about to dig in when something tickles my skin.

The Black Beauty's fur coat brushes my bare arm as she drags it behind her. A few mink hairs float in the air after her. Ah, a chink in her image. Fur doesn't come off unless the leather's drying out. That means it's an old coat. But the scent of Joy perfume wafts around her, an expensive perfume, and my favorite in the Dale days. The Black Beauty's a contradiction.

She holds her head at a haughty angle, not granting us a look as she glides out of the restaurant, her middle-aged companion scampering behind.

Edward stands up, drops money on the table, and draws me to my feet. He helps me put my coat on and squeezes my shoulders, like a friend. My nipples bloom, not like a friend. I have to stop this. Edward Osler's married.

But, he's also a man with secrets. Who was that Black Beauty? How can he afford to give away a thousand dollars just like that?

The man gave me a job. I should be grateful. I am grateful. And I should mind my own business, and stop being suspicious.

13

DECEMBER 23   8AM

A t 10 pm, I retrieve the kids, bleary-eyed and cranky from sugary treats at Cheryl's. I knew she'd do it. Now, their bedtime's a battle of whining and begging for more treats, calling me the meanest mommy in the world, howling that Cheryl would have given them a cookie. Good Mommy, Bad Mommy. But which is which?

In the morning, after dark scowls they finish their Red River cereal, and we whisk off to St. Ives to get those library tests. Paula, the librarian, who dotes on Edward, shoves a sheaf of unmarked tests from her desk.

"I need these marked right away. I hope you won't have any questions, Mrs. Forsyth, as I'm very busy today trying to get all this work done before noon when we close for the Christmas break!" She turns her head smartly and recommences pounding on her computer.

I realize I'm at the level of a gofer, a dog's body, but I don't care. I'll do such a bang-up job on these tests, she'll be begging for me to do more.

I round up the kids, who are running their hands along the shelves and shelves of books. On our way out, I peek into Edward's office. He's not there. He must have called Paula after our dinner to get the work ready for me. Too bad I can't say thank you in person, but I'll thank him by getting all the tests done before the school closes today.

I rush back to the house, put the kids in front of a large LEGO set, and sit down at my small hall desk. The tests are hand-written. The kids are used to keyboards, not penmanship, so it's time-consuming deciphering their scrawls. They also have to lose marks for spelling, grammar and punctuation. I note commas and apostrophes where they should be, and delete them where they shouldn't be.

Through gritted teeth, I apply myself and in record time, two and a half hours, I circle the last apostrophe error. I feel my brain burning. How does Paula survive this? How will I?

I pack everything into my brown book bag, shut off *Elf*, the movie Stevie's turned on, and bundle everyone into the van. When we get to the office, everyone's in a tizzy. The principal, Victoria Lomboni, is looking way up into the angry red face of Joseph Irondale.

Since Irondale owns Tic Tock Travel agencies, he's never late for anything or allows that in anyone else. Apparently, Edward Osler's a no-show for their earlier appointment. Disaster.

Normally, the Directors' office is a noisy cacophony of teachers asking for impossible favours, secretaries ticking on their computers trying to get the Board paperwork done, and phones ringing with impossible requests from well-heeled, impatient parents. But, in the presence of Irondale's fuming, all have fallen in a frozen silence.

"I missed an important meeting at my company to be here to talk to Osler about my boy and he's an hour late." He leans down into Victoria Lamboni's stricken face. "If this is how he handles school meetings, maybe he isn't fit for his job."

Victoria Lamboni cautiously steps closer to him. She wants to contain the public spectacle, and she also wants Edward's job.

"Why don't you and I have a chat in my office, Joseph?" She parts her bright red lips in a coy smile, but Irondale prefers a broader audience for his rants, especially about Edward Osler. Irondale despises Edward for upsetting his meticulously laid plan for getting his son, Jeremy, into Harvard.

Three years earlier, Edward was one of the school staff who took a group of students on a field trip to Washington. Jeremy Irondale was already on probation for smoking pot in the washroom, which meant a curtailment of privileges, like field trips.

But Irondale insisted Jeremy be allowed to go to Washington because he'd already arranged for him to have lunch with the Administrative Assistant of a Congressman.

Edward reconsidered the ban, thinking this opportunity might focus the boy on bigger goals than smoking pot to impress his friends. However, to protect the school, he forced both Irondales to sign a behavior contract the gist of it being, No Drugs.

The trip went smoothly until the night before they were to fly back to Toronto. It was Edward's turn to supervise lights out. Edward, he decided on a surprise inspection of the students' rooms.

Even in the hall outside Jeremy Irondale's room, Edward could smell marijuana. When he opened the door, he saw a faint cloud of smoke in the air and four students lolling half on, half off each other on the carpet, giggling.

The light from the hallway startled them. They looked up and saw Edward, scowling at them like an angry RCMP officer. A lit joint fell from Jeremy Irondale's fingers.

"Irondale, pick that up now and hand it over!" Edward ordered. Instead of obeying, Jeremy dashed to his suitcase on the bed and snapped the locks shut.

Edward shook his head. "Irondale, open up that thing. I'm hoping you weren't stupid enough to bring pot across the border."

Glaring at Edward the whole time, Jeremy threw open the suitcase to reveal several fat joints, rolling paper, and a baggie of marijuana.

"You idiot!" Edward snarled. "If you were caught bringing this crap back by Customs, we'd all be detained, and you might even be jailed. How would that look on your record? How might that affect everyone in this room's university entrance opportunities? Did you give any thought to your father at all?"

Jeremy smirked and sat on the bed. "He'd get me out of everything."

Edward grabbed the joints, stepped between the scared-quiet kids on the carpet, and flushed the whole mess down the toilet.

When they got back to Toronto, Edward chose not to report the incident to the police, but he got Victoria Lamboni to suspend Jeremy for 10 days. Within an hour, Joseph Irondale was in the Board office with a lawyer.

The lawyer threatened to sue the school and Edward Osler personally for false accusations. Jeremy had denied having drugs on him. And even though the other students supported Edward's version of events, because there was no physical evidence of drugs, Irondale forced the school to rescind its suspension and remove it from Jeremy's record.

Irondale wasn't stupid, of course. He knew Edward might be asked for a recommendation by the Harvard admissions office, so he was now working single-mindedly to get Edward Osler fired. Missing this date with Irondale was tantamount to job suicide.

No one in the office could fathom why Edward would miss a meeting this morning with him, but I'm afraid I know why. The baby monitor incident. I interrupt Irondale's rant.

"Sir?"

He glares in my direction. "Whooo aaaare yooooou?"

He sounds like the Cheshire cat in Alice in Wonderland, but meaner.

"I'm Sara Forsyth, technical assistant to the Library Head." Irondale stiffens. He thinks libraries are a waste of money. If it hadn't been for Edward, the library at St. Ives would have become a computer lab focused on business subjects alone.

"I know why Edward isn't here."

Irondale levels his furious black eyes on me, livid Edward has a defender. I rush on.

"He's so sorry for missing today's meeting with you. But he had a family health emergency late last night, and he called me knowing I'd probably be up late with my baby who's sick, which's why I'm so tired this morning, and forgot to relay the message to his secretary."

"Rea-a-a-ally?" Irondale drawls, unconvinced.

Stevie looks up at me. "Mommy, was Sally sick last night?"

Children will make liars of their parents given any chance at all.

I smile down at him. "You were asleep, dear." Sally coughs. End of interrogation.

Irondale writes down my full name to intimidate me, which it does. Then he stomps out of the office, furious at Edward's excellent excuse.

Once he's out the door, Victoria turns on her heel and marches into her office, slamming the door. I hand the marked tests to the secretary to be logged into the marks program. She hands me $40 from Petty Cash, on Edward's orders.

I wish everyone a Happy Holiday and gather the kids back into the car. I creep along the road slippery with ice. Twice I skid, slipping sideways towards cars in the next lane. My all-season tires are bald, rather like Dale. But this is no time for gallows humour. I've no money for snow tires. Yet if I don't get them, I'm going to have an accident, I know it, with the kids in the car.

Cautiously, I veer off into a grocery store parking lot to take a breather from the tense driving, and also to pick up a few Christmas goodies for our early celebration. Dale gets the kids for Christmas this year, so we're celebrating tomorrow.

At a Salvation Army kettle inside the door is a teenage Santa Claus singing "Joy to the World," pumping his arm up and down like he's at a rock concert. I have a job, I have a few dollars in my pocket. I feel especially joyous at this moment, so I send Stevie over with a quarter.

When the teenager smiles at us, I walk over to him and whisper, "Hey, Santa Honey, Momma needs new snow tires."

14

DECEMBER 23   1 PM

B y the time we get home on those slippery roads, my back's in a tension spasm, it's lunch time, then naps. I usually try to take a nap with them, but not today. I have to get ready for Christmas.

In no time, they're done with their grilled cheese and pickle sandwiches, and lumber off to dreamy time. My back's still sore, so I lie down on the couch for a minute, but just for a minute because I have to get going on Christmas.

Last year, without Dale's income again, I realized I had socks and underwear as presents for the kids, but nothing fun. I scrounged around in the mall until I found a baseball wallet for Stevie and a sequined purse for Sally.

The gifts turned out to be bigger hits than I expected. When we left for our family excursion to the Science Center, they each insisted on bringing their new wallet. Stevie also insisted on putting in it his $20 cash, a gift from Ronnie.

After creating songs in the music studio, talking to each other from across the vast room even though we were whispering, and watching Sally's hair stand on end at the electricity ball, the kids decided they needed a drink.

Stevie insisted on spending his own money for his apple juice. He pulled out his Christmas wallet, placed his $20 on the counter, watching the cashier as if she were a thief, and tucked his change and receipt back in his wallet. That accomplished, he handed it to me for safekeeping.

That set my panic bell off. The August before, Stevie, Sally, and I had been at a park, lying around on a plaid blanket.

"Mom," Stevie had jumped up, "I want to race around those trees like baseball bases. Can I?" He'd been desperate to play baseball but the fees were so high.

"You want to race me?" I'd been desperate for him to say no.

"No, you'd win. And the grass has too many bumps for Sally. I'd be picking her up the whole time."

Stevie had been comfortable in his big brother role. Sally relied on him one hundred percent. She'd rolled on her stomach and nodded. "I fall down." Instead, I'd offered to time him to see how fast he could go.

"Okay," he agreed, "but use my new watch."

Ronnie had given Stevie $60 as a birthday gift, and he had purchased an Ironman watch, much too big for his thin wrist, and much too complicated for a five-year-old. But that's what he wanted. I still had no idea how to use this techno monster.

"Stevie, I might break it." Family joke. Dale used to say I broke electronic things just by looking at them. "I'll use my own watch." Then I'd slipped his into my purse, and waved my arm to start the race.

On the drive home, Stevie had said, "Mom, can I have my watch?" I'd reached into my purse, but couldn't find it.

"Here, Stevie, you look in Mommy's purse." He hadn't been able to find it either. I pulled to the side of the road, and turned the purse upside down. The watch wasn't there. My purse had an open top, so we figured it might have fallen out on the grass. I'd swerved a U-turn, and sped back to the park. We searched, but the watch was gone.

I'd been mortified. I was not a safe haven for my children. Of course, I had replaced it though I had to dip into the grocery money to find $60. That made me feel like an even bigger loser. And now, here was Stevie, trusting me again with his wallet, his newest treasure.

I stored it in a safe place. So when Stevie asked for it, to my horror, it was nowhere in my purse. Once again, we returned to the scene of the crime, but there was no wallet left on the table, under the table, on the floor or in any pocket of either Stevie or Sally. It wasn't in the Lost and Found. Someone must have picked it up.

Stevie wouldn't make eye contact with me. Sally began to sing, "Rise, Sally, rise," her scared song. No, I wasn't a safe haven for my children. As Dale always said, "You never do get things right."

Lying with my eyes closed on the couch, I remember the dream I had last night. I saw bedraggled parents scouring thrift shops to find Christmas presents for their kids. No doubt it was a reflection of my own worries. I realize that in my murky basement is a cornucopia of unwanted or outgrown toys from the rich Dale days. Maybe I can ease the heartaches of other parents struggling this Christmas.

I slip downstairs, a large plastic bag in tow, and quickly snatch up four now ignored stuffed animals, a too-short hockey stick, a forgotten doll, even a neglected toy oven. Eager to donate everything I can, I reach for a small box behind the furnace where it lies in the dust. It once held a child's calculator. Maybe it's still in there. I pull out the contents and stare in disbelief at what's in my hand.

My legs give way and I sink down on the basement steps. It's Stevie's Christmas wallet. I peek inside. There's the receipt from the Science Center for his apple juice, and the $17.20 in change.

The children were too young to have done this and why would they? Dale didn't live here at the time the wallet went missing, and I certainly didn't put it in a calculator box and hide it in the basement.

How does that song go, Scarlet Ribbons? "If I live to be 100, I'll never know from where came those lovely scarlet ribbons." How had the wallet gotten into this basement?

I'm not a religious woman to put it mildly. God never helped me during my difficult childhood, or my weight issues, or my bad husband or my children's negligent father. What has God ever done for me? Nothing. So, I don't believe this gift has anything to do with Him.

But maybe it's some kind of vote from the universe. Maybe I'm not an inadequate mother after all? I do mean well, and I am doing the best I can.

Or, maybe this is a reward for thinking of someone else for a change by gathering all these toys for other parents and their kiddies.

I clutch the wallet tightly, and lug the bag of used toys upstairs. I feel better about myself than I have in a long time.

15

DECEMBER 23   3PM

O nce the kids are up from their naps, Stevie suggests making a snowman and I agree. It takes quite some time to get both of them into their extra sweaters because their snowsuits aren't that warm, and extra socks because their boots aren't that warm, but we manage to stumble out of the house while there's still daylight.

Across the street, Cheryl and her girls are just getting out of their brand new Jeep with their bushy Christmas tree tied to the roof. Cheryl's husband, Stewart, bounds out of the house with a dolly. And in the center of their lawn's an enormous snowman he and his girls made earlier. It has eyes of coal, where do you get that nowadays? A carrot nose, and thin branch arms. My heart sinks in defeat.

Stevie senses the undercurrent. He solves the situation handily. He picks up a snowball and throws it across the street. Stewart whoops, and throws one back. His girls only giggle and grab onto his legs, no fun at all. Stewart has no son. I do. And a daughter. I smile. Twice lucky, me.

70

Once Stevie has vanquished Stewart, we build a lovely snowperson. S/he has button eyes, a button nose, and lipstick. Sally insisted.

Then we head back into the house to prepare our Christmas feast. I won't see them for a week now. One more reason not to divorce Dale.

We apron-up, and prepare a Christmas dinner that can't be beat. The menu's international. Tomato Egg Drop Soup from China. This recipe was from a senior Asian student at St. Ives who traded me recipes for English tutoring after school. I got the better deal.

I dice the tomatoes, Sally drops them into the warming water. I break the eggs, and Stevie scrambles them with chopsticks, slopping over the edge of the pot. He's an enthusiastic cook. I measure and slice the ginger and green onions and they dump them in. This takes at least twice as long as doing it myself, but it's twice the fun.

Now we start on their all-time favorite, Christmas Chicken from Morocco. This dish was the first solid food Stevie ate. And he ate two helpings of it.

To accompany that, a breath-tingling Italian Caesar Salad with homemade garlic croutons. What can I say? My kids prefer savory to sweet. How are they my children?

That connection becomes clear in their choice of dessert: Jamaican Pineapple-Coconut Squares, enough sweet to knock out a whole village. These are my kiddies after all.

What with filling up the gas tank and buying the groceries, I've spent all the money I got through Edward. Luckily, for the next few days, the kids are eating on their Dad's dime. He's taking them to a ski resort in Collingwood. Not that they ski. They do toboggan, so I hope he'll take them, he and Chloe-the-Very-Thin.

I freeze the leftovers and let the kids finish watching Elf. I haven't given them any presents. They haven't noticed that, yet. Then I remember. I run over to the bag of toys I left in the hall closet. There on top of Stevie's baseball wallet.

"Stevie, look what I've got," I sing.

He runs in the room and gapes. "My Christmas wallet! We didn't lose it! This is the best Christmas ever, Mommy." He grabs me in a tight hug.

Sally toddles over, sees the sack of toys and yelps, "Santa! Santa!" She dives into it and spots the forgotten doll. She cradles it lovingly in one arm and hugs my legs with the other.

"Best Christmas Mommy ever."I couldn't have planned this better if I'd been the one who planned it. I'm on a roll. Stevie yawns.

"Time to get ready for bed, sweethearts, and sweet dreams."

"Sweet dreams, Mommy," he replies.

"I'll be up to read you a story in a few minutes. And then Mommy will tuck you in."

Stevie straightens his little back. "Okay on the story, but I'll tuck myself in. I'm the man of the house, you know." And he climbs the stairs slowly, heavy with a responsibility he doesn't deserve, a child trying to handle his parents' mess.

Why does this remind me of my late father and me?

I suffered an incident on my last day as librarian at SunnyCare. Elke, the German secretary, she said Swiss, didn't even bother to drill me with her gimlet eye as I left early carrying nothing but my overstuffed French clutch.

Though it was only four o'clock, it was already dusk. The depressing weather was in direct opposition to my mood. I was going to join Edward Osler at St. Ives Private School as the Head of their Library.

The wet snow piled up on the street turning to brown slush the instant cars drove over it. I inched my way carefully along the icy sidewalk. The people ahead steered around the snow piles and steaming sidewalk grates. We edged down the slippery subway steps, being careful to hang onto the rough metal railing. I hadn't fallen since I was a kid and didn't want to start again. I passed by the blank ticket-taker, an overweight man with thick, wet lips.

Round-shouldered commuters clogged every square of the white and black subway floor. I navigated up the platform to the first car as the train screeched into the station. Everyone surged forward carrying me on a tide of damp overcoats. We all made it in the doors before the second whistle blew, except one man.

He was standing near the mouth of the north tunnel, swaying, an empty liquor bottle in his shaking hand. His soiled topcoat hung loose about his thin legs. His face was expressionless under the ragged white hair mated on his head. His rimless eyeglasses reflected the red signal light inside the tunnel. He looked like my father on a bad day. And there were many bad days as a gambler.

The crowd stood against the glass panels of the doors, watching him. The train lurched forward. As if hypnotized, the man stepped towards the edge of the platform. The closer the train got to him, the closer he moved to the track. He was going to jump.

I struggled against the pressing bodies, raised my heavy purse, and hit the glass as hard as I could, repeatedly. The man looked up long enough for the subway car to slip past him into the tunnel.

He crumpled onto the platform, safe, prevented from dying by my purse. I couldn't do the same for my father, though I'd tried. He died when their house burned down, a punishment for unpaid gambling debts.

"You saved the poor old drunk," a soft British voice said behind me. I turned to see a man with a salt and pepper beard, and a leather briefcase.

"This time," I answered, my voice tight. His brow wrinkled. He didn't understand addiction was endless dying.

The bad and good part of my father's untimely death was on the day he lost his life, I found my husband to be.

16

I met Dale in the most painful way possible. That weekend, Ronnie and I, both in our mid-20s at the time, were booked to go see a famous, local psychic. We loved that sort of thing. I always felt better after pouring out my problems and getting a promise of better things to come. This time it turned out differently.

We parked on a side street because the spaces in front of the house were all full. Business was booming at the King Street Tearoom. We entered the crowded alcove with ten round tables packed closely together. Each had a red-checked tablecloth, and cracking vinyl kitchen chairs. Every table was full of women chatting excitedly to each other, pouring tea into chipped china cups or nibbling at their cookies.

The law didn't like psychics pretending to predict the future, so they hid in tea rooms and when you paid, it was for the strong tea and the stale cookies.

An elderly waitress hurried over. "How many, dear?"

"Two," Ronnie answered. "We have a reservation."

"Of course." She smiled. "I'll be by with your tea and cookies in a minute. When they call your table number, it's your turn. Oh," she paused, "do you want a special person?"

Ronnie nodded emphatically. "Stewart Dore."

The waitress nodded sagely. "He's the most popular." She whispered, "He's so famous for his predictions, the TV people were here last month. They're making a documentary on us, well, mostly him." Beaming, she handed us two green cards with numbers seventeen and eighteen on them, and bustled away.

In a minute she was back with the teapot, two teacups, and a plate with the regulation cookies, one oatmeal and one vanilla sandwich for each of us, both stale. Ronnie ate all four.

"Drink the tea down to the dregs, dears. Then turn the cup upside down on the saucer and twirl it three times to the left, and then three times to the right. Don't disturb the tea leaves in the cup or on the saucer. When they call your number, take both in with you. And have a nice reading." She scurried away.

The tea was tepid and too strong. After a few sips, I wanted to pitch it out, but I drank it down to the dregs, as ordered, even though my stomach heaved.

At the bottom of my white cup was left a pattern of tea leaves. I could imagine all sorts of things, much like finding shapes in clouds.

Ronnie took out her cell phone and began texting away to any number of people. I leaned forward to survey the women in the room more closely. A few looked young and happy, but most were older, round-shouldered with worry.

These were women who had tried other ways out, and were desperate for relief from some trouble that hadn't yielded to platitudes or the comforting homilies of religion. Just like me. I long ago rejected the gods of religion, which declare ludicrous ideas like genuflection, no bacon, sin, holy wars.

I preferred a stranger with "special" powers as an advisor. The steady buzz of women in the room, the warm stuffy air, and the strong tea made me woozy. The next thing I remembered was the waitress shaking my shoulder.

"Dear, your number's been called. Pick up your teacup and saucer, and follow me." Ronnie gave me a thumbs up and bowed her head in texting again. The waitress checked back on me as we walked down the dark and narrow hall. Was she worried I'd get lost on the way? If she only knew how bad my sense of direction was, she'd have checked more often. I can get lost in an elevator.

We stopped at what had once been a bedroom door. The waitress knocked. A thin voice beckoned us to enter. There he sat, Stewart Dore.

His long hair was silver. He was wearing a western shirt and string tie, and a dark brown vest and jeans. That wasn't the look I'd expected. He was seated at a square table, shuffling Tarot cards, and watching me steadily through gray blue eyes. Most psychics I'd met had gray or blue eyes. I've often thought that coincidence odd.

Dore's pale hand absently waved me to sit down while he reached for my teacup. He looked deeply at the pattern there. Then he looked up, his eyes serious. "Do you know the phone number of the fire department?"

Dore went on. "There's criminal behavior in an older couple." He couldn't know my father was a gambling addict who stole the premium checks his clients made out to SunnyCare insurance. And my mother covered for him when the police raided our house. Even I covered up for him against the police.

Then he folded his hands, smiled, and said, "You'll marry a short, dark stranger and be rich, for a while."

I cackled out loud at that one. Psychic readings always made me feel better.

Ronnie's reading had been less charming. She told me he spoke of a serious illness for a slight, well-educated man. Her husband, Marshall?

Then he startled her by lowering into a gravelly voice and intoning, "Double trouble, double murder."

After which he told her she'd be going on a long journey to a beautiful place with lots of money to spend.

Ronnie drove us to her house then loaned me her car to go see my parents. Their phone had been ringing unanswered since the night before.

I knew on Friday nights they often went to bed early. On Saturday mornings they were at their curling club. When I

76

remembered they'd switched to Sunday morning curling, I realized their phone had been ringing unanswered for two days.

It took almost an hour to get to my parent's, normally a fifteen-minute ride, but in my panic, I kept missing the streets, endlessly turning the wrong way.

When I finally screeched up, there were two police cars, their red and blue roof lights revolving lazily, a parked ambulance, and multiple fire trucks whose firefighters were wrapping up long, wet hoses. My parents' house was burned to the ground.

The only thing left of them was their car parked on the street, black and gleaming. A trench-coated, stocky man approached me. He opened the car and reached in to shake my hand.

"Dale Forsyth, Forest Real Estate."

"I'm Sara Walsh."

He dropped his eyes, and then mumbled, "I was your parent's real estate agent."

"Was?" Hot tears swamped my eyes.

He reached in to help me out of the car. His hand was dry, hard, and warm. He was short for a man, but solid. He had small brown eyes, weathered skin, but a beautifully-shaped mouth, even sensitive.

"We had a meeting today. They were thinking of selling up and moving to Florida."

"What? I had no idea." But it was probably precipitated by some gambling mess.

I faced what was left of the house. It looked dead as a doorknob, as Mom used to say. Used to say? My knees buckled. A strong arm caught my elbow.

"It's bad," he said softly. "They're in there." I started crying, big, noisy gulps. He rushed on. "But the fire chief told me they didn't suffer, what with smoke inhalation." He put his arm around me, holding me up. "The fire chief also said their furniture was turned upside down, a safe broken open. Do you have any idea why?"

I gritted my teeth. I had a very good idea why. Mom and Dad must have been paid a visit by an irate creditor. When he couldn't force Dad to pay up, he set fire to their house during the night as a warning to other welshers.

"Listen," Dale Forsyth said, "let's not talk about this now. What's your first name?"

"Sara."

"What a beautiful name."

I blinked through the hot tears in my eyes. Was he flirting with me, at a time like this? Somehow it felt nice, safe, and normal. He took my arm and began to walk towards his car.

"There's a box I found. It was thrown out of a window and landed in the backyard. Sara's written across it, with a lot of little x's. Would you like me to ask the fire chief for it?"

I nodded, and he was gone. I wanted to turn my back on the house, but I couldn't. It reminded me of Ronnie's dead father. He'd died of evil. His body in the casket was shrunken into a mummy shape, only a husk left. That's how the house felt.

In a few minutes, Forsyth was back. "Here it is." He lifted the lid for me, and inside was the most beautiful camel's hair coat I'd ever seen.

His eyes were sad watching me. I slipped the coat out of the box and pulled it on top of mine. In seconds, its warmth surrounded me. I tucked my hands into the deep pockets, and felt a slip of paper. When Forsyth was called to confer with a police officer, I turned my back and quickly opened it.

Sara,

Dad has borrowed quite a bit of money lately. You know why. Someone called about an hour ago to say they were coming to collect. We don't want to be home for the visit, so we're locking up, and going on vacation. We need to talk to Marshall about our wills.

The note ended there. In spite of wearing two coats, I shivered. Forsyth was returning, so I ripped the note into tiny pieces and stuffed it in the pocket.

I couldn't tell anyone I knew who burned my parents' house because they'd find out about Dad's gambling. Wasn't it better to have all their dirty secrets burn with them?

Dale Forsyth said gently, "Do you have someone to call?"

I nodded. I had Ronnie, but I no longer had the parents I loved. I stifled a sob. He took my arm gently. "Let's go for coffee."

Here was an attractive, law-abiding real estate agent offering support. He was wonderful during the horrible aftermath of disposing of the lot the property had been on. He helped me get through the paperwork, the loss, the mourning. We were married four months from that day.

When I remember this, all I want is to have him back.

17

DECEMBER 24   6AM

C hristmas Eve morning dawns bright and sunny, clear blue
    skies and icy air. The Arctic vortex sits heavily on us. Dale will
be here shortly to collect the kids for their Christmas time with him
and Chloe-the-Very-Thin.

I tossed all night in a terrible nightmare about that gruesome
episode I overheard on the baby monitor. I kept trying to reach
Ronnie on her cell phone to no avail. In the dream, I asked her,
"Why don't you buy a new phone where you are?" That still niggles
at me.

I check the time. I want to bake a lemon cake for Dale before he
picks up the kids. It's his favorite. I'll woo him back with food. It
worked before. And I won't eat one bite of it. I won't.

I turn on the radio to the Talk News while I race around the
kitchen making his cake. If there has been a murder, they'll be the
first to make a frenzied report of it. I listen for an hour, but nothing.

Is it possible I misinterpreted the whole thing? Maybe it was a
couple making love, all that heavy breathing which's only a faint

memory for me. But, Dale will be here soon. And where there's life there's hope.

If he's a good father, he'll shower Stevie and Sally with the big gifts since he's a big earner. Stevie wants an iPod, just like all the other five year olds. Sally wants that electronic frog reading thing. Multiple bucks.

Once Dale picks them up, I'll be alone for the rest of the holidays. Well, not exactly. I'll be at Ronnie and Marshall's tonight for Christmas Eve dinner, and stay over for Christmas morning. Their lack of kids keeps me from getting too depressed though it depresses Ronnie.

The doorbell rings. Dale's way early. The kids aren't even up. I dust flour off my black sweatshirt, which tries to hide the painfully obvious. Dale peers though the door window, his eyebrows puckered in irritation. I'm keeping him waiting.

"Sara," he says formally as I pull open the door.

"Dale." I dimple up. "Your timing's perfect. Come right in."

He takes a step back, startled. He hasn't always gotten this warm a greeting when he's shown up, hours or days late. But this time he's early. That's interesting. A positive behavior. Maybe he wants to repair our marriage, too.

I want my old life back, where I could be the fulltime mother and not have to worry about facing bills and bank accounts and solo decision making and popcorn alone on the couch.

"Please, come in. I have a little present for you. Don't worry, you didn't have to buy me anything. I didn't buy it, either, I made it. Your favorite lemon cake," I finish breathless. I'm nervous.

He steps in briskly, not one to linger over subtleties. He's gained weight. Too much cruise food? On him, it looks good. How maddening.

He's wearing his contact lenses today. This means he's here to flirt. In order to do that well, he wears his contact lenses because he thinks they make him look sexier. Unfortunately, they irritate his eyes, making him blink so much he succeeds only in looking nervous.

I realize he hasn't worn his contacts here for a long time. Are we on the same wavelength? Have we both had enough of this separation, this breaking apart of a family? Isn't the point of life to have a family with both parents and two children of each sex to replace us? If not the whole point, surely it's the main one.

Stevie, dressed in his jeans and Leafs' sweatshirt, shoots past me to hug his Dad. Dale holds his arms up, keeping a set of keys away from Stevie's face. Does he still have a key for this door? What does that mean? Likely it means I should change the locks. So why haven't I? One, I can't afford it. Two's becoming obvious: A.B.D., Anything But Divorced.

"How are you, Stevie?" Dale asks, bending down to pull the boy's arms from around his knees.

Sally's wearing her little jeans and her yellow goldilocks sweatshirt, backwards. Stevie must have dressed her. She toddles over and also goes for Dale's knees, but he darts to the side. He pats her head absently. He wasn't there for her birth or for anything else, so there's little bond on either side. Sally simply imitates her brother.

"Stevie, why don't you go upstairs with Sally and get your suitcases?" I suggest.

"I can bring them down. I can bring down hers and mine," he boasts.

"No, sweetheart, they're too heavy. Just call me when you have them, and we'll do it together."

Dale smirks. "You have noodle arms, Sara. Stevie, you call Dad when you have them, and I'll help you."

I'm dumbfounded. Dale has never lifted a finger to help the kids with anything. I look at him more closely. His camel hair coat's rumpled, even a little soiled.

"Did Chloe lose her way to the Laundromat?" I ask. That's a running gag he sometimes allows between us. As if it's cute that Chloe-the-Very-Thin never does housework. Unlike me, they have a cleaning lady, send out their laundry, and stock a whole raft of take-out menus for meals.

He stiffens. "Chloe's none of your business." I'm put in my place. Dale clears his throat. "I'm going out west to see Mom." I nod. He said that on the phone. "She's just been diagnosed with Alzheimer's." Tears spring to his eyes. I reach out my hand automatically to comfort him. To my shock, he grabs it. "With Dad gone, I'm all she has. I have to be there with her."

I wrench my hand from his. "No. You want to take the kids and leave me here."

What fantasy had I been spinning for myself? It's the new Dale in front of me.

He rushes on, "...or move her here, move her here." His voice's strained. Unasked, he makes his way to the couch and sits down heavily. "I'll know what to do after I've visited." He drops his head in his hands. "I've ruined so many things. Now, my mother's alone and sick."

Did he mean he ruined our family, our marriage, me? This emotional display's so uncharacteristic, I wonder if I'm being manipulated. Since when does Dale want the kids? Is he trying to please his mother before it's too late, a mother who could never be pleased? This is too complicated.

"Dale, your mother has never shown any interest in the children."

His eyes narrow slyly. "She will, though, once she spends more time with them. And us." Red alert. "Chloe and I want to get married, Sara. We want to have a family, and, we want to live in the most beautiful province in Canada."

He isn't here to invite me to join him on his adventure. So dies the dream of a reunited family. I was clutching at straws, and a straw man.

"You think you can steal my children, dump them on your— wait a minute. I want to see proof of your mother's diagnosis."

He smirks. "I don't have to provide that to you."

"You rotten animal! You want to move to British Columbia not to help your mother, or show her the kids…"

"Look, Sara, what I want is none of your business. What you have to realize is that you do not have the financial resources to care for my children. You don't work. Your paltry B&B pays squat."

"If you'd give me the child support our separation agreement calls for—"

"It's in a trust fund to keep you from squandering it on yourself. Anyway, you should be earning enough to run a household but you don't. And worse, you're putting my children in danger every time you let strangers come into this house to stay overnight. You have no idea who these people are, or what they might do to my sleeping children."

Said that way, the B&B will sound bad to the courts. I have to get the money to put in that enclosure of the staircase, but from where? He stares at me with his mouth set in the grim line I've seen him use in negotiations when he's playing hard ball.

"Sara, my mother wants to spend time with the kids. Okay, she isn't suffering from Alzheimer's, yet, but she's getting older." He stops speaking. He knows he's said too much.

"Your mother's an alcoholic."

"She's not!"

"Your mother never has food in the refrigerator, doesn't cook, and drinks booze all day. You'd subject your children to her care?"

"Who told you that nonsense?"

"I was there, remember?"

I met her once when we flew to Vancouver to tell his parents about our wedding. Dale's father wasn't home. He was at a conference. Conference was the family euphemism for "his latest mistress." Maybe that was why his mother drank so much. When we entered the house, she was leaning against the kitchen counter, a highball glass full of clear liquid in her hand. It was 10 am.

"Would you like a drink?" she asked me, pleasantly.

If she'd offered me chocolate cake at 10 am, I wouldn't have blinked, but vodka? When I shook my head no, she pushed off the counter, sauntered languidly to the kitchen table and sank down.

"See what's for breakfast in there, Dale, dear," she said, tilting her head towards the fridge. Then she stared at me. After awhile, she slowly and carefully got up, tottered out of the room, and was never seen again.

Dale broke down. He said as a kid there was never food in their refrigerator for breakfast or any meal. His mother was always busy with committees, meetings, or causes. She didn't cook or shop for food. They ate out or ordered in.

What kind of an awful family did he come from, and what kind of a partner and father would he be with these people as his role models?

"But you, Sara, you cook and especially for me. You ask me my favorites and you make them." He looked up at me adoringly with starved puppy eyes, and I melted.

He never uttered a word of criticism about my cooking, only about my packing on the pounds. He rarely gained an ounce. Unfair male metabolism.

"The kids'll love her. And they'll love BC, and Chloe."

Any vestige of desire to reunite with him evaporates. I rage, "You want my children to live with the woman who stole my husband, who doesn't like them, to be babysat by a raging alcoholic grandmother? Why are you making a play for children you and your fling-a-ding don't want?"

He jiggles his knees, looking away, clearly eager to get out of here. Fortunately, the kids are running around upstairs. This gives me time to get to the bottom of this crazy turn of events. I decide to try charm.

"Dale, your mother misses her grandchildren? I have to admit, that sounds nice."

His shoulders relax and he faces me again. "She'll be a big help for us once Chloe and I start our new business."

Bingo! I continue calm questioning. "You're starting a business and with Chloe? How nice. What kind of business?"

He grins widely and I see his teeth have been recently whitened. He used to scoff at that. "An Amway distributorship."

I'm stunned. "You're leaving real estate to sell kitchen supplies?"

His laugh booms out, hearty but humourless. "No, Medusa. As usual you're out of touch. Amway's a multimillion dollar company now and sells everything from dish soap to appliances. Real estate's too competitive these days. I'm working 20 hours a day and that's no life for Chloe. Plus, her family lives in BC."

"This still doesn't explain why you want the children."

"Because Amway is a family-oriented company. They want their distributors to be a part of their family philosophy."

I brace myself. "You mean our children are a ready-made family for you to show off to get a business deal?"

His smile vanishes replaced by a grim line. "I want custody of the kids. You're putting them in danger in this house full of strangers and you don't have a stable income. You don't stand a chance against me."

"Daddy, we're ready," Stevie and Sally call from the top of the stairs.

"Coming," he calls. To me, he hisses, "I'll see you in court."

He bounds up the stairs, grabs their small plastic suitcases under one arm and a giggling Sally under the other.

At the bottom of the stairs, she pats his face softly and burbles, "Good job, my Mommy." She's seldom had use for the word Daddy.

I'm drowning in feelings. My husband who said he loved me plans to leave me, and take my darling children, too.

That's what he thinks.

THE POINT

87

18

DECEMBER 24   4 PM

I pack my canvas weekend bag ready to spend Christmas with Ronnie and Marshall. I still haven't reached her, but she's scheduled to be home from New Mexico by now.

I'm leaving the stillness of my lonely home, preferring the messy days of Christmas at Ronnie's. One Marshall coughing, two women chatting, three wine-soaked smiles, four courses for dinner, and a dramatic black Christmas tree. Ronnie's way out-there in decorating.

I'm desperate to talk to her about what I heard on the baby monitor. Who was the evil-whispering woman? I need to air it all out in front of someone who'll listen, add her two cents worth, and then let me muse on it. Ronnie's famous for forgetting things people say shortly after hearing them. She's a perfect sounding board.

I back our geriatric van out of the garage. And what to my wondering eyes should appear, but a small band of pre-teen boys mounting my neighbour's front steps.

Sweet pubescent male voices, like angels in the crisp winter air, begin to sing, "We wish you a Silent Night." In all the years we've been living in this house, no one has ever caroled on the street. Maybe it's the new Catholic elementary school around the corner.

But my neighbours are new to Canada, straight from China. They're certainly lovely people, quiet, smiling, neat, but their English isn't the best nor is their understanding of Canadian customs. They used to watch Dale for hints of what to do with the garbage, when to water the lawn, even what kind of car to drive. There's a chance they'll shoo the boys away.

I idle in the car to see what will happen, thinking maybe I should run back into the house and scrounge up some cookies to repay the boys for their sweet voices.

The curious parents and the 9-year old daughter appear in their doorway. All are smiling, and after much squealing excitement from the daughter, the boys are presented with a box of Lindor chocolates and waved on to the next house.

Tears spring to my eyes. Love from unexpected quarters.

I set off for Ronnie's. As I drive, I order my phone to call Edward so I can leave a voice mail. Blue tooth technology in the car's another luxury left over from Dale days. He doesn't pick up. Probably busy finishing up at the school.

I hope he'll at least check his voicemail. "Edward, it's Sara. I'm calling to warn you Irondale's on the warpath because you missed a meeting with him this morning. He might use the Christmas break to persuade the Parent Board to fire you. You know him. Any excuse to get rid of you. Call me back when you get this message."

I'm approaching Ronnie's brick and wood home when I pull to the right quickly. Two ambulances, red lights flashing, rush by. No sirens? That usually means it's too late to save the person.

Wait a minute, they're stopping at Ronnie's house. What's going on? Parked in her driveway are two black and white police cars, red and blue roof lights flashing around lazily. I see yellow crime scene tape surrounding the house.

Memories of the screaming voices on my baby monitor flood back. Did Marshall finally do it? After that radio show, he threatened to kill Ronnie. I grab my purse, then slip-slide over the snow-packed sidewalk to their driveway.

A pack of police are blocking the entrance to the Stohl's front door. I feel light-headed being this close to cops.

"Stop there. No one's allowed past the tape," a young policeman with short blonde hair says, his breath visible in the cold air.

He moves towards me. I stand rigid. I want to hide, but something bad has happened at Ronnie's. I have to help.

I say the first thing that comes to mind. "I'm expected for dinner."

The officer shakes his head. "Sorry, but no one's allowed behind the police tape."

I want to push him down in the snow, rub it in his authoritarian face, and freeze his eyeballs out, but I restrain myself for Ronnie's sake.

"I'm her sister," I lie. The officer looks away. "Please," I beg.

He purses his chapped lips. "Wait here." He tramps through the snow to a tall man in a dress coat and nods in my direction. The tall man waves at me. Do I know him? Both men stride over.

"Miss Forsyth?" says the tall one.

I don't bother to correct him about my marital status. I'm not sure what it is myself. "How do you know my name?"

"I'm Detective Garry Clere of the Toronto Police, and this is Officer Erika Cochran." The officer nods, her face blank. Ms. Robot. "Mrs. Stohl said you'd be coming. You can see her in a moment, but I'd like to ask you a couple of questions first, if you don't mind."

Garry Clere, probably mid-thirties, has impeccable taste in clothes. He's wearing pressed, dark green slacks, a light green checked shirt, and a tartan green tie inside his open black wool topcoat. Ronnie would be impressed. His clear brown eyes stare into my face. Officer Cochran's fussing with a tatty black notebook and a small pen.

Clere says, "Do you know exactly what time Mrs. Stohl arrived here after the murders?"

I hear it. I hear him. But, it's so cold. My hands are freezing. Where are my gloves? I remember. They're in the car with my wool hat. I think I'll just get them because I feel so cold.

"Mrs. Stohl says you knew Mr. Stohl was murdered yesterday. How did you come by this information?"

I pitch forward, knocking Detective Clere off balance. He throws his arms around me, and rights us both. I'm shaking all over now. A policeman touched me.

"Mrs. Stohl also says you knew that his nurse, Kim Park, was murdered at the same time. How did you come by this information, Miss Forsyth?"

My legs give way. Detective Clere catches me before my knees hit the snow.

He puffs, righting me once again. "We'd better go inside." He stamps his brown leather boots to warm his feet. They must have been out here for some time. And he starts again.

"Mrs. Stohl told me you knew about these murders before her. Yet she's the one who called the police. Can you clarify how you knew, Miss Forsyth? Were you on the scene?"

I can hardly hear him for the racket my heart's making. What a time to have a heart attack, which I've never had. But it's constantly on my mind because of the tachycardia. Any stress starts my heart pounding. The doctor says I likely won't have a heart attack. But right now, my heart feels like it's about to explode. I'm stunned silent and wobbling.

"No more falling, please," he begs. "Let me help you inside." I struggle to get out of his grip, but Clere's one of those strong wiry ones. He helps me into the bright foyer of Ronnie's house. Officer Cochran pushes a chair behind me and I sit.

Ronnie's crouching on the floor, waiting. Her cheeks are mottled, her eyes fiery, her red hair flying out at all angels. "You said you'd check on him," she hisses, and she springs at me.

Clere darts in front of me, suddenly, my protector. With one arm, he blocks Ronnie's attack, while with the other he grabs my hand for comfort. I can smell his damp, wool coat , lime cologne.

I peek around him at Ronnie. She looks dazed. She slips down to the floor, her white leather pants squeaking on the hardwood. She sobs.

I slip around Clere, get on the floor. She crawls to me and pulls me into her arms, and we begin to rock.

Ronnie whispers, "The real estate lady found him. I got home, Sara. I was home, but when I came into the living room there was this small woman in black, blonde-tipped hair sticking all out like lightning. She was on her cell. I had no idea who she was.

"'Luba Kotash. Remax,' she said, and grabbed my hand in hers. Sarie, she had so many rings, all diamonds, I think. She said, 'You know, Mrs. Stohl, the house is only in Mr. Stohl's name, so it has to be him who signs the listing agreement. The last time I was here, he promised me an exclusive sales agreement for a week. I won't show the house without it being signed, no, it's not legal and it's not right.'

"She was about to go on with her tirade when I said, 'You can't sell my house. I just decorated it.' That stopped her. But she stared at me like I was nuts. Didn't she know I got it into House Digest?"

Ronnie's starting to sound nuts to me, too. I nod, afraid to say anything.

"'Anyway Miss Remax, you are mistaken,' I said. 'Mr. Stohl's very ill at the moment. He can't sell this house. When he wakes up, I'm sure we can clear up this mess.'

"'My name's Luba Kotash from Remax real estate. And what do you mean, Clear up this mess? Is he considering another real estate agent? Really, that's a breach of trust.' She twirled in a circle. 'I've advertised Sunday's Open House at my own expense, I might say, great expense, in the Executive Homes in the Globe and Mail, online and print. Do you know how much that costs? I don't think so.'

"She leaned so close I could smell her spearmint breath and whispered, 'I have an out-of town buyer who insists on seeing this place today.' She beamed at me. "Yes, I do!" Then crossed her arms over her big chest. 'But, Mr. Stohl has to sign the Exclusive

Agreement before I show it to her. He knows the rules. He's a lawyer. I could have him up on charges…'

"She was talking so fast I couldn't get a word in, so I shouted, 'You're fired!' That got her attention. But she barely paused for a breath.

"'I'll just pop into Marshall's room for a second. You see,' she straightened her jacket, 'my contract is with your husband. And I have a signed a purchase offer based on the description alone. The offer price, which I cannot reveal as per a real estate agent's code of ethics,' she leaned closer, 'is tens of thousands over your asking price. Rich ain't the half of it with this babe," she shook her head in awe. "She even sports a full length Blackglamma. The hairs on that thing are longer than my legs,' she snorted.

'Over asking?' I said. I thought maybe selling wasn't such a bad idea what with Marshall being so sick and his income being so low lately. 'Miss Remax, give me your client's offer. I'll talk to Marshall.'

"'My name is, oh never mind. I can't give you this offer unless Marshall signs the exclusive listing agreement. I am sorry.' Again she crossed her short arms over that huge chest.

'Mrs. Stohl, let me get Marshall to sign my listing agreement. It'll take one second. Then we can go over the offer together, and I know I can sweeten it in any way you want. Just take a second.'

"I couldn't think straight. I didn't know what to do, so I nodded. She turned so fast her heels make a cracking sound on the hardwood. She ran up the stairs to Marshall's room. Then she screamed. Again and again. They were blood curdling. I wanted to run somewhere and hide. She stumbled back down into the living room.

"'Mr. Stohl has a bloody nose,' she whispered.

"'You nut! You scared the life out of me with that screaming.'

"She stood there, not moving. 'And he's dead.'

"I grabbed her arm."

"She shrieked, 'He's dead! He's dead!'

"I ran upstairs calling 'Marshall. Marsh?' He didn't answer. I tiptoed to his bedroom. I looked at Marshall. It looked like he was sleeping, but his head was at a funny angle."

Like a child, Ronnie's eyes are wide with disbelief and terror. "His pillow was beside him not under his head. And there was something smeared on his face, Sarie. I touched it. It was dried blood!"

Ronnie looks at her leather pants. There are smears of blood where she'd wiped her fingers. "The dry cleaners charged a fortune the last time I took these in, Sara. How will I pay now?"

I feel a chill. Had Marshall become just her meal ticket?

"I called for Nurse Kim. She would be able to help us because she's a nurse, you know. I ran all over the house calling. Then I went to the basement door because her bedroom's down there. I shouldn't have looked down there, Sarie. Nurse Kim was at the bottom of the stairs. Her neck was bent funny."

"I turned back and saw that ReMax person. 'You killed my husband! You killed them both!' I grabbed for her, but she got past me and ran out the door."

"Poor Ronnie," I soothe. I wrap my arms around her, but she jerks back.

"Are you trying to smother me?"

She starts giggling and she doesn't stop.

19

Detective Garry Clere pushes off the wall where he's been leaning, listening to Ronnie. "Miss Forsyth, do you know who the family doctor is?"

"Dr. Subrisco. He's my doctor, too. Here's his number." I scroll to his number and hand him my phone.

Clere gives it to Officer Cochran who leaves the room. A male cop steps in.

"This is Police Constable Michael DeBraie. He'll be helping Mrs. Stohl to her bedroom."

The officer looks doubtful. "Sir, I believe her husband is still...."

Clere corrects himself. "Not the master bedroom." He turns to me. "Is there a guest room?"

"Ronnie's room's at the other end of the hall. She and Marshall have had separate bed rooms since his illness." Before that, too, but he doesn't have to know. Now, why don't I want Clere to know that? Maybe because I'm not sure Ronnie didn't do it. What about her phone, the spa, and the timing? But I'll never let the cops in on this.

"Do you feel up to staying the night with her, Miss Forsyth?"

I feel sick. Marshall Stohl was a friend and he's been murdered. I'm in the house of murdered people. And I'm getting more scared that what I overheard on my baby monitor was Marshall being suffocated. That I heard his nurse shoved down the basement stairs to her death.

Clere takes something from Officer Cochran and holds it up.

"Miss Forsyth, would you mind taking a look at this glove we found in the hall? Mrs. Stohl says it isn't her husband's, but then, she's upset right now. Is it Mr. Stohl's?"

I recognize the glove like a slap in the face. It's a dark brown leather man's glove with a fur lining from The Bay. I gave that glove and its partner as a present to Edward Osler.

"Miss Forsyth, do you or don't you recognize this glove?" He leans close to me. "It's important."

Of course I know it's important. Anyone who's watched TV murder mysteries knows it's evidence. Wasn't it a glove that finally connected O.J. Simpson to the murder of his wife?

This is the first evidence of the murderer. But, Edward wasn't the murderer. It was the woman, wasn't it?

Clere warns, "Miss Forsyth, if you know who owns this glove and don't tell us, added to the fact that you seem to know a great deal about what took place here last evening, I'm going to charge you with being an accessory to murder."

I step back. "I had nothing to do with any of this."

He goes on, robotically. "If you have knowledge that a crime's being committed, if you're helping the criminal in some way, even if you're simply concealing information, Miss Forsyth, you're an accessory to a double homicide."

Do modern women really faint? My knees buckle. Clere's arm shoots out and steadies me, and then he guides me to the white leather couch Ronnie adores.

If I tell Clere who owns that glove, Edward will be arrested for murder, especially if I reveal my baby monitor story. I don't know how involved Edward is in this monstrous thing. I don't know if he did one murder or both, just helped that woman, or tried to stop her, if he's the dupe, the victim, or the architect?

Even the suspicion of involvement will lose him his job if Joseph Irondale gets wind of it. He could lose his license to practice law and worse, his treasured teacher's credential. After what he's done for me, how can I do that to him?

I shake my head no. Clere squeezes my arm with his thin, strong hand.

"Mrs. Stohl tells me you're a mother. If you have a criminal record, Miss Forsyth, how will that look to your children?"

My heart constricts. If I have a criminal record, Dale will get custody more easily. What kind of a life would the kids have with their father ignoring them in favour of his mistress? Just like his daddy did.

Detective Clere's voice comes from what seems far away.

"Do you understand, Miss Forsyth, that if you're involved in these murders in any way, you could also be in danger? Your children might be in danger?"

I slide off the smooth leather couch. The last thing I hear before my head hits the hardwood floor is a curse from Garry Clere.

20

DECEMBER 25   1 AM

A voice hisses in my ear, "Sara? What are you doing here?"
I wake up at once. Child training. Ronnie's sitting bolt upright in a bra and panties, and I'm lying beside her in her canopy bed.

"Sara, why are you in my bed? Is something wrong at your house?"

Ronnie's sedative has worn off and it seems she has no memory of Marshall and Kim Park being murdered in this very house short hours ago. And I'm not going to be the one to remind her. I'll distract her, and I know how. We aren't best friends for nothing.

"Ronnie, it's Christmas morning! Let's have our cookies."

"That's right! Christmas morning tradition." Ronnie claps her hands. "And I've got chocolate fudge cookies and chocolate crackle ice cream."

In a flash, she's on her feet, though she sinks back down quickly, dizzy. Sedative hangover. "Geez, is this still jet lag?"

It's going to be a bad blow when she remembers.

"Chocolate-chocolate-chocolate," I sing. "Beat you."

She's off like a shot. Powerless to prevent the return of her misery, I slink down the stairs after her. Ronnie has wrapped herself in the rose duvet from her bed. She's almost to the kitchen when P.C. DeBraie steps out of the shadows near the front door.

"Who are you?" Ronnie screams. "Marshall, call the police! Marshall!"

The officer tenses, ready for anything. "Mrs. Stohl, I'm Officer DeBraie, here to protect you."

Ronnie backs away, her hand pressing on her chest. "How do you know my name? Marshall!" she cries. "Marsh?" She turns to me, confused. "Sara, why isn't Marshall answering me?" She pauses, and then bursts into tears. She remembers.

Officer DeBraie melts back into the shadows while I help Ronnie onto a kitchen chair. I grab the chocolate cookies, the chocolate crackle ice cream, and two spoons. There's no need for bowls. And we go at her.

I have to stop halfway through because of brain freeze, but Ronnie plows on, finishing the litre. Barely breathing, she mumbles, "More cookies in the pantry."

I snatch the bag of Oreos, milk from the fridge, and two glasses. This is like the night Dale walked out on me for Chloe-the-Very-Thin. I ate a whole litre of chocolate and hazelnut ice cream, but at the end of the binge, my problem was still there. My husband had left me. Ronnie will have a sugar high for about an hour, yet at the end of it, her husband will still be dead plus she'll have a binge headache to deal with.

"Sarie, I can't stay in this house. Can we go to your house, Sarie?" She topples off her chair and lands in a heap on the floor, the rose duvet cushioning her fall. Just like a drunk.

"Marshalllllll," she moans.

Officer DeBraie peers into the room, scrutinizes the scene and says, "Ladies, enough with the booze."

"We are leaving," Ronnie over-enunciates. "Going to Sharie's." She uses a chair to help her stand back up. "Have to pack." She wobbles off towards her bedroom, but veers into the living room, drops onto the white leather sofa, and passes out.

Officer DeBraie whispers into his cell phone, then jerks his chin at me. "Detective Clere's picking you up in 10 minutes."

Detective Clere? What do I remember about that guy? I can't picture his face. I do recall the smell of his damp wool coat, and his arms holding me up when I couldn't do it for myself. A strong man who lets me lean on him. But he's a cop.

I sink onto a kitchen chair. Who knew emotions could be this exhausting.

"Would you like to go for a drive, Miss Forsyth?"

I look up. Garry Clere's already here. How much time has passed? I stand up quickly, too quickly. Clere's arm snaps around me, holding me steady, a worried look on his handsome face. Can I fall into this man's arms, like a heroine in a romance novel, and let him take over, save me from Dale and Chloe, and the murder of my friend and his sweet nurse?

He helps me on with my coat and we're in the dark then in his police car. I watch as our breath freezes on the inside of the windshield. He leans over to adjust my seat belt and I can smell his lime aftershave. I haven't kissed a man in years, and I'm not sure Clere's allowed to on duty, but I bob my head forward and kiss him on the lips. I miscalculate and our teeth bang against each other.

"Lord," he gasps, rearing back. "I'm gay!"

I blush. Clere's gingerly feeling his swelling lip with the edge of his finger.

"It's my position. It has this effect on women, at least that's what my mother says. That and my snappy dressing." He grins lopsidedly. "Hey, are you alright?"

I splutter an embarrassed apology, which he accepts with a nod. "Please, can I me go home now? I'll talk to you about it all later. I need to prepare a bedroom for Ronnie. She's going to stay with me for the next few days."

He shakes his head sympathetically. "That poor woman." Why oh why is he gay? He scoots around to open the police cruiser door for me. He watches as I climb into my cold car, and pull out onto the street.

But I need to know what really happened before I talk to Clere again. He watches me until I turn the corner towards my house.

When he can no longer see me, I change my route and head to Edward Osler's condo.

21

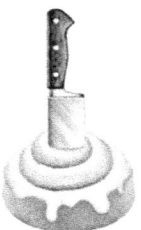

DECEMBER 25   7 AM

T he snow-banked roads have long shadows from the faint
  streetlamps. I drive the short distance to Edward's building.
There's no one around. Well, small wonder. It's early morning on
Christmas Day. I drive into the parking lot and scout for his Ferrari.
Not parked outside, because of course he'd have an underground
spot.

I leave my barely heated van in the Visitor's parking, enter his
foyer and search for his intercom number. No answer. I can see his
mailbox near the entrance. There are a couple of envelopes leaning
against the window. Looks like he hasn't emptied it for a couple of
days.

The door behind me swings open letting in a cold draft. I
glance over my shoulder to see a smiling Detective Garry Clere. I
didn't spot him tailing me. Well, he's an expert.

"Visiting a friend?" He isn't smiling.

"Yes, much like you."

"I thought you were on the way to set up a room at your house
for the distraught Mrs. Stohl."

"Are you following me?"

"What would your kids say if they knew the danger of what you're doing, Mrs. Forsyth?"

So, he's done an Internet search on me since our talk, scant minutes ago. But, it's so easy to do on with a cell phone and a data plan. Now he thinks I lied to him about being a Miss vs. Mrs. Forsyth. And if I lied about one thing…

"You know I'm not.…"

"Married," he finishes my sentence. "I know. Mrs. Forsyth, listen, I care about your safety and even more for that of your children. I know you know something you're not telling me. But, please, leave the murder investigating to the professionals. Murder's a dangerous business."

Why did a cinnamon bun pop into my thoughts? Oh for sweet oblivion. Clere tucks my arm into his and escorts me back to my van. He shuts my door, nods, and ducks his hatless head down against the whipping snow and dark. Why doesn't the man wear a hat?

Without another glance at me, trusting I'll go home this time, he strides back into Edward's building.

I pull out of the parking lot, aim in the general direction of my house, but veer into a small all-night coffee shop. I've research to do.

I'd been content seeing Edward Osler as an exceptional school administrator, someone who helped me when he didn't have to, someone whose his staff respects, even adores him.

But, I have to know more about his background, his problems, anything that might link him or unlink him from Marshall Stohl and Kim Park's murders. What's Edward Osler's whole story?

I settle into a dim booth next to an old-fashioned wall jukebox actually working. The customer before me chose "Stand by Your Man," which plays softly at my side while I pull up Google on my cell phone.

I search the name Edward Osler. The top hit's Senator Edward Davis Osler, a big player in the Conservative Party who now has a seat in the Senate, still active and working even at 78. There's a slight physical resemblance to Edward, something in the chin. So, this is the powerful "His Lordship." Once the owner of thousands of acres of prime Ontario land, but no longer? What happened there?

I scroll to the next hit. This is Lawrence Edward Osler. He's older than my Edward, but younger than the Senator. Must be the dad. Lawrence Osler's a lawyer running for a seat as the Conservative provincial candidate for our district. Since the Forest Village area is a Conservative stronghold, there isn't much doubt he'll get elected.

Ronnie and I like some reigns on the budget, but compassion for the needy. We're Liberal supporters except when the New Democrats have a better platform. A Left divided. No wonder the Conservatives get in so often. Dale votes Conservative. He likes tight reigns on any budget as long as he and his wealthy friends get tax breaks. Dale and I went to vote together, but didn't talk about where the x went. We were a house divided.

The provincial election hasn't been called, but it's expected within the year. There's a tag under Lawrence Osler's name announcing a fundraiser this very Christmas Day at the Forest Village Golf and Country Club. That's maybe fifteen minutes from here.

I read farther. The next hit's Edward Allen Osler, my Edward. School administrator. Known for his innovative educational ideas. Creator of the innovative Jane Finch Storefront School for disadvantaged students for which he won Provincial Teacher of the Year twice in a row. He didn't tell me that.

A theme's developing on the name Edward Osler: old money, power, respect. Yet they all work for a living. Do they have to? And is the missing land part of that puzzle?

Edward's still not picking up on his phone, so I have to find him before Clere does. But where is the man?

I look out the wide plate glass window of the coffee shop. Heavy snow's mounding on the ground. My car was clean when I came in, but it's now heaped with snow. I glance back to the computer page. If Edward's anywhere, he'll be at the breakfast fundraiser for his father.

I hunch up against the wind and snow, but on the way to my car what to my wondering eyes should appear? Detective Garry

Clere. Am I the little goose girl he got stuck to? I turn my back to him as he approaches.

"Need a snow brush?" he asks, all innocence. I ignore him, swipe at the snow with my gloved hands. "Try this." He waves an orange plastic brush. "Or let me do it."

I whirl on him. "I haven't done anything wrong. What law gives you the right to follow me?"

"Law of attraction." He grins, sweeping my door clear.

I hide my smile. He'd make a fun friend if he weren't a cop. But I have to find Edward before he does. That means getting rid of him.

I scowl. "Stop following me or I'll take you on a wild goose chase the likes of which you've never seen."

I struggle into my snow-covered car, praying my windshield wipers are industrial strength. They do the job of clearing the snow off the glass, but barely. I crawl away from his alert face onto the freshly cleared road. Snow plows are wonderful.

But when I check in my rearview mirror, Garry Clere is driving right behind me. Fine, then. He asked for it. I'll take him on a trip to Hell.

I head North on Bayview out of Forest. The lashing snow makes it hard to see. I glance out my back window. Though I can't spot him, I know he's there. I concentrate on my driving. All I can hear is the wind whipping around my car, and the crunch of my bald tires on the packed snow. It's slippery out there.

Gradually I come to the outskirts of town. I make a right turn heading for the small, out of the way Belle Lake at the farthest end of Forest Village. Years ago it was a fetid pond, choking the fish in debris. But the wealthy landowners sunk lake lungs, two accordion-style billows, to stir things up. Now it's alive again.

The morning sun's shimmering on its icy surface. I steer into the ploughed parking lot to settle my nerves after that harrowing drive. I'm a mother of two little ones, a part time librarian, and a Bed and Breakfast owner. Why on earth am I pursuing Edward Osler who might be a murderer?

A tremor goes through me. My breath clouds in the cool car interior. Soon it'll create ice on the inside of the windshield and I'll need Clere's scraper.

There's a knock on my frozen side window. I can't roll it down, so I open my door a crack.

"Garry Clere at your service. Car trouble?"

I laugh. How can you not like the guy?

"Sara, it's really not safe for us to be driving north in this weather. Can we turn around now? Follow my tail lights and I'll help you home."

If I could have, I'd have kissed him again, gay man or not.

THE POINT

109

22

DECEMBER 25   9 AM

C lere takes the lead as we squint through the pelting snow back to Ronnie's house. When we arrive, exhausted from the concentration needed to stay on the slippery road, I invite him for fresh coffee and a treat, if there's any left.

He peers in the picture window at Ronnie, who's staring out at us. He bites his lip. "Will you take good care of Mrs. Stohl?" What's this interest in Ronnie? I thought the man was gay.

"I'll get her calmed down at my place, don't worry."

He blows out his breath, which frosts in the cold. "I don't like women being left alone without protection. I'll send a police officer to your house to keep watch on the two of you. And now, I have a murderer to catch. The longer I take, the less likely the success." His boots squeak as he trudges through the snow to his police car.

I turn to go into her house when I notice Ronnie pacing up and down in front of the picture window, hugging the phone against her shoulder and talking passionately. She sees me, and waves for me to go away. I take another step towards the front door, but Ronnie glares at me through the window. Are those tears on her face? She mouths, "Go away!"

I check behind me. Clere's tire tracks are clear in the snow, away from the house. The Forest Village Golf and Country Club is just two blocks over where there's the Osler Christmas fundraiser happening right now. I get back into my car. This time, I make it to my destination without Clere on my tail. I shove my wild hair as well as I can under my hat and slog into the building.

There's a rush of warm, pine-scented air coming from the cluttered Christmas tree standing ten feet tall if it's an inch. An array of beribboned packages are strewn under the bushy green branches, though I bet it's all for show, empty boxes tied up in expensive wrapping. Do I know something, that is, someone else who fits that description?

The rest of the foyer's festooned with restrained Christmas paraphernalia. Members of the Forest Golf and Country Club are the wealthy villagers, or those who want to appear so. The sign at the front desk lists only one event today, the Traditional Osler Family and Friends Christmas Brunch. I can hear a hubbub of voices coming through the large double doors.

The light's dim in the hallway, so I shrug off my bargain bin coat and hat and leave them on a bench. A speaker has just finished to a round of loud applause and fist pumping. The fist pumpers are middle-aged men wearing suits. Politics brings out the strange in people.

Above the podium from which the speaker has just departed is a large swag of white satin with a giant C and a red maple leaf inside it, the colours and logo of the Conservative Party. A fundraiser on Christmas Day. What would Jesus say?

The speaker's being glad-handed and slapped on the back as he makes his way from the podium. He's wearing a black suit with a white shirt and a red power tie. He looks like Edward in height, same broad shoulders, the cleft chin, but his hair's graying around the temples.

This must be Edward's father, Lawrence Davis Osler, the eager Conservative candidate for Forest Village, Ontario. I search the room for Edward. He should be near his father if he's here at all, but I can't spot him. So, my only hope's waylaying his father for information of his son's whereabouts.

When Lawrence Osler passes me I reach out to shake his hand, then I hold on tight.

"I'm Sara Forsyth, a friend of Edward's. He might be in trouble." Lawrence Osler freezes.

"Then let's talk." He grabs my elbow and pushes us over to a quiet corner amid more back slapping. We're immediately joined by a dignified, elderly man.

"This is my father, Senator Davis Osler. Father, this is a friend of Edward's, Sara Forsyth."

"I'm impressed with your name recall, sir. I couldn't have done it," I say.

"It's a gift, though a necessary part of the job, Miss Forsyth."

"Where's Edward?" the old man interrupts.

"I thought you knew," I say.

The Senator eyes me suspiciously. "Excuse me, Miss, uh, Foster. But how do you know my grandson?"

"It's Forsyth, Dad, Sara Forsyth."

"Edward's the Chairman of the School Board at St. Ives Private School where I work. I want to alert him to a problem which might impact him." This is true, in part.

Senator Osler rubs his chin. He has a cleft in it, clearly a family trait.

"What problem?"

I go into Irondale and his vendetta. Both men sigh deeply, and then Edward's father says, "I know where he's supposed to be."

Senator Osler looks me in the eye, nods, decision made, and rasps, "We could use your help. My grandson's in Hawaii, about to go on a cruise with his wife."

"Of course, of course," I say, but I'm suddenly depressed. I know he's married, of course, but because he never wears a wedding ring, or refers to his wife, I've been deluding myself into thinking he's divorced, translation, available. Because he's still my crush.

But Edward has helped me when I needed him, so whether out of love for him or friendship, I'll help him out of his trouble, even if it's murder. In the meantime, I'll keep as much of it secret as I can to avoid upsetting his family or destroying his career.

Lawrence Osler's talking. "We're worried about him. He hasn't called or texted. We don't trust Elena." He spits out her name like dirt on his tongue. "Now that she has him to herself, on a ship where he can't communicate with us, who knows what she'll do?"

I feel the hairs on the back of my neck stand up. Was she the woman I heard on the baby monitor arguing with Edward?

A group of men barges into our corner, surrounds Lawrence Osler, and though he protests, but not too loudly, sweeps him away to another group of men in the center of the room.

Senator Osler steps closer and leans his face towards me. I can smell spearmint on his breath. "Miss Foster, do you care about Edward?" He hurries to add "…as a friend?"

"I do." Why am I smiling? It sounds like I'm at the altar in a wedding ceremony. What an immature woman I can be.

"Sara, is it? Sara, I wonder if I paid your way, would you consider going on that cruise, and reporting back what's going on with Edward?"

I purse my chapped lips, so dry in this cold winter weather.

"You want me to spy on him?"

"Help him," Senator Osler says, then clutches my shoulder. He has big hands, like his grandson, but thin, bony. "Please," he whispers urgently. "He's in some kind of trouble, I know it. But I can't help him if I don't know what's wrong."

I chew on my lip. Can I really leave to go on a cruise? Of course, the kids are with Dale, so they're taken care of. And if I go on this cruise, I might see something to explain and excuse Edward's possible involvement with the murders.

His father and grandfather have no idea that Edward might be in far more trouble than they suspect.

"I'll do it on the condition that if I see something I don't think is any of your business, I won't tell you."

The Senator nods and hands me his credit card and begins to pat each of his pockets. Finally, he grunts in satisfaction and pulls out a black cell phone covered in lint.

He proffers it to me. "Take this."

I smile. "Senator, I don't need your phone, I have my own."

"But mine has free long distance, and ship to shore calls can be very expensive. Two years ago when I used this on a cruise vacation, I had to pay $8 US a minute."

I blanch. I can't afford that kind of phone bill. I can barely manage the one I have which is as basic as it gets.

"I want you to call me from anywhere the minute you see something important. I'll take yours for now, if you don't mind. You know your own number, I presume?"

Can I trust this old geezer with the lint-covered phone which he can't find half the time with my expensive cell? I don't have the money to replace it. On the other hand, I certainly can't pay for $8 a minute phone calls.

I take his phone and reluctantly hand mine over and we exchange passwords.

"My Administrative Assistant will book your flight to Honolulu where the cruise originates. It's just a short cruise around Oahu, three nights. You can use the credit card for things you need for the trip."

He has no idea what temptation he has just put in my hand. Things I need for the trip, like new boots for Stevie, a warm winter coat for Sally? This, of course, would be spending money that wasn't mine, but hey, it's what I learned at my father's knee.

Osler nods his head as if he's reading my mind. "I'm not a rich man, Miss Foster, but in this case, I'm willing to buy you whatever you need to go."

"You're not a rich man?" I blurt, caught off guard by his candor.

He sucks in air. "We were rich, once. Now, as you see, my son, my grandson, and I have to work for a living. Things changed a few years back, but that's another story which doesn't concern us now." He blinks rapidly, showing the lie.

"You go on that cruise, and report back to me. Edward's my only grandch…," he pauses for a fraction of a second then corrects himself, "…grandson."

I don't know how to interpret any of this. What changed a few years ago? Edward got married. Is there a connection between their money and Edward's wife? How could she bring about such a drastic change to the Osler fortune?

"Don't look so gloomy, Sara. Welfare for the Osler family's a step or two away yet. If you'll help us, you may be doing more for your friend Edward than you can imagine. When my mind's at ease about my grandson, I'll be better able to help my son run for office.

Like me, he wants to pay back some of the good fortune our family has enjoyed in Canada, and serve his fellowman and his country. It's the Osler way. We pay back the good we have gotten from this wonderful land."

Honestly, I want to applaud and start singing O Canada. Then something pricks at me. "Senator Osler, how do you know Edward's going on this cruise if you haven't talked to him recently?"

He looks so distraught I think he might cry. "That isn't something I can tell you, at this time." Then a jowly man taps him on the shoulder and pulls him away to a clutch of serious-looking men. He calls over his shoulder, "Call Cheryl, my Administrative Assistant. She's on speed dial on my phone. She'll make all the arrangements."

He hobbles off. A 78-year old duffer has my expensive cell phone. What if he loses it?

I turn on his phone and navigate to Settings. I click Find My Phone and set up the app. Now if the old codger loses my phone in his glad handing, I'll be able to find it.

I head back out to my car. Once again, it's blanketed with snow. Once again, I have to use my arm as a brush. Tiny things can make life so difficult, like not having a snow brush when you need one. Can I afford a trip to Canadian Tire? Do I have the time?

After all, I have to get ready for my Hawaiian cruise. A cruise in the middle of winter. I can't help it. I giggle, just like Sally.

When I get back to her house, Ronnie's curled up on the couch, crying.

"Marshall's life insurance's $1 million dollars. I have all the money I want now. But my husband is dead. That money's like sawdust in my mouth."

Since I know she and Marshall were at each others' throats until he got sick, I question her sincerity. Furthermore, as soon as his diagnosis was made, Ronnie hired a nurse so she wouldn't have to do all the "icky stuff" Marshall needed.

And as soon as she got control of the family platinum credit card, she was off like a shot to that spa. Suddenly she's in mourning? Suddenly she's feeling guilty because she has a fortune?

I won't acknowledge her crocodile tears. I mount the stairs to the guestroom and collapse on the bed. My best friend lost a husband and inherited a plump bank account.

I jolt upright. Why couldn't I get hold of her by phone at the spa? She said she dropped it in the toilet and would buy a new one when she got back home. Why didn't she buy it there? The place is crawling with high end stores, and she has a platinum credit card.

How do I know she didn't sneak home early and dispense with the weak Marshall and his tiny Korean nurse for the million-dollar life insurance?

This gives my friend Ronnie a compelling motive for murder.

23

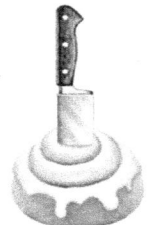

DECEMBER 25   3PM

D id my best friend murder or arrange the murder of her husband for money? How could she? My stomach lurches because I have to ask myself the same question. If it meant a million dollars, would I dispose of Dale Forsyth, that philandering wretch? A million dollars is a lot of B & B advertising, winter clothes, maybe private schools for the kids.

I shake my head to rid myself of such negative ideas. Dale's the father of my children, albeit a totally absent and completely neglectful one, not to mention an insulting husband. The better question might be why wouldn't I trade him for a million dollars?

The pain in my stomach might be hunger. I have to head home soon. Not only are cookies there, but so's my suitcase for my all-expense paid Hawaiian cruise.

When I walk into Ronnie's house, she asks, "What do you want to do now?"

"Pack."

She moans. "Noooo. Why are you leaving me?" Shades of me and my last night with Dale. She runs after me into the guestroom,

118

glaring. "I can't be left alone. Where are you going? Can I come, too?"

"Ronnie, I have to…" What on earth can I say, 'Go on a cruise to spy on a friend?'

A trip like this would be good for her, get her mind off her tragedy. It would even make it less obvious as to why I'm on the cruise, coincidentally with Edward.

On the other hand, Ronnie will persist in finding out the reason for this sudden trip, and as Ronnie has an open mouth policy, that won't work. On the third hand, I'm not leaving her home alone.

"Sarie, you can't leave me alone!" She collapses on the rug. She's right. I can't leave her in this state.

"Ronnie, do you want to go on a cruise in Hawaii?" I expect any number of responses but not what I get.

She sweeps out of the room, and is back in seconds with her brown overnight bag. "I'll buy us anything else we need. Let's go."

I'm surrounded by other people's wealth. Which reminds me of Ronnie's new found, suspiciously gained money. How do I broach the subject of Ronnie possibly murdering her husband to Ronnie? If she did it, she won't admit it.

Well, I'm her best friend. She tells me everything else. What if self-preservation turned her into a killer? I blink back a bad idea. If I broach the subject, will I be in danger?

She's sitting at the end of the bed, her arms clutching her overnight bag.

"Ronnie, why didn't you buy a new phone at the spa when you couldn't use your old one?"

Her eyes swivel in my direction. They're red-rimmed, but also frightened. "I didn't think of it," she says, quickly.

That does sounds like Ronnie. On the other hand, she could be pretending to be the old Ronnie, clueless Ronnie, hiding her newfound slyness. I try another tack.

"What made you think you could leave Marshall in his condition?"

This time, she turns her whole body and stares at me. Her eyes, which a minute ago were shot with weariness, are now focused.

"What are you trying to figure out, Sarie? If I suffocated my husband and then murdered his nurse?"

My hands quiver. I'm sorry I started this. But I have to know. If it was her, maybe I can help her, somehow.

"Ronnie, did you do that? Did you say you were at the spa, incommunicado, then race home?" She bursts out crying. That's no answer. "Ronnie, stop that caterwauling." She stops on a dime. She was playacting. I shift away from her on the bed.

"I have to know. I'll help you; I'll hide you, or plead your case. But you have to be honest with me. Now, did you yourself, or did you arrange for someone else to kill Marshall, and Kim Park?"

She stands up menacingly, arms outstretched, long sharp nails aimed at my face. I duck. "Ronnie, stop!"

She collapses on the bed. "I wasn't at the spa when you called. I was in Toronto, seeing Stewart Dore."

"Come on, Ronnie. Really?"

"I'm addicted to that guy, you know that. I need him to figure out what to do about my life, Sara."

I shrug. What can I say? Ronnie and I have been seeing psychics ever since we could afford them, but this guy, Stewart Dore, is the best, eerily accurate. But because Ronnie has a habit of exaggerating the truth, lying, I can't be sure this is true. I'll have to call the tearoom and check her story.

"I had an appointment to see him at 4 pm the day Marshall was...."

She still could have returned to her house in the wee hours of the morning when Marshall was killed, but if she was at the tearoom, it lends credibility to her story.

Once Ronnie leaves to pack her little suitcase, I make a quick call the King Street Tearoom.

"King Street Tearoom. Mary speaking. How can I help you?"

"This is Sara Forsyth. My friend says she had an appointment with Stewart Dore on December 23. Can you tell me if she was there?"

"If you want to make an appointment, we'll see if we can find out what you want to know."

"I'm not asking for a psychic appointment, I just want to know if…"

"You have to make an …"

"And ask Stewart Dore if my friend murdered Marshall Stohl and Kim Park?"

She doesn't miss a beat. "Come in right away."

24

DECEMBER 25   4PM

While Ronnie takes a nap, I head off to the King Street Tearoom.

An elderly waitress hurries over. "How many, dear?"

"I'm Sara Forsyth who called to find out if my friend was here on December 23."

"I can't tell you that. It's confidential. And if you don't have an appointment, we could use your table."

I note there's now a small line waiting at the door. Business is booming. "But Mary, you said to come right away. Did you make me an appointment? "

"That's what I do." She hands me a green card with number seventeen on it, and bustles away. In a minute she's back with the teapot, teacup, and a plate with the cookies, one oatmeal and two chocolate sandwiches. I don't like the oatmeal, though I'll eat it anyway. Who turns down a cookie?

They are only up to Table Eight. I have a wait ahead of me. A few women look young and happy, but most are rounded-shouldered with worry. The sugar from the cookies and the strong tea make me feel dizzy. Add to that the buzz in the room and the fact that I haven't slept much and I doze off. The next thing I know, Mary's shaking my shoulder.

"Your number's been called, dear. Pick up your teacup and saucer, and follow me down the hall."

We stop at a bedroom door. Mary knocks gently. A thin voice beckons me to enter. There he sits, Stewart Dore, looking a little older than the last time I saw him. But, he's still wearing a western shirt and string tie, and that dark brown vest.

He's shuffling the Tarot cards, and staring at me. I sit opposite him.

"Mr. Dore, do you happen to remember a short, curly red-haired woman who came to see you a few days ago?"

"Double, double, toil and trouble. Double murder."

"Yes, that's right. You predicted the last time and you were right."

He blinks, startled. "Do you mean there were two murders?"

"That's exactly what happened. Can you tell me who did those murders?"

His eyes close and his voice gets low, gravelly. "Watch out for the dagger. No, not again! Where are the children?"

I'm terrified. "Whose children? My children?"

His eyes pop open, and he smiles. "How was that for you?"

I don't care about Ronnie's last visit; I don't care about Marshall's murderer. I run out of the room, pulling out Senator Osler's old cell phone and call Dale. He has the children.

He doesn't pick up. I click off only to bobble the phone when it suddenly rings. Maybe it's Dale.

"Are the kids alright?"

"This is Senator Osler's secretary. I've been asked to book a flight to Hawaii and a cruise cabin for you. It's done," she says in a bored voice. "You can pick up your ticket at the Air Canada counter in the International terminal, and your cruise documents at the cruise ship terminal."

Now I have to persuade her to let Ronnie come. "I'll be bringing an assistant."

There's a pause on the other end then a sigh. "I'll update the arrangements. Might I ask if your assistant's a man or a woman? That is, do you need two cabins or one?"

"One cabin will do. My assistant's Lorraine Stohl."

She perks up instantly. "Is she the woman on the news whose husband was murdered?" She barely pauses, and then continues in her bored voice, "Anyway, her travel will be at your expense."

I hope Ronnie has the bucks for this because I certainly don't. What am I thinking? She's a millionaire now.

"It's an overnight flight, so your taxi will pick you up at your house at 10 pm tomorrow evening." And she disconnects.

Ronnie and I are winging our way to Hawaii to cruise in the sun. Plus, I'll be with Edward Osler. It's my fantasy. I've no right to these feelings. He's married, I'm technically married, and I'm a mother, for heaven's sake.

When I get back to her place, Ronnie's asleep on the couch, snoring, or more like purring, the overnight bag draped on her stomach. Through the open zipper I can see only two things, her jewelry box and a photo of Marshall. She loves him again now that she's lost him? Will I feel that way about Dale once we're divorced? I don't think so.

P.C. DeBraie's sitting in a chair in the hall, keeping one eye on Ronnie, and one on his cell phone. Maybe he's watching a movie. It must be mind numbing sitting there all day, watching for something that never happens. Police work equals drudgery in my book. He looks up as I approach.

"Officer DeBraie, you won't have to stay on duty for the next few days. Ronnie and I'll be going to my house shortly, then away for a few days."

He nods, punches a number into his phone, turns away from me, and holds a lengthy, whispered conversation. Then he says, "Detective Clere wants to know where you're going and the exact dates."

My police-hate rears its head. "I don't have to report my every move to the cops. I'm not a suspect nor is my friend."

The officer stands up. He's tall and bulky with the gun in his holster and a black leather belt. I take a step back, intimidated.

"Detective Clere's worried for your safety is all. Now, tell me the details of your plans, Mrs. Forsyth." P.C. DeBraie makes notes, gathers his gear then drives off in a police car.

I can breathe easily again. I bundle Ronnie into my car for the short trip to my house, and lead her dozy self to my guest room. She flops on the bed, asleep in no time, and I close her door softly.

A few minutes later, I fall on my own bed in an exhausted sleep, unable to fend off images of me strolling arm in arm on a cruise ship with Edward Osler.

25

DECEMBER 26   11 AM

B oxing Day appears crisp and sunny, making a wonderland of yesterday's snowstorm. Ronnie jumps into my room, wildly energetic.

"Sarie, would you like me for a permanent roommate?" She's pale, drawn, and near hysterics. "I can help with the B&B." Then she shakes her head. "No, I can't. But, I can help with the kids while you do the B&B stuff. And I'll pay you rent!"

Ronnie for a roommate? Bring in the clowns. She sees my reaction.

"Sara, I can't move back into my house. Two murders happened there. I'd tear it down and build another one, but I don't have the energy. I have to get rid of it even though I'll lose a ton selling at this time of year. I don't care. Please, can I live with you?"

I recognize desperation when I hear it. Like the night Dale told me he was leaving me. "Please, stay with us. For the children." I would have demeaned myself more to keep the illusion of a happy family. But he left anyway.

I say, "Sure, we can be roommates."

Ronnie chokes me in a fierce hug. The doorbell rings. Who can that be? It's way too early for the taxi. Ronnie darts forward. "I'll get it. See, I can be helpful right away."

I cut in front of her. She's in no state to deal with anything at the moment. "Why don't you start brunch? How about waffles?"

"Waffffffles," she sings and darts to the kitchen.

I tug open the heavy door, andI'm hit by a blast of frigid air, and a barking Detective Clere. "Where's Mrs. Stohl?"

"She's out," I snap. Now, why did I lie? Because I'm facing a police officer and it's an ingrained habit. Clere's demeanor's so ferocious he scares me. Where's that Good Cop from yesterday?

His black coat flaps around him, open in spite of the cold. His brown leather pants and creamy striped shirt look great. I want his clothes sense and budget.

"Someone has just set fire to the Stohl house," he snaps.

I breathe a sigh of relief. That solves so many problems! Now, Ronnie's never going to have to return to the house where Marshall was murdered. She doesn't even have to worry about selling it, and she'll get the insurance money. That reggae song starts in my head. "Don't worry, be happy. 'Cause every little thing's gonna be alright." She has a big "alright" coming. My lips twitch in a smile. Detective Clere is not as amused.

"What are you so happy about, Mrs. Forsyth? Do you know anything about this, as you seem to know about everything else in this case?"

"Bad cop," I mutter under my breath.

He narrows his eyes at me and steps inside. He steps in close, his body adding to his menace. I step back.

"The forensic evidence on the murderers of Marshall Stohl and Kim Park burned up in that house fire." He glares at me. "Obstruction of justice's a crime, Mrs. Forsyth. Arson's a crime, Mrs. Forsyth, no matter what the motive."

When I don't respond, he growls, "When Mrs. Stohl returns, my officers will bring her in for questioning, along with you." He storms out and speeds away.

I realize he didn't say we had to stay in town. Maybe in the chaos of this new development, he forgot. Or not. In any case, I'm not changing our plans.

Ronnie drifts out of the kitchen singing, "Waaaafles a-comin' soon."

"Ronnie. Come here and sit down for a minute." She looks at me warily, and then plumps down on the sofa.

"Ronnie, someone burned down your house last night."

Her vacant face lights up with joy. She jumps up, throws her floury hands in the air, and twirls around in the cloud.

"I don't have to go back there ever again!" Then a sly smile creases her cheeks. "And I get all that insurance money."

Well, Clere certainly has a suspect in Ronnie. Oh good heavens, now I'm suspecting my best friend of arson as well as murder. What next? My children poisoning their father? I can't help it. My lips twitch up at the corners.

She flies back to finish the waffles while I settle on the couch to think. Who besides her has a motive for torching that house?

Of course, Edward Osler's a lawyer, and knows burning evidence is a great way of getting rid of it. Might he have done it? How deep's he in this? Or, maybe it was the mystery woman from the baby monitor, the one who seemed to have done the murders. She'd want that house gone for the same reason.

Clere thinks it might be Ronnie, but he's grasping at straws. First of all, both Ronnie and I were sleeping here all night. Of course, if Ronnie had left the house, I wouldn't have heard her. I was so exhausted I wouldn't have heard an ice cream truck.

He says he wants to interview me, too. Why? I have no reason to burn down her house. Except, if he knows the glove they found belongs to Edward Osler. He could think I'd try to protect Edward by burning other evidence.

At the moment, I don't know if he even suspects Edward of anything, but if he keeps catching me going to talk to him, he may grow suspicious. I'd better be careful.

We have lots of time before the taxi arrives tonight to take us to the airport. I want to see her burned house for myself. Maybe the police missed a clue.

Ronnie's still in the kitchen, loudly banging pans. Suddenly, she pops her beaming face out of the kitchen.

"Sarie, you only have Mrs. Butter's table syrup. Now that I'm rich, let's splurge on real maple syrup. Will you go get some?"

Perfect. "Will do."

I rush to my car, hoping there's no cop waiting to follow me. Clere's always popping up where I don't want him.

The firemen are packing away their equipment when I arrive at the site. All that's left of Ronnie and Marshall's place is black, smoldering charred wood and tangled wires.

A quick twitch of a window curtain next door tells me Ronnie's long-time neighbor, Mrs. Trimble, is on guard. That creepy old woman and her spinster daughter know everything about this neighbourhood. If anyone saw something, it would be them.

I step onto their fire hose-dampened front porch and press the buzzer. Old Mrs. Trimble opens it a crack.

"Who's it? Nobody home," she cries in a shrill voice and tries to shut the door. I stop it with my shoulder.

"Mrs. Trimble, it's me, Sara Forsyth, Ronnie's friend. Your next door neighbour?"

"No next door," she caws, and slams the door in my face. I press the buzzer again. There's a scuffling on the other side, then a strong arm yanks me inside. Tina Trimble, the daughter, is facing me, her beady black eyes gleaming in the murky hall light, a cigarette hanging off her lips.

"Isn't it terrible?" She pulls me into the living room, the morning light hazy with dust, cat fur and cigarette smoke. The house smells of stale tomato soup, and unchanged cat litter.

Her small, dark face's bright with glee.

"We're so sorry about that fire. They wanted us to evacuate, afraid our place would go next, but Mom and me says we're not going nowhere. We can see the fire just fine from here. It burned straight up," she says in wonder, "like a bonfire."

She frowns. "They said they'd come back and check on us, but they never did. Did they, Mother? And we saw something, didn't we, Mother?"

Mrs. Trimble whispers conspiratorially into Tina's ear. Tina twitches away from her, hissing, "Soon." She turns back with a sly smile. Her teeth are stained with tar, unevenly spaced, smaller than normal. Like a child's set of teeth.

"So, how's Ronnie? We saw her load up and leave a few days ago. Is she back?" Tina asks, her voice innocent. I know she probably recorded Ronnie's every coming and going in a formal ship's log.

"We tried to tell a fireman we saw something, but he was so busy putting out the fire, he ignored us."

She sucks in her thin cheeks. "Would you like some refreshments?" Her face takes on an avaricious look, as if she's waiting for me to feed her. "Mom can get it while you and I have a little chat about the fire, and Ronnie, and…" Her voice trails off. Even she can't be casual about the murders.

"A woman done it," Mrs. Trimble snaps. Tina glares at her mother then jumps in, wanting to tell the gory details herself.

"Dressed all in black fur, like a bear. Hard to see at night. She dumped something, or threw something," she lowers her voice "and the house burst into flames like an explosion." She claps her hands in uncontained delight. "Then I called the fire department."

"No, it was me," her mother gripes petulantly.

The woman, the murderer, had come back to the Stohl's house. If Ronnie'd stayed there last night, she'd have been burned in her bed. My knees buckle. Tina's strong hand whips out and catches me.

"Oh dear, we'll have to sit you down." She bustles me over to a couch. I sink onto the stained yellow sofa. "I'll get us some, uh, refreshments. Would you like some, uh, gin?" Her hands clasp, her eyes shine.

"Perhaps brandy if you have it."

Tina squints up at the ceiling and purses her lip up against her nose. "Uh…" Then she brightens. "Got beer!"

No kidding. Ronnie used to count the empty brown beer bottles rolling around in their backyard after a night of mother and daughter hurling insults and bottles at each other.

Mrs. Trimble snarls, "Tea, you ninny. She wants tea. Don't you know anything? Didn't you learn anything at that school I sent you to?"

"You sent me? You sent me? I paid my own way through beauty school."

"And never earned a cent out of it in your life."

"No, because I have to take care of you." They've forgotten me as they lock onto each other, shoving toward the kitchen. "I'll see if we have tea bags," Tina trills. The swinging door wobbles back and forth. I hear a scuffling and someone yelps.

A woman in black torched Ronnie and Marshall's house. If it wasn't Ronnie, and it couldn't be Ronnie, it must've been the woman on the baby monitor. She came back to destroy any evidence she left. It had to be. But was she working alone? Was the man from the baby monitor with her?

Since no one was staying at the Stohls, the police had left their crime scene tape and left no guard. Why would they? The Trimbles alerted the fire department, but not in time to catch the arsonists.

It sounds like Clere knows none of this. He's after Ronnie. I have to get home to protect her. How much do I need to reveal to save Ronnie but avoid telling him about the voices I heard which will implicate Edward?

All the Trimbles saw was a woman in black set fire to the house. That's all I need to tell him. Maybe I don't even have to do that. I can suggest he visit the Trimbles. Maybe he can get more info from them.

Of course, I'll get taken to task again for interfering. Surely he'll interrogate the neighbours now that the fire's out. If Edward did this, I want to report him to Clere. I have to. Murdering my friend Marshall, burning down Ronnie's house—the man has to be stopped. But, I'm running away with myself. I don't know any of this for sure. Once I spy on Edward, though, I will.

I stand up, take my purse from the floor, and call out, "Thank you for your hospitality, Tina and Mrs. Trimble. I have to go now."

Tina bursts out of the kitchen, her mother skittering behind, hoisting a round tray with three sweating brown bottles. "I brought beer. Opened!" she bawls.

"Another time," I say as I back out the door. Tina's shoulders sag. She knows there will be no other time. I feel bad. "You can expect a visit from the police though," I promise.

Mrs. Trimble shoots a thrilled glance at her tittering daughter.

THE POINT

26

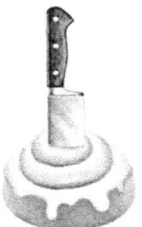

DECEMBER 26   10 PM

Ronnie wanders into the living room, patting her newly done hair. She must have gone to the hairdresser's while I was gone. She's talking a mile a minute about the fabulous Ala Moana mall in Honolulu.

"Ronnie," I interrupt, "I have to stay on the ship to do the job. But, when I'm not working, I want to eat the local foods, walk the side streets, get a feel for the locals, and maybe listen to the ocean."

She stares at me, wide-eyed. "What kind of vacation is that?"

When the taxi arrives, we climb into it with less luggage than any two women ever took on a trip. Ronnie strong-armed me into leaving most things behind by promising to buy me anything I wanted. That started my brain whirling. Would new underwear for Stevie and Sally count?

We pre-clear U.S. Customs and head to U.S. Immigration. The agent questions me closely on why I have so little luggage, grudgingly accepting the excuse that I'm going to Hawaii for a short work project.

Waiting in line to undress and re-dress from the security check takes over an hour, but finally we're through. We head to the busy cafeteria to get a snack. We each order coffee, almond and chocolate croissants, and muffins in three different flavours.

The evening bustle of the airport's exciting. People leaving, others seeing them off, either happy or sad. Children and parents thrilled and electrified by the prospect of the trip ahead.

We eventually go to sit in the waiting area, and suddenly reality clicks in. We're about to board a plane to Hawaii. One minute I'm agonizing about past-due bills, and the next I'm on my way to a cruise. What a bizarre turn of events in the last few days. All because of my old baby monitor.

When I was a kid, Dad promised to take me to Disneyland, but the fever was bad that year. So, I pretended to be on the plane, imagining blue sky above white clouds.

Our flight's called, and we board after the Business Class passengers. Our seats are comfortable enough, but with a couple of steps, we could have walked into Business Class. It looks so simple to do, but of course the airlines have safeguards against that, like public humiliation. Ronnie found that out the hard way a few years ago.

She settles herself, storing her Gucci bag under the seat. She's pale, but she's chattering steadily. I lean back and let her words and the hot air in the plane eddy around me. Two flight attendants move along briskly, adjusting seats, answering questions, smiling. It's a job I never wanted, too much traveling. They used to have terrible reputations, too. If a man said he had a date with a flight attendant, a leer went with it.

But those days are long gone. Most of the crew on this flight are older employees, gray hair on some and wrinkles on others. Ronnie once told me Marshall assured her every man could tell if a woman was a virgin by the way she walked. Ronnie believed him. She's oddly naïve about sex.

There's no guesswork about these women, with the exception of one. She's young, pert, and wiggly. I would guess she's not a virgin, but then, who cares anymore?

My mother, on the other hand, had a completely different notion of virginity. Women from her era remained virgins until marriage. Mom was 29, unmarried, and still a virgin. By that age, the men she met expected a woman to have experience.

So, practical woman that she was, she moved to Montreal, thinking the French could handle this "sort of thing." And within a year, she was no longer "burdened," as she put it. It didn't mean she'd had a love affair; it was more like corrective surgery. Then she returned to Toronto. That year, she married Dad.

Ronnie grabs my arm tightly. "Sara! I forgot my toothbrush!" She wrings her hands. "It's my favorite pink one with the green thingy on the handle."

What can I do? I pat her hand.

People are pushing their way awkwardly through the crowded aisle, their cameras swinging wildly from their necks. I can almost convince myself I'm on a real vacation, not a business trip, or a distraction from murder.

When everyone has finished boarding, Ronnie and I are approached by the pert steward. She rattles pages on a clipboard, finally bending down to us. "Mrs. Forsyth, you're on our VIP list since you're one of the Osler family. You're in luck. We've overbooked the Coach section on this flight. If you two will transfer to Business Class, it would help us out."

"But," I protest, "I'm not a member of the Osler family."

"Well, Senator Davis Osler's office made the arrangements, and when we have the room, we give him upgrades."

"Come on," Ronnie grabs my arm and pulls me behind her into Business Class before I can object. "This is more like it," she breathes, settling into the roomy, leather seat.

So this is the way the privileged live. The Business Class section is airy, fewer people in a larger space. There's a winding staircase in the middle of the area. A sign posted above it reads, "Sky Lounge."

A beautiful steward saunters over, and says, "I'll be back with your rum punch as soon as the flight leaves the ground." Within seconds of the take-off, she's back, as promised, with two fruit

136

drinks. I refuse mine. After all, this is a business trip. Ronnie drinks both in quick succession.

"That was delicious," she says, and pushes the Call button to order more. When the steward arrives, she asks, "Are the drinks in Business Class free?"

The steward bends down and whispers, "They used to be. Now they're only for nervous flyers. Are you a nervous flyer?"

Ronnie purses her lips, and then says, "I may be." The steward smiles and waits. Ronnie takes out her credit card and orders two Bloody Mary's, pretending one's for me.

"Ronnie," I say, nervously, remembering our New York experience, "there's a lounge. Let's go and see it."

We're about to mount the stairs when we notice a huge buffet laid out on a corner table. It's crowded with baked goods.

Ronnie makes a sharp turn, and begins to graze her way along the offerings.

She grabs a mini cheese Danish, takes a bite, and makes a face, "I don't care for this, but you will." She hands the remains to me and takes a different flavour, moving down the line, testing one item after another, handing me the ones she doesn't like.

She's still sampling when a bell signals us to return to our seats. Ronnie clutches my arm with a sugar-coated hand.

"I'm a nervous flyer. She said they give you free drinks if you are."

What kind of insanity is this? She offers to buy me everything in Hawaii, she's just inherited a million dollars, yet she's lying to get free booze. Is it greed or is it grief?

No matter how bad her relationship was with Marshall, she loved him once, and now he's gone. She's drowning her sorrows in alcohol, and soon she'll be pushing her feelings down with food. That won't work for long. I know.

Ronnie gulps a Bloody Mary. "Yum. Tangy and spicy. Since you aren't drinking yours…." She reaches over to my tray.

"Ronnie," I warn. "You're going to be very sick very soon."

She nuzzles my cheek with her soft nose.

"M-hmm, Sarie juicy."

On the other hand, what if this drinking isn't about sorrow, but guilt? I never did find out why she wasn't at the resort when I called, and why she didn't buy a new phone there.

What if she'd returned home early, sneaked into Marshall's room, and smothered the life out of him for the money? And then she had to get rid of Kim Park because she saw something.

With her brain pickling in alcohol, Ronnie may actually tell the truth. It's worth a try.

"Ronnie, did you do something bad?"

She looks at me shamefaced. "I threw up on you in New York. 'Member? You were grumpy after that."

I certainly do remember that fiasco. It was my one and only trip to New York, right after Dale left. Ronnie said she didn't want to go alone, and it'd cheer me up.

"And I got hold of Marshall's credit card, so the trip is on him."

The first thing she did was try to crash Business Class. She stood at the curtain and tried to lure me to crash it with her.

Luckily, I refused because the steward noticed, darted over and said, I thought unnecessarily loud, "May I see your boarding pass, please." A red-faced Ronnie scuttled back to sit with me in Coach.

Simply having time away would have been luxury enough for me, but she insisted I get myself a present. So, I bought a pair of shoes at Chandlers, dove gray suede, on clearance. Ronnie bought two suits from Saks Fifth Avenue with matching everything, put my home phone number on the bills, just in case they called Marshall.

When we went out to dinner, she ordered all the appetizers on the menu, and tried to get me to eat the ones she didn't like, as usual. She snored all night. And on the flight home, she got drunk on red wine, and threw up. On my new gray suede shoes.

But, she also secretly bought me a bottle of Chanel No. 5, and a Givenchy wallet into which she stuffed a $100 bill. And when we got home, she gave me the biggest hug and the sloppiest kiss I've ever had to endure. Now, how can you not love a girl like that?

"Night-night," she whispers, and dozes off in a drunken stupor.

As it's midnight, the lights in the cabin have been lowered. I want to read, but I don't want to disturb her, so I get up quietly and head for the Sky Lounge.

There's a narrow flight of stairs leading to a large room surrounded by windows. Several captain's chairs face each other, like the old days of train travel, and a few passengers are sitting in them, conversing softly. On one side of the lounge's a counter with several open bottles of champagne. Ronnie would have made short work of these if she'd seen them.

I settle into a swivel seat facing an enormous window, and watch as the dark whips past at six hundred miles an hour. I shiver but not from the cold. Someone I know, someone who once was my friend, is dead, murdered. And more, I'm on my way to spy on someone dear who may have been involved.

I stand up abruptly and return to my seat. Ronnie's head is lolling against the back of her seat. There are three more little bottles of alcohol empty on her tray. As I sit down, she wakes up, her face flushed, tears streaking her cheeks.

"I was a bad wife." She's breathing raggedly. "I no longer loved Marsh. I stayed for the money, the status, the appearance." Then she curls up in her roomy Business Class seat and falls back asleep.

Ronnie didn't know Marshall was planning to divorce her, only I knew that. Should I have told her? Should I tell her now? Will she feel less guilt?

I lay back in my seat, tired and sad. I don't wake for hours. Then we're in Hawaii.

27

DECEMBER 27   6AM

"Aloha," a breathy voice comes over the PA. "Shortly, we'll be arriving in Hawaii, land of lovers."

What irony. Dale and I are getting divorced, Ronnie's mourning a dead husband, and though she's my closest friend, in my mind she's somehow involved in his death, and the only man I care for may be a murder suspect. Love couldn't be farther away.

"The time's 6am Hawaiian time. Please lower your trays for a light snack which will be served immediately." There's bustling all over the plane.

Ronnie looks around in excitement. "Breakfast!"

We're served strong Kona coffee and pineapple sweet rolls. I eat everything nervously because in a few minutes, I'll be boarding a cruise ship to become a spy. And for the next several days I also have to keep an eye on Ronnie, who is not herself. What fun.

After a long descent, the pilot lands the plane so smoothly the passengers applaud. Outside on the Honolulu tarmac, the stewards hand a white, fragrant orchid blossom to each Business Class passenger.

"Does a flower over your left or right ear mean you're available?" Ronnie whispers, tucking the flower on the left side.

"On the right, I think," I answer.

She repositions it. "I'm available," she trills.

This Ronnie frightens me. One minute she's begging for her dead husband, and the next, she's ready for a new man. She links her arm in mine and breathes deeply.

"Smell this heavenly air."

She's right. Even with the fumes of the airport, perfume scents surround us. A flutter of hope springs in me. Maybe Edward didn't do it, and Ronnie didn't, or anyone I know. Maybe the murderer's in Toronto right now, with Clere, being jailed. This shoots a bolt of joy through me.

Ronnie says, "We go over here. See the sign? Go to the Wiki Wiki bus, whatever that is." I smile at her and at the world and get on the bus. It has hot pink plastic seats.

Ronnie says, "Google says to eat mahi-mahi! It's porpoise."

My stomach flips. "But porpoise's another name for dolphin. You don't eat dolphins."

Ronnie looks into her phone. "The Aloha Hawaii site says to eat mahi-mahi."

I try again to keep my pineapple sweet roll down. "Porpoises are mammals. Like us. You can't eat dolphins!" I say louder than I mean to.

"Excuse me," the bus driver says. He's wearing a military cap, but sporting a thick flower lei over a floral shirt. "I eat mahi-mahi all the time."

That's it. I might throw up right on the bus.

"It's not what you think," he rushes on. "Mahi-mahi is a fish. It's just shaped like a porpoise."

"See?" Ronnie squeaks. She grabs my hand and squeezes it. "It's a fish, Sarie. Not a friend."

The bus jerks to a stop. "Try mahi-mahi with poi." The bus driver grins, but Ronnie grimaces.

"I've heard of poi. Glue, isn't it?"

The driver laughs loudly. "No, not really, lovely lady."

Ronnie smiles, dimpling at him. "People are so friendly here."

"Hawaii does that to you. I'm from Illinois, and I never spoke to strangers before I moved here. The place softens you."

We arrive at the end of the short driveway surrounded by tall, thin coconut trees facing a coral building with a wide, white wraparound veranda.

Ronnie points excitedly. "What's that gorgeous roof?"

The top of the hotel in front of us has a large, low overhanging lip. It looks like any wind might carry the whole thing into the sky.

The bus driver laughs. "It's okay, it's like that on purpose. It's called a hip roof. It catches the cooling winds and funnels them through the vents to the inside. Very useful before air conditioning. And very modern now. Wind power!"

The bus driver grins at each of us in turn as he hands us down the steps. "Welcome to the Halehawaii Hotel which means the Doors to Heaven."

Ronnie gives him a big kiss on his cheek.

"Mahalo!" he laughs loud with delight. "That's Thanks in Hawaiian. You have the Hawaiian spirit already."

After he drives off, we stay standing in front of the hotel.

"Oh, smell those flowers." Ronnie sighs. "Are those the ones they use in the leis everyone's wearing?"

I don't answer her because I'm craning my neck to take in the riot of colourful flowering plants. From pictures in National Geographic, I recognize a purple amaryllis big enough to eat a hand, and the mildly pornographic red althurium.

A short, big-bellied man wearing a white flower lei on top of his orange shirt steps forward.

"Aloha! I'm Puyi, your All Pleasure Cruiseline guide. We've been waiting for you. You're the last to arrive. But that's because you came all the way from Toronto, Canada! O Canada," he sings, in tune. "Please join the rest of the group in the minibus which will take you to your cruiseship. Once you check in there, you'll have until 4pm to wander around Honolulu. Your wonderful Hawaiian vacation has started!"

Never in my wildest dreams did I think I'd be on a Hawaiian vacation at this time in my life. Cheryl and John Andersen are home, in the cold, in the snow. I can't help it. I smile. Then I feel guilty. Then I feel hungry. In other words, I feel normal.

At the cruiseship terminal, a Pleasure Cruiseship crewmember in a crisp white uniform is at our sides in seconds.

"I am Oleg. Please follow me right this way, Mrs. Forsyth and Mrs. Stohl." He escorts us up a separate gangplank far from the crowd. He offers us chilled glasses of what I think is orange juice, but when I take a sip, it doesn't taste like any orange juice I've ever had.

He smiles at my startled expression. "Are you enjoying our champagne and passion fruit cocktail?" Before I can answer, he says, "Here's another Hawaiian tradition."

He drops a thickly-flowered lei over my head and kisses me on both cheeks. The lei lands on my shoulders, heavier than I expected, rich with velvety purple and pink hibiscus and white gardenias.

I check around us. None of the other passengers are getting leis or champagne. We're Oslers now. Oleg waits until we have finished our delicious cocktail, and then marches us down a long corridor.

"You have one of our best cabins." I doubt that. Surely Senator Osler wouldn't waste money on his spy. But when the cabin door opens, I'm dazzled. The sun's streaming in huge sliding glass doors bathing it in warm sunlight. Instead of only one room with twin beds, I see two rooms, a living room, couch and all. On a ship! And around the corner a good-sized bedroom with two beds.

"Sara, all this furniture's premium bamboo," Ronnie the decorator enthuses. The cushions are vibrant red, orange and green. Flower arrangements top every surface. And there's a huge fruit basket and a bottle of wine waiting on the small wood coffee table.

Oleg smiles at our gaping mouths. "When Senator Osler or his guests sail with us, we give them first class treatment. Your concierge will be up in a moment to see to your needs."

Ronnie asks. "What's a concierge?"

Oleg says, "He's a Joe Friday, here to get you extra pillows, bring snacks from the kitchen, or even breakfast in bed. If there's nothing more I can do for you at the moment?" He nods smartly and slips out.

Ronnie squeals. "We're in Hawaii! What should we do now?" She ponders a second, and then claps her hands. "I know. Let's buy real Hawaiian dresses, the long flowered ones in the colours of the flowers here."

In one fluid movement, she stands up, loops her purse over her arm and is out the cabin door. By the time I get over the shock of her change of mood and catch up with her at the bottom of the gangplank, she's hailed a cab.

It arrives in seconds because there's a line of them waiting expectantly. The cabbie comes around to help us in and we wind onto a quiet Hawaiian street. All the car windows are wide open so we can see and smell the glorious scenery.

"Is that coconut?" I ask.

The cabbie smiles. "And mango, and guava and bananas." With the perfumed air, the sound of swishing palm fronds, and the rumbling of the ocean below, I have to fight a nap. Now that I'm in Hawaii, my fantasy vacation spot, I'm not going to miss it.

The cabbie turns around. "You pretty ladies want a wikiwiki tour of our beautiful island?"

"What's wiki wiki again?" Ronnie whispers to me.

"Quick! Quick!" the driver laughs. "Like the wikiwiki bus that brought you from the airport.

"A tour? Why not!" Ronnie throws her arms out. "Then to the best mall in town." She pats my arm. "Don't worry, Sarie, I'll pay for it all. I'm rich."

I look over at the beatific expression on Ronnie's face, and I'm desperate to stop suspecting her of murdering her husband and his nurse, so I'll stop. Let Clere do that dirty work.

THE POINT

28

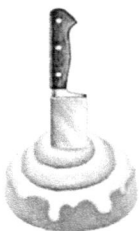

DECEMBER 27   10 AM

T he sun glints off the windshield, the soft, fragrant breezes
rifling our hair as the cabbie sweeps his arm in front of him.

"Look at that view. In front of us are the famous black rocks of
Diamond Head and the vast blue Pacific Ocean."

A gleaming white apron of sand sits next to deep blue water and
a contrasting black mountain juts into the azure sky.

Everywhere are deep pink flowering trees, delicate ivory orchids,
brown and green cacti, and red tile roofs on white stucco houses.

The birds are singing, strains of a Hawaiian guitar drift from the
beach on a breeze. A day in paradise. A delicious lassitude steals over
me. Why don't I live here?

After our impromptu tour, the cabbie slows down and deposits
us at the door of the huge Ala Moana Mall.

"Please wait. We'll be back in an hour," Ronnie says, tipping
him royally.

Inside the doors we're struck dumb by the architecture. It's as if
the outside has been transported inside. Tall coconut palms reach to
the high glass ceiling, lush flowerbeds surround delicate mermaid

146

fountains, and wind chimes tinkle in the tropical breeze that flows in through the open glass shutters.

At the first shop, Ronnie picks out clothes for me. Over her arm she drapes a gorgeous muumuu, purple, blue, and white with a fitted bolero jacket. She adds silver sandals and a pair of long silver and shell earrings to finish the Hawaiian look.

The dress fits perfectly, landing just at my ankles. The purple brings out the pink in my complexion. The earrings bring a dreamy look to the outfit. Ronnie's a designer, after all. The dress is three hundred dollars, but the cotton's as soft as a kitten. The sandals are a bit large, but with sandals, who can tell. I hope Ronnie's really going to pay for this because it's way out my snack bracket.

When I walk out of the dressing room, Ronnie's waiting there like an indulgent mother. She claps her hands. Then she grabs up her outfit, a golden yellow sundress, white sandals, and a white picture hat.

"Got to keep that burning Hawaiian sun off my fair winter skin," she titters.

When she comes out of the dressing room, she looks like a movie star. The shop assistants applaud. She orders them to find her the same long muumuu outfit I have, but in ivory.

The bill comes to over two thousand dollars. I've heard of people spending indiscriminately after a death because they feel they've lost something priceless. Ronnie sees my look, and shakes her head airily.

"We have a large income. Marshall and I ..." She stops and shivers. I bite my lip. Do I encourage her to cry, or distract her? I decide distraction is the kinder cut.

"We still have a few hours until the ship leaves, so let's go to the beach!"

Ten minutes later, we're trying on swimwear. Ronnie's red hair looks glorious in the first bathing suit she tries on, shiny gold. It has secret elastic, which pulls her in and pushes her out skillfully. She looks Rubinesque.

I choose a similar style in black. A blonde in a black bathing suit's eye catching, especially with my cleavage. Good thing the kids are nowhere near.

An hour later we're completely outfitted in suits, cover-ups, flip-flops, and sun hats, both of us smiling. Retail therapy has its charms.

Our cabbie waves as we walk out of the store. "Is everyone happy with Hawaii?"

Ronnie blows him a kiss and sings, "Next stop, Waikiki Beach, please."

We leave our bundles of new clothes in the cabbie's trunk, exacting another promise of his return in an hour or so, and we hike down to the beach.

The sand's like warm white sugar. The perfume of the flowers, the heat of the sun, and the rumble of the waves do their work. My fatigue will be denied no longer. Resisting the distant calls to join her as Ronnie skitters in and out of the surf, I make a pillow of my beach towel and sink into sleep.

I dream of shadowy figures running up and down stairs. I'm running after them, but I can't see who they are or catch them.

Ronnie's shaking my shoulder. "Sarie, stop shouting. You're scaring everyone. What's the matter?"

I feel muzzy-headed from the sun, the fatigue, even the heady Hawaiian air.

Ronnie plops down on the beach beside me. "Sarie, look at this." From the beach bag she pulls a discount coupon. "For Your Next Purchase." Ronnie laughs. "Do they know me or what? When Marsh and I traveled, I always went back to the same..." She breaks off and looks around, confused once again.

I say the first thing that springs to mind, "Cake?"

Ronnie wobbles on her feet. "Yes, cake, on the ship, right Sarie?"

We hike out of the sand to the street where our taxi's waiting. She gets in and lays her head against the back cushion, limp.

"I don't want Marsh to be dead," she says in a child's voice, and closes her eyes. She's breathing calmly, but her face is plaster white.

148

That's it as far as I'm concerned. Ronnie had nothing to do with Marshall's murder.

We re-board the ship, refusing another offer of champagne and passion fruit juice. Lugging our shopping bags up and down corridors, we locate our cabin once again, no easy task. All the doors look alike. Once inside our lovely room, we drop everything on the floor, and flop onto our beds.

Ronnie sighs. I think she might fall asleep, but that isn't why she's sighing.

"You promised me cake, Sara."

I'm so tired but dessert wins out every time.

We hunt down several corridors in search of those famous cruise buffets. Finally, we spot a sign directing us to an all-day buffet. Ronnie giggles like a teenager. She has regressed as far back as she needs to forget her present situation.

She grabs a nearby table, her face as untroubled as a child's waiting for cake. I line up to get hamburgers. I like the taste of American beef better than Canadian. It has fewer hormones. I opt for double French fries because fries make Ronnie happy.

And for dessert, I forget about cake and head for chocolate waffles. I smother two in smooth French vanilla ice cream, topped with hot fudge sauce and sliced almonds.

My tray's now so full, I have trouble balancing it as I dodge between other guests back to our table. A few of my fellow passengers look like Pillsbury doughboys. If I'm not careful, that's how I'll look soon, I know this, but I can't stop myself.

Ronnie and I start with the waffles, hamburgers be damned. She eats fast, but I eat faster. Child training. If I don't finish my desserts quickly, the kids sneak bites.

Also, the faster I eat, the less full I feel, enabling me to go back for second helpings, which I do. At the bakery end of the buffet I pick up four chocolate brownies, two syrupy butter tarts, and iced tea as only the Americans do it, without sugar. It's for the best.

I place the platter on our table. Finished with her waffles and all the fries, Ronnie's face's flushed from eating so many carbs. But she dives into the new sweets anyway, soon hyper and chattering like a monkey. I'm too full. In fact, my mind's swimming in so much sugar syrup, I can barely think.

Ronnie says, "I want to hit the stores on board."

"We've each just bought three outfits. Isn't that enough for you?"

She looks at me seriously. "It never feels like enough."

We both want more. The eating and the buying seem to fill a hole inside me. And I have found no other way to fill it.

We make fast work of the shops, buying t-shirts with nautical logos, and captain's hats. We trudge our happy way back to our cabin, now finding it easily since I had to ask the steward to hang a red ribbon on the door handle.

We drop the bags on the neatly-made beds, and soon we're sitting at an outdoor pool, getting closer to Hawaii, sipping the drink of the day which happens to be Whiskey Sour. Who doesn't like sweet and tart? Ronnie likes it five times. Then she slides down on a lounge chair to take a nap. I cover her with a towel to protect her from sunburn, and leave her purring.

She misses the casting off ceremony, which amounts to strangers waving at us from the shore. No more streamers like the old days. The small sign on the railing explains they made too much mess.

I turn to scan the cruise passengers for Edward Osler. I have spying work to do.

THE POINT

29

DECEMBER 27   5PM

I need to find Edward. I have to warn him about Irondale on the warpath and I need to spy on him for his grandfather.

After the casting off ceremony, I head for the casino. That would be my first stop. Genetics. But I'm not here to gamble, though there are already a handful of people sitting on soft cushioned bar stools playing blackjack. Everyone's smiling and laughing, and drinking. That's what casinos like. Edward isn't one of them.

I wander through a couple of the bars, also already in full swing. I even take a peak in the gym. No takers yet. And no Edward.

Turning the corner on the way back to my cabin, I spot a little cubby-hole of a room which the ship calls The Library. But he's not here, either.

However, over in the corner of the room I see a shiny black piano. I'm drawn to it like a child to candy. Before the music lessons had to be stopped because one of Dad's creditors popped the piano to pay off a gambling debt, I learned to play two things well:

Beethoven's 9th Symphony, and Bach's Air on a G-string from his Suite in D.

I sit down on the smooth black bench. Though most pianos have plastic keyboards these days, this one's old like mine was. The smell of ivory keys thrills me.

As I plink out the first few notes of Ode to Joy, a man and a woman enter the room quietly, and begin setting armchairs in a circle. I play a few more notes, then switch to Bach's Suite in D and start in earnest. I'm almost through the first movement when three more people straggle into the room and sit down in the empty chairs. I expect them to ask me to stop playing, but they just smile over at me.

One of the men says, "That's beautiful. Please don't let us interfere with your playing. We can move to another part of the room." And they stand up.

How considerate. I was here first, granted, but now there are three men and two women who are clearly about to start a planned meeting. And yet they're willing to relocate for my convenience? Well, I'm Canadian. I can out-polite them.

"No, no, I'll go. I was just noodling around anyway."

"Don't leave," a middle-aged woman says, gently. "If you're a friend of Bill W.'s, you're welcome to join us."

I run through my file of friends. Though there was a Computer teacher at St. Ives named Bill Wapsowich, I couldn't call him a friend. But I'm curious. Who are these gracious people?

I sit down beside her, and she smiles at me with lovely blue eyes. I always used to comment when I met someone with blue eyes, but I don't say anything anymore. It got me into trouble a few years ago.

Dale and I were at a professional meeting in Kingston, and went out for dinner afterwards. At a table near us was a group of about 20 men. They were of various ages, though all looked street tough. From several sidelong glances, I noticed they all had blue eyes.

Were they a family? Since several were about the same age, likely not. My curiosity got the better of me, and on our way out of the restaurant, I stepped over to the table and addressed them.

"You're such a large group of men, all with blue eyes. I was wondering if you belonged to a club or had some other interesting connection." I smiled.

Every one of them stared at me, but not one of them smiled. Finally, one guy broke the embarrassing silence and asked coldly, "Why would you want to know that?"

Dale grabbed my arm, apologized and rushed us out of the restaurant. "Don't you know who they are?" he hissed.

"No. That's why I asked, dear. They all have blue eyes. That's highly unusual since blue eyes are a recessive gene. Stop squeezing my arm, Dale."

"They're likely prison guards from Kingston Penn. They wouldn't identify themselves because you might be a family member out to get them. Who knows what they could've done to us, you idiot. Why don't you keep your crazy ideas to yourself from now on?"

I had read that Moses had blue eyes, and this unusual colour was part of his power over the people. And Jesus had blue or gray eyes. That's two legendary religious figures with the recessive gene of blue eyes. What could it mean?

I figured maybe blue eyes were a sign of some sort, or a special gift, a sixth sense. Prison guards could use all the senses they could get. Of course, Kingston Penn's closed now, but those guys are probably still prison guards somewhere, and using their blue eyes to know when to duck.

Edward has amazing deep blue eyes, which change to ice blue when he's upset. And he seems to read my mind regularly.

I check out this group of people, but the only one with blue eyes is the woman sitting next to me.

The men range in age from 30 to probably 60. They have a serious air about them. One looks like a professional, one's a crew member dressed in his ship uniform, another's wearing jeans and a T-shirt which says, Serene Gene. Two of them look tough like the prison guards, as if they've been through the wars.

There are also two women, one plump blonde, maybe late 20s, while the one beside me has to be 40, dark and slim.

I decide to stay and hear a little more. I can always leave if it gets too boring.

The man who appears to be the leader says, "Shall we start with the Serenity Prayer?"

Not religious zealots! I force myself to calm down. I'm still curious.

Everyone latches onto another person's hand. The two women on either side of me smile as they reach for my mine. I don't like being touched by strangers, but they look to the center of the room, ignoring my reluctance, and begin chanting,

"God, grant me the serenity

To accept the things I cannot change,

The courage to change the things I can,

And the wisdom to know the difference."

I scowl. God has no place in my life. At all. If there's a God, where was He when Dad spent the money for my scarlet fever medicine at a poker game? As a result of that, I'm left with a damaged heart. And where was he when I got a soft, round body and my handsome husband changed his preference to long and lean?

"So, the topic tonight's Step 1."

Well, well. This is a 12-step meeting. I've heard of these. I saw a sign at a casino where I'd once gone in search of Dad.

"*If you have a problem with gambling, we have a solution. Call xxx-xxxx-xxx. Gamblers Anonymous.*"

I suggested it to him, but he said he wasn't that bad. He clucked his tongue sadly. "Some people just don't know when to quit." Right.

The leader opens a big black book and reads, "'Step 1: We admitted we were powerless over alcohol, and our lives had become unmanageable.'

"Who would like to start the sharing?"

I feel a jolt of fear. Sharing? I'm not going to share anything. I was invited, but I'm not a member. I don't plan to even talk never mind bare my soul.

The young man dressed in khakis, a red and blue checked shirt says, "I'm Jim, alcoholic. And Lordy, there's a lot of drinkin' on this ship and we've hardly set sail. This is our first cruise," he smiles at the blonde woman sitting next to me, "and my wife and I are having a rough time resisting, me the alcohol and her the food."

I perk up. Resisting food?

"That's why we came tonight, and will keep coming. I need the support of the group for me to stay sober and for her to stay abstinent. We want to enjoy this holiday, not regret it."The man who looks like an accountant with wire rim glasses, a neat yellow polo shirt, and blue pressed slacks clears his throat and says, "I'm Tony, a cocaine addict. I feel powerless and ashamed today because my wife criticized me in front of our kids, again. I said nothing, just slunk away as usual. I don't deserve to be treated that way. But I didn't use over it. Tonight I'll write on Step 2, what would a sane Tony do next time it happens?"

His wife demeans him yet this Step 2 stops him from getting high? Could it stop me from bingeing? I snort. No one and nothing's going to stop me from enjoying my brownies.

Then it's the turn of the woman on my other side.

"I'm Monica, a compulsive overeater, recovering by the grace of God. Tonight's my fourth anniversary in Overeaters Anonymous, and I'm maintaining a weight loss of 80 pounds."

I'm impressed. That's some good dieting to keep it off for four years. I look more closely at Monica. Her face's full but she has the lovely, doe-shaped eyes you used to see on love comic heroines.

"One year ago, my husband of 10 years left me for a younger, thinner woman."

I feel myself flush. No one notices. They're all listening to her.

"We went to marriage counseling, but he wouldn't deal with his problems. Last year, he bought a red Corvette and began an affair with a woman half his age. A blonde, of course."

Monica takes in a deep breath. "Now she's pregnant. Though we have two of our own children, a boy 8 and a girl 5, and we're still married, he doesn't see any of this as a problem. He's in denial, but I'm not."

I'm spellbound. It's like watching my own home movie.

"With the help of my OA sponsor, and doing a 12-step inventory on this, I realized I don't need to stay where I'm not loved. I'm a loveable child of my Higher Power, and worthy of being in a mutually loving relationship. It's best for the family that I get a divorce."

My throat tightens. That's the opposite of what my plan was. I wanted Dale back to keep the semblance of a relationship if I couldn't have the real thing. I wanted the financial security so I could stop worrying about the basics. I was willing to take the illusion of the picture perfect family if that's all I could get. It would have been better than what we have now, I was sure. But Dale wasn't interested. He has his thin bimbo and a new business and now he wants my children, too.

"When I came into OA, I'd have eaten myself silly over this. The bakery down the street would have been wiped out, and my kitchen cupboards emptied. Food was my friend then, my best friend. It was always there. It always listened. It never left me.

"But now I have a better way of dealing with my problems. I call on God and my OA support people, and the food thoughts stop and the craving and the bingeing and the pain go away."

That was impossible. Not having food thoughts, never bingeing? The woman's lying.

"I'll wrap up by saying that through all of this, I've maintained my abstinence which's no wheat, no sugar, and weighing and measuring three moderate meals a day. I eat healthy food in healthy amounts at healthy times. And I haven't gained one pound, and for that, I'm truly grateful."

Not gaining weight when her whole life is crumbling? I've gained at least 20 pounds since Dale left and I'm still gaining. I don't believe one word she says.

When no one else wants to talk, they end with the same mumbo jumbo prayer. I quickly excuse myself and escape. All that gobbledygook Higher Power stuff. What some people will go through to fit into a pair of jeans.

While I admit Monica's story's uncomfortably like mine, I've more important things to think about. For example, should I warn

Edward, and exactly where was he the night of the murders? I hope I can spot him at dinner. Maybe his grandfather's secretary arranged for us to be at the same table. If so, I'll get a look at the elusive Elena Osler, Edward's wife.

I head back to the pool to find Ronnie, but she's gone. I don't have time to wander the huge ship in search of her. I have to get ready for dinner. The cruise suggests a casual outfit for the first dinner at sea. All I have is the muumuu outfit I got this afternoon, which is too dressy. I'll embarrass myself since this evenings is supposed to be casual. On the other hand, my only other choice is my travel clothes, the rumpled slacks and top I'm wearing.

We'll be in a dining room, possibly at a table with Edward Osler and his gorgeous wife. It has to be the muumuu.

30

DECEMBER 27   7 PM

A s soon as I open the cabin door, I hear rattling shopping bags. Leaning over her bed, rooting through a pile of new stuff she purchased in my absence, is little Miss Retail. I wonder if there are 12-step groups for compulsive shoppers.

Ronnie twirls to show me her new shimmering gold blouse, no, it's a dress. No matter a few excess pounds, with her red hair frothing on top of this rich outfit, she looks like a cherry flan.

She croons, "And look what Mama bought her little girl." She dives into her magic sack and out comes a small black sparkling blouse.

"Isn't it a great dress?"

"Ronnie, that's not a dress. And there's no way on this green earth I'm going to wear something that short in public. My underparts will be on display the minute I move."

"It goes with these black tights and leather boots."

"What, no whip?"

With a flourish, she dumps out a pair of black silk tights and red ankle boots. I feel dizzy. That outfit would have paid for two weeks of children's camp.

"Please, Sara," Ronnie whispers. "Let's pretend it's last week when nothing bad had happened."

So, her memory's back. I pick up the new clothes and slip them on. As a buxom blonde in black with red boots, I look like a slice of black forest cake.

Arm in arm, we walk through the long corridors to the dining room. We have been assigned to Table 4. We spot it near the center of the room. There are three people sitting there. Yes, it's Edward, and who I imagine is his wife. From a distance, she's a stunner, long black hair, white skin, and languid elegance.

What a perfect Kodak picture they make, wealthy, socially prominent, and gorgeous, individually and as a couple. So why does Edward look so miserable?

Ronnie isn't wearing her contacts. She hisses in alarm, "Sara, who are those people at our table?"

"That's my Edward."

She squints. "Oh yah, Marshall's lawyer friend."

"What? You and Marshall know Edward Osler?"

"Of course! Marshall met in him law school. He's been to our house a few times. He was working with Marshall on a trust, or breaking a trust, I can't remember. Marshall didn't go into detail. But who are the other two?"

"I'm guessing that woman is Edward's wife. Didn't she come to your place with Edward?"

"No, he always came alone."

"She looks vaguely familiar to me. Maybe I saw a picture of her on Edward's desk or something. But who's the other man?"

He looks familiar, too. As we approach, Detective Garry Clere shoots to his feet. Is he, a gay man, alarmed to be approached by two buxom women? He acts more amused than scared. Maybe he likes drag. Edward, on the other hand, is all eyes.

"Mrs. Forsyth, what a pleasant surprise. And Ronnie is Marshall with you?"

He doesn't know about Marshall? No, of course he wouldn't if he hasn't heard a newscast recently. Ronnie slides into a seat, looking down at her lap.

I spout my rehearsed pretext. "I'm here because Ronnie wanted company on her short vacation."

Edward looks me up and down with heated absorption. I haven't had this much attention from a man in a long dry time, and from Edward, never. It's intoxicating.

Elena breaks the spell with a high, tinkling laugh. "Down, boys, there's obviously plenty for everyone."

Mocking our weight. How charming. Wait a minute. Isn't she the woman I saw at the restaurant I went to with Edward? If not, the resemblance's remarkable. But she can't be because Edward said that woman was a colleague, a hostile colleague while this woman's his wife. Still, the resemblance is remarkable.

"Keep your thing inside your pants at least during dinner, husband, dear."

Edward's lips thin. Garry Clere turns his laser stare on the couple. I turn my laser stare on him.

"Detective Clere, what are you doing here?"

All heads swing to stare at him. Clere smiles serenely. "Even detectives get a vacation, Mrs. Forsyth."

We seat ourselves, and I'm about to question him in more detail when our waiter arrives, carrying a tray of huge, puffy bread balls.

"What are those giant things?" Ronnie gasps in delight, her attention riveted.

The waiter grins, "Popovers a la Hawaii. You each have to eat a whole one or you don't get dessert."

Everyone laughs except Ronnie who says, in all seriousness, "But if I eat two, do I get extra dessert?"

The waiter beams. "Madame, if you can eat two of these, and still have room for dessert, I'll personally introduce you to the Pastry Chef. Now, please, ask for whatever you like from our evening menu. I'll be back to take your orders," he winks at Ronnie, "however large."

Ronnie snaps up the heavy white card, and silence reigns as we consider our options. Ronnie and I read menus like contracts, seriously, whispering to each other about this sauce or that reduction until, frustrated, Elena snaps her elegant fingers at the waiter.

"I want dinner before the cruise is over," she snaps. The waiter leans towards her. "Bring me the shrimp linguine," she says, her voice dark and husky, her long, black lashes fanning her light blue eyes. She's a stunner, alright. The waiter drifts closer to her face. Is he going to kiss her?

Ronnie and I order in unison, "Cold raspberry soup, endive and parmesan salad, then Duck l'Orange."

The waiter begins scribbling.

The men choose French Onion soup, Caesar salad, and filet mignon wrapped in bacon. With the waiter's hurried departure, quiet reigns.

Then Clere smiles at Ronnie, his eyes soft with compassion. "Mrs. Stohl, this is my first cruise. Do you have a suggestion for how to spend tomorrow?"

"Eating!" jumps out of her mouth.

We all laugh, but I know when she's serious. The meals come in no time. The cold raspberry soup's chilled and topped with a dollop of crème fraiche. The salad's crisp and salty. And the Duck l'Orange is sticky with basted orange juice and brown sugar.

The men shake their heads in amazement as their steak knives slide through the miraculously tender meat. Elena pushes a shrimp around on her plate. She bends over her purse for a few minutes, rooting around while the rest of us concentrate on eating.

She winks at Edward. "I have something tastier in my cabin, don't I, darling?" His face darkens. She flashes her ice blue eyes at Clere, like a challenge, and then stands up languidly.

No one can stop watching as her long, slim body winds gracefully out of the dining room. She's magnetic. But Edward's face's red, his mouth tense. Something's rotten in the state of that marriage.

Our waiter appears with the dessert menu. Ronnie licks her bottom lip as she reads out the offerings: "Chocolate Cheesecake with Raspberry topping, flaming Christmas Figgy Pudding, Peche Flambé with soft vanilla ice cream melting under a hot peach half, drizzled with chocolate sauce, flamed with Grand Marnier liqueur." She explodes. "I'll have all of them!"

The waiter doesn't flinch. He must have served on cruise ships for a long time.

"I'll have what Ronnie's having."

Edward laughs along with Clere, thinking she's joking, but the waiter knows better.

"I'll bring enough of everything for the whole table." He dashes away. Before I can explain the necessity of choices to the stunned men, a ship's officer approaches our table.

"Bonjour, mes amis."

We turn to see a large, stocky man, dark hair, Mediterranean complexion, and a handsome face.

"I'm Capitaine Andre Monet, the captain of the Aloha Adventure, at your service. Quel qu'un parles francais?"

"Un petit peu, seulement," Clere says, embarrassed.

The captain continues in his deeply accented English, "But, I sot you're Canadiennes. Yet you don't speak French?" Our entire table of mature adults blushes.

The captain gives a Gallic shrug. "C'est la vie. I speak wis English. I am Captain Monet, great nephew of the great French painter." His eyes light on Ronnie. "I don't know to garden or paint, mais, madame," he places his hands on Ronnie's plump fingers, "I know what I love, and that's beauty. S'il vous plait, may I ask you to permit me a dance?"

Ronnie bursts into tears. Edward and Clere look at her in consternation, not sure what to do. I reach over to console her, but she turns and grabs the captain's large palms.

"Madame, please. I know, I know." He gently helps her to rise, and expertly guides her onto the dance floor.

Our waiter returns balancing a huge tray of desserts. Clere asks, "Does the captain spend a lot of time with the women passengers?"

The waiter shakes his head. "No-no. Never. But since his wife died two years ago, he finds those who have suffered a loss and he, how shall I put it, attends to them."

"How did the captain know about her loss?" I ask, now worried. What else does the man know? The waiter shrugs, deposits the tray of shining, oozing desserts, and scurries off.

Edward says, "Whoever made the reservation might have mentioned her recent widowhood."

I gape at him. How does he know Marshall's dead? He didn't know only hours ago when we first boarded the ship. Or at least, he pretended not to know.

I have a bad feeling. I reach for a piece of the chocolate cake, and eat it quickly. The bad feeling continues. I reach for a dish of peche flambé and am about to shove some in my mouth when I notice the men watching me in astonishment.

If I don't stop, my secret eating life will be secret no more.

31

DECEMBER 27   10 PM

S ugar drunk amid the chatter of a thousand happy cruisers, I
totter out of the overheated dining room bent on finding a
computer. I need to write my first report to Senator Osler. After all,
those desserts were on his dime. I turn and turn until I finally find
the computer room.

At 10 pm, the room's occupied by only a couple of teenage girls
in the corner giggling over a picture of Captain Monet on Facebook.

I settle behind a computer and begin my email:

*Dear Senator Osler: I have seen Edward and had dinner with him
tonight. He looks well.* That alone should ease a grandfather's heart.
He's sharing a cabin with his wife, Helen.

No, not Helen. I try to remember her name through my brain
fog. Oh, it's Elena.

Should I indicate that Elena probably has a drug addiction? I
recognize the ruse about going back to her cabin for something
tastier than dinner. She's definitely the woman in the restaurant who
was licking white powder off her top lip. Then I thought it was Icing
sugar, but I've seen enough TV shows to know it was probably

cocaine. But Senator Osler didn't ask me to report on Edward's wife, and since I have scant proof, I'll say nothing. Should I mention my dessert addiction? My snort disturbs the teens, who squeal, trying to conceal their hilarity.

Back on topic, I type: *Our table mate, to my surprise, is Garry Clere, the detective investigating my friend's…*

Should I write murder? Am I going to start crying? Poor Marshall. Did Edward have anything to do with it? Edward, my hero? Tears trickle down my cheeks. I sit up straight, pull myself together, and continue my email.

… death. I haven't had a chance to talk to Edward alone yet, but I'll definitely do that tomorrow first thing. Sincerely, Sara Forsyth.

That's all I can manage. I'm starting to experience the low that comes after the high of a sugar binge. I leave the computer room wishing for a Snickers and make slow progress back to our cabin.

I open the door and see a towel puppet in the shape of a swan on each of our beds. On its back's a chocolate truffle. I perk up. I pop the truffle into my mouth, and then since latecomers are losers, eat Ronnie's, too. Now I have the energy to take a shower and crawl under the soft covers for a much-needed sleep.

But, I lie in bed, unable to calm my mind. Edward, Marshall, Elena, Kim Park, Clere, Ronnie. What happened that night? Was that gasping and choking I heard on the baby monitor Marshall? Was it his nurse, Kim Park who screamed, "What you do? You suffocate him!?"

Those words are emblazoned in my memory for life. I heard my friend being murdered. I feel nauseous. I make it to the toilet just in time.

When I crawl back into bed, my body's exhausted, but my brain's still in high gear. Who was the woman who murdered two innocent people? And who was the man who threatened to tell her secret or kill her if she didn't keep his. What secrets? Were they were blackmailing each other?

Edward has a secret. I know that from his interaction with Elena Osler in Scatter! Why did he insist she was merely a colleague when she was his wife? What on earth's going on with that man?

Ronnie said Marshall was working on a trust for Edward. It must have been vital to bother such a sick friend. What kind of trust? The only ones I know of are financial, like keeping money for a young person until they reach a certain age. Or, trying to break a trust to get money early. Why did Edward need help with a trust?

I can't stand it anymore. Maybe the late night air on the deck will help me think more clearly or calm me down enough for sleep.

I dress quickly and walk down our corridor. There's shouting coming from one of the cabins. It's Edward and Elena. I hate the sound of fighting. I heard too much of it as a kid, and more recently, experienced too much in my marriage. In a knee jerk reaction, I bang on their door.

The yelling stops instantly. As I hurry down the hall, I glance back and see their cabin door wrenched open. I slip out at the nearest exit in a panic, afraid Edward or Elena will catch me.

The night breeze's fresh and cool. Though it's dark out, the sail halyards are festooned with coloured lights. Christmas on the sea. I feel my way along using the rails of the deck.

No one knows where I am at this second. A peace descends on me. I don't have to make anyone's meals, fight with errant husbands. My only job's to keep an eye on a man I'm attracted to, who might be a murderer.

As I round the stern for the second time, I freeze. A woman screams, "Don't, please!"

I rush toward the voice. I see two silhouettes struggling near the rail. It's Edward grappling with Elena, bending her over the side of the ship.

My legs start shaking, but I run forward shouting, "Edward, stop!"

To my relief, his head turns in my direction, but his eyes are glazed. Edward isn't in there. I step closer and twist his nose.

"Ow!" he yelps, slapping my hand. Elena twists away from his grasp and runs into the dark.

"I was just trying to scare her," he says, panting.

"You were about to pitch your wife overboard, Edward, I saw you."

"She's not my wife."
"Edward, please, I know the whole—"
"She's my sister."

32

DECEMBER 28   2 AM

"**Y**ou'll catch flies if you don't close your mouth," Edward says. "You heard me right, my wife, Elena Osler is my biological half sister. I didn't know that when I married her," he rushes to add, shamefaced. "Incest, the last taboo."

I feel squeamish. Incest is the last taboo. But, he's a friend. I need to help him. I slip my arm into his.

"Incest's an ugly word, Edward, barely accurate in your case. Let's get something to eat and a coffee since neither of us is going to get any sleep tonight."

I lead us to the ship's café, open twenty-four hours a day. A tired young waiter mixes two lattes, but I forget to order a sweet roll.

As we sit down at a table, Edward rubs his hand over his face, stopping to prod his swollen nose.

"I'm sorry. I didn't mean to tweak that so hard."

He grins ruefully, and takes a sip of his coffee. To my surprise, I don't touch my latte even though I can see it's topped with whipped cream and chocolate sprinkles.

"Now that you say it, I see the physical resemblance between you. Both of you have blue eyes, black hair, and the Osler chin cleft."

He looks down. "I know I should have noticed it, but she was so alluring." I wait for him to go on. "I didn't know I had a sister. That dirty little family secret was kept from me until it punched me in the face.

"In my parent's early days, things weren't going well with their marriage. My mother wanted a baby, but they were having trouble conceiving, in large part because when my father wasn't busy building his law practice, he was working for the Conservative Party.

"Being the town's only immigration specialist, he met many attractive foreign women. He started taking them out, hiding behind the shield of client-solicitor conferences. None of them meant anything to him, that is, until he met Beatriz Magyar.

"I've seen the pictures of her from that time. She was a knockout, a light-eyed, dark-haired 20-year-old Hungarian refugee. She'd survived a three-week journey on turbulent seas only to arrive with no papers, both her parents dead on the voyage, and little chance of remaining in Canada.

"All she had left of them was her father's World War II Hungarian dagger. He had been an officer in the Air Force, apparently. Dad showed me a picture of the weapon once. The blade was sleek, nickel-plated iron with a spread eagle of solid gold. Must have been a dress model. It had a secret blade-releasing button on the scabbard, lethal. Her father had even taught her how to use it.

"But a dagger-toting immigrant didn't faze my father. Beatriz was alone, destitute, a wild bird with a broken wing who was oh so appealing. He set her up in her own apartment. Their affair lasted for two years.

"Things finally got better with my mother and him when she got pregnant with me. That was when Dad tried to break it off with Beatriz, and that was when she told him she was pregnant, too.

"He believed her for awhile, until he found a cache of half empty bottles of alcohol hidden in a spare bathroom cabinet. She didn't drink in those days, so someone else must have been enjoying it.

"He hired a detective to follow her and found out she had Hungarian refugees visiting her whenever he wasn't around, day and apparently, night. So he figured he wasn't her only sex partner.

"There was no chance of an abortion. She was a devout Catholic. So he assumed responsibility for her care until Elena was born, then arranged a paternity test. That removed any doubt. He was the father. Even if he hadn't done the test, just looking at the baby photos would have been enough. She was the spitting image of my father as a baby, right down to the cleft in the chin."

I was so wrapped up in my own needs at the dinner with him at Scatter, I didn't notice the similarities then. Though now I recall while Edward's eyes are deep blue, hers are Nordic blue.

Edward continues, "Once I was born, my father made the decision to cut off all ties with Beatriz, in spite of baby Elena. Not good, I know. But, he was honourable in one way. He went to court and settled a one-time payment on her of $300,000 in lieu of alimony and child support."

I blink. "That was a lot of money back then."

"Yes, if she'd gotten professional investment advice, she and Elena could have lived a middle class life. But no, she couldn't resist the money. She rented a penthouse apartment, dressed in furs and jewels, dressed Elena in designer baby clothes, if you can imagine such a thing."

I shrug. Ronnie bought designer clothes for Sally and Stevie as if it was a must.

"And she threw extravagant, boozy parties for her Hungarian friends, and lovers." He grimaced. "So, when the money finally ran out, they had to resort to Food Banks, and what she could finagle from her Hungarian men friends. She started drinking heavily then, paying for her liquor by God knows what means.

"When my father found out about this, he paid for a full time nanny to care for Elena. Then he put additional money into a small trust account to mature at age 18, which would allow Elena to attend a local university. He made sure Beatriz couldn't touch it.

Finally, he referred Beatriz to Welfare, and stopped any further communication.

"But the booze changed Beatriz. She began publically accosting my father on downtown streets, screaming about her poverty, his child neglect, his betrayal. Once he got a restraining order against her with which she complied, she took another tack.

"My father was elected Mayor of Forest Village. Beatriz taped his TV appearances. Then she showed them to Elena over and over, saying my dad was her father, but he didn't love her. Sometimes, if I was in the clip, she'd say I was her brother, but I didn't want to play with her.

"She pointed out my clothes, new and expensive while hers came from thrift shops. She pointed out our big car while they had to ride the bus, even in the winter."

Edward's voice's ragged with fatigue and emotion. I glance out the window. Ronnie and Captain Monet stroll by in the moonlight, shoulders touching. When I look back to Edward, his expression has changed.

"You don't really want to hear any more of this, Sara. You're on a vacation. Come on, let's get some breakfast."

My heart thumps. I love breakfast. Poppy seed muffins with lemon zest, cinnamon buns drizzled with melted butter and honey, warm croissants, maybe chocolate, and of course waffles and whipped cream. I'm so distracted by the thought of food, I lurch from my chair before I notice Edward's face. It's tortured.

I sit back down immediately, and put my hand over his. I try to squelch the food thoughts in my mind, but they fight back. They're like leeches.

I manage to say, "Edward, tell me all of it."

He looks at me, his eyes suddenly ice blue with rage. "It gets much worse." My stomach tightens. Is he going to admit to murder? "Beatriz and Elena waited until I graduated from law school. As a graduation gift, my grandfather bought me the Ferrari."

"So, that's how you afforded it."

He smiles. "No young lawyer could have bought it. Plus, my parents were so thrilled I was doing what they wanted, they gave me a Mediterranean cruise as well."

I take a deep breath. So, this is how the rich live. I see why Beatriz and Elena were jealous. I feel a twinge of it myself.

"It was on the cruise where I met Elena. Beatriz followed all my family's comings and goings, so she found out about my trip. Years before, she'd talked Elena out of going to university in favour of a long-term financial plan. I was their stock. They used the trust fund money to pay for the cruise. Elena's stunning, you'll agree?"

I don't like hearing this man compliment another woman. He waits for my nod. I won't. Childish of me, I know.

His smile is brief. "Elena made sure we spent every waking minute together, and soon, every sleeping minute." My stomach roils. Incest. But a split second later, I'd like to pinch him and leave a bruise. "The romance of Europe, the ease and indolence of a luxury cruise, the relief of finally finishing school all combined and before I knew it, Elena and I were standing in front of the ship's captain being married."

Edward stares at me. He's a lawyer. He knows it's against the law to marry a sibling, even a half sibling. A child of the union's almost guaranteed to have birth defects. He was tricked. But why?

"When we got back to Toronto, we went right to my parents' house. My mother ran into the living room, and I introduced her to my new bride.

"'Mom, this is Elena, my wife.'

"She took one look at her, and collapsed. Elena laughed long and loud. My mother suffered a stroke and never recovered. My father grabbed me into his study where I got to hear about the family shame in detail."

I shiver. I'm a witness to evil.

"Of course we separated immediately, but that didn't change the fact that I had consummated a marriage with my sister. How would that affect the career of a young lawyer, or worse, a teacher, if I ever got back to it? How would it affect my father's dream of moving up in provincial politics? And how would it affect my grandfather's reputation as a Senator? My mother was already dead from the shock. We didn't want more losses. That's why we agreed to pay the blackmail. And we've been paying it ever since. That's why the Osler empire's no more.

"Beatriz died last year of alcoholism, and Elena has become crazed with revenge, bent on ruining us for good."

I'm startled when two ship's officers interrupt us at our table.

"Edward Osler?"

Edward nods.

"You're under arrest for the attempted murder of Elena Osler."

33

DECEMBER 28   5 AM

S tunned, I watch as Edward's escorted out of the cafe between the two security officers. He tried to kill Elena, and now I finally know why. She's blackmailing his family, keeping their careers in constant jeopardy, their reputation as an old respected Canadian family hanging by a thread, and caused the death of his mother. This gives him a king-sized motive.

I fold my arms on the table, drop my head to think better, and fall asleep. I have a bad dream. It's a replay of the voices on the baby monitor, but this time, I can hear the woman's voice clearly. I swear it's Elena Osler.

Is this Edward's other secret: he knows Elena murdered two people? But in order to keep her from spilling her guts about their incestual marriage, he's keeping that under wraps. If this is so, he's made a deal made with the devil, and devils are not known to honour them.

Yet I'm flooded with relief because if Elena did the murders, Ronnie didn't, and Edward didn't. It was Elena Osler on her bloody own. Could she have killed two people herself, in quick succession? Of course. Yes, I'm sure she could have. Why not?

Now, should I tell? If I accuse Elena, will she reveal her marriage to her half-brother, effectively ending the grand old Osler family? No more future MLA for Lawrence Osler; no more Senate position for Davis Osler; and no more the Chairman of the Board at St. Ives or any school for Edward Osler. Not to mention the family will be ostracized socially. That one little secret has the power to ruin so many lives.

Edward's unable to catch out Elena at the moment, but maybe I can. If she's jailed, no one will believe her wild ravings about the Osler family. Now, I just have to find her.

The sun has risen, and it's time for breakfast. How convenient that I'm still in the café. I belly up to the early bird buffet where I see a fresh plate of warm cinnamon buns. I take three. The muffins are next to it, and I chose a blueberry, a poppy seed and a bran, for health.

With my plate full, I'm about to slither back onto the blue plastic chair when a voice behind me says, "You don't have to eat over it."

I whirl around and there's Monica, the woman from last night's meeting. She has a simple coffee in her hand.

"Would you like to talk about it?" she asks.

I look down at my plate of muffins, which crowd every inch that isn't taken up by the croissants. The urge to devour them is overwhelming, so what's stopping me? A stranger with doe eyes?

Monica says, "There's no problem so great it can't be lessened." Oh-ho, little does she know. "I have a fail-proof recipe." Now she has my attention. I like recipes. "May I join you?"

I've never been one to confide. With parents like mine, secrets were a rule of survival. Self reliance is my motto. On the other hand, she's a stranger. I'll never see her again. Maybe a little brain rinse will help me decide my next step.

Monica nods to a quiet table in the corner near a window. I leave my plate full of untouched goodies on my table. That's a first. I settle onto a chair facing Monica and scrutinize her. Her almond-shaped eyes are clear. She has an air about her, is it enthusiasm, peace, well-being? In any case, she looks happy and healthy while I most certainly am not.

She says, "Do you want to talk about it?"

The thing is, whether or not I say a word to Monica, I've left a plate of food I love uneaten. This complete stranger has an eerie effect on me.

"I saw you at the meeting." Monica smiles warmly. "It was a mixed bag of AA, CA, and OA that night, I know, but on a ship we're all Friends of Bill W."

I'm curious. "You asked if I was a friend of Bill W at the meeting. What a coincidence that all of you know him."

She laughs. "I think we're talking about a different Bill W. Our guy's the founder of AA. Meetings for friends of Bill W. on a cruise ship keep everyone on an even keel when there's temptation." Monica laughs again. "And for a compulsive overeater, a cruise is serious temptation."

I like her sense of humour. I thought 12-step people were serious and glum, holding onto their new healthy habits with white knuckles.

Monica continues, "I came into OA, that's Overeaters Anonymous, after trying every diet out there, not to mention fat farms. I was even considering bariatric surgery. Before OA, I weighed 210 pounds." I gape. Monica is slim.

"But, with the help of a group of like-minded people, cleaning house of my character defects and making amends to those I hurt, and asking for help, help, help," she grins, "I've maintained an 80-pound weight loss for fifteen years, one day at a time."

That gets my undivided attention. "And how did you do that, exactly?"

"My abstinence's healthy food, in healthy amounts, at healthy times. That and a healthy relationship with my Higher Power whom I choose to call God."

I drop my eyes. So she's a Born Again something. Asking a supernatural mythical being for help help help's no recipe for me.

God might work for her, but I learned a long time ago the only person I could rely on for help help help is myself.

"Thanks, Monica. I want to talk longer, but I'm quite busy. My friend, Edward Osler, is in trouble."

Why did I tell her that? But I won't tell her he's being held on suspicion of attempted murder of the woman who smothered his friend then stabbed his nurse.

"And I have to watch over another friend who's on the cruise to recover from a shock." I didn't need to tell her that either. What's wrong with me? Am I confiding? That stops right now.

Speaking of Ronnie, I glance out the glass doors to see her with Captain French Fries, bumping hips as they stroll along the promenade deck.

I turn back to face OA Monica. "I don't have time for God at the moment, thanks."

Plus, I'm ravenous. I pretend to be looking at my watch as I surreptitiously glance back to the table where I left my plate of baked goods. Someone else's eating them. I groan.

Monica observes the whole charade. She shakes her head. "After the food's gone, the problem will still be there. Sharing your worries is the best way to solve them, but maybe you aren't ready. If you ever do want to talk, I'm willing to listen."

I sigh with relief. Anything to get away from her and back to my real friend, food. That's what'll make me feel better, think better. I offer her a pacifier.

"Why don't we exchange phone numbers?"

We each write on a napkin. I shove hers into my pocket impatiently. All the goodies might be gone by the time I get back to the buffet.

We part with promissory smiles, at least on her part, and I rush back to the buffet for muffins and croissants. There are still a few of my favorites left, and a huge plate of fresh chocolate waffles. Oh, water for the parched.

I give a cursory look at the other offerings on the table, a bowl of hard-boiled eggs, a plate of whole-wheat toast, hot oatmeal with coconut, and a batch of herbal teas.

Unbidden, my hand reaches out and takes two eggs, a piece of whole-wheat toast, and a lemon spice tea bag. I sit down at the closest table and eat that food and enjoy it. I can't explain it.

Ronnie drifts by the window again, alone this time, looking blissful. I run out of the cafe and intercept her on the deck.

"Ronnie? What's going on?"

She drapes her arms around my neck and leans her head on my shoulder.

"I feel so much better. Captain Monet's a wonderful listener."

Maybe that's what happened to me a few minutes ago. However, I find this conversation far more to my liking than the one I had with Monica.

"Is he married?"

Ronnie tears up. "His wife died two years ago of leukemia."

"Oh, that's right, the waiter told us that."

"He says he's trying to learn to live without her, but he says he needs me to help him. And I don't want to go home, Sarie."

I'm quiet, digesting this idea. Finally, Ronnie picks up her train of thought.

"His next cruise's to Holland. When he has time off, he says he'll show me the tulips and the windmills, to get my mind off ..." Her voice trails to a stop. "Will you come with me?" She adds hurriedly, seeing my long face, "I can pay. I have the money from Marshall's life insurance. Please. It'll take you away from your worries about being in love with a married man."

I blanch. "I'm not in love with Edward! We're just friends, like you and Captain Monet. I like him, sure, of course, but we aren't, we've never...." I'm babbling.

Ronnie puts up her hands in surrender. "Whatever you say. I still want to take you on the cruise. Okay? Dale can mind the kids."

If I could have thrown her over the ship railing, I would have. Ronnie's life has changed dramatically and maybe for the better, but mine hasn't.

"Ronnie, I can't leave my kids with Dale to go off on a two-week cruise. It would give him more ammunition to get full custody. No, until the kids are grown up, my life's over for things like that."

Ronnie leans towards me. "I already signed us up and put down the deposit. You deserve this."

I jerk back in horror. That was what the woman on the baby monitor said just that before she stabbed Kim Park.

Maybe it wasn't Elena Osler whose voice I heard on the baby monitor after all? The coast's uncomplicated and clear for Ronnie and a new man now—a manly man.

34

DECEMBER 28   9 AM

I have to report Edward's incarceration to Senator Osler. It isn't going to be easy on the old man. What can he do from Toronto?

At the moment, we're pulling into the port of Lahaina on the island of Maui. I can see passengers ambling towards the gangway for a day of pina coladas at the beaches. I turn away from the horrible sight of so many winter-white legs in shorts.

I don't know what to do with myself. I noticed one shore excursion that interests me. It's a tour of the government buildings, which are so old they're made of pink granite and cooled by those hip roofs like that hotel in Honolulu.

But how can I be thinking of enjoying myself when my friend Edward's under arrest? The detention cabin on the crew level still houses a drunken passenger who swung a bottle of Sir Frog tequila at a passenger agent. So they're detaining Edward in his own cabin.

I head to the computer room to write an urgent email report to the Senator. Poor grandpa.

Dear Senator Osler,

You're right to despise Elena Osler. She and Edward had a violent quarrel. At the end of it, she reported him to the captain, saying he'd tried to throw her overboard. The captain believed her. Edward's presently sequestered in his cabin until we return to Honolulu where he'll be delivered to the local police. If you can arrange to have legal support for him there, it would be a good idea. I don't know if he'll be returned to Canada right away or kept in the U.S. for a while.

Edward told me about your family tragedy regarding Beatriz Osler, and I fear it makes him a suspect in the murder of....

I can't tell his grandfather that. Clere hasn't charged Edward with anything, or Elena for that matter. I delete the paragraph and instead type.

Unfortunately, Detective Garry Clere of the Toronto Police's on board. He's got his nose into this business now.

I'm sorry to have to send such a sad report. I'll update you again tomorrow, I hope with better news.

I hit send.

Though most people have left the ship on various shore excursions, Edward, I know, is still on board. I'm sure Elena has been moved to an empty cabin several decks away, so I wonder if I can get in to visit him.

Though my key won't work, the chambermaids will be around making up the rooms. I can say I left something important in his cabin. What? I can wink and say, "My earring." Who doesn't love a love affair?

As luck would have it, the cabin steward's opening Edward's door with a food tray as I round the corner. I stand on the opposite side. When the steward comes out, I wait a second until he has walked a few steps away before I slip through the slow closing door.

He's sitting at the desk, staring out the window, the food steaming in front of him, untouched. Without meaning to, I notice what he chose: eggs, Canadian bacon, whole-wheat toast, fresh red grapes, and a sweet roll. In my bad old days, that sweet roll would've made my mouth water, but once again, my reaction to food's weird. I'm more interested in Edward. He's so deep in thought, he hasn't noticed me.

"Edward," I whisper.

He jerks around, banging his knee against his food tray, knocking several grapes onto the patterned carpet.

"How did you get in here?" he says, his voice low. Then he's up and out of his chair, grabbing me in a tight hug. A cry of despair escapes from him. We hold each other, each in our own sorrow, so many different sorrows.

Exhausted, we collapse on the bed. Here's where I'd like the romance to start, but I don't have the heart for it. He's loved, but he's also a friend in trouble. Now is not the time.

"Sara," Edward says his voice husky. "I was going to throw her overboard. Marshall was altering my inheritance trust to save me. When I turned 35, which was a few days ago, I was to come into the last of the family money, one million dollars. Elena was ready to blackmail us to get it all so we'd go bankrupt. That's been their plan all along."

He drops his head into his hands. I put my arms around his shoulders. I notice how broad his shoulders are, and I get that squiggling feeling in my stomach, or thereabouts. Focus, focus!

He exhales. "Marshall was trying to break the old trust that had me inheriting the money at age 35. We planned to change the age to 50. We figured if we added another 15 years, Beatrix would certainly be dead of alcoholism by then, and Elena even before from her cocaine habit.

"Beatrix beat our prediction by dying this year, but there was still Elena. Marshall was sick, but he insisted on doing it for me. But being so ill meant he couldn't get all the documents done until the last second." Edward stands up and paces in the tiny room. "It took him until the night before my birthday, his last night alive…." Edward shakes his head, unable to go on.

I glance out the cabin window. Detective Clere strides past. Is he on his way to talk to Edward? I jump up.

"I have to go."

Edward ignores me. His voice has taken on a flat droning quality. "I was to show up before 11:59 pm and sign in front of a witness, his nurse, Kim Park. Then the trust would be locked, safe from that woman."

I look out to the deck again. Clere's no longer visible. Is he in the corridor?

"When I got to Marshall's house, just before midnight, Elena was standing in the front foyer, smirking. 'Your lawyer's permanently incapacitated now, and so's his witness, that little nurse. This means the old trust's still in effect. You have access to all that money now, and I want it. All of it. I'll finally have the money we should have had all along. If only my mother were alive to see this day.'

"I pushed her aside and ran up the stairs, but her voice screamed after me. 'If you don't sign over the money, I'll let the whole world know your filthy secret. And ruin you, Daddy, and dear Senator Grandfather.'

"I ran into Marshall's bedroom. He was laying still, his head at an odd angle, his pillow obscuring his face. Someone, Elena, had smothered the life out of him because he was too weak to defend himself.

"That blackmailing contemptible witch murdered my friend, and my only chance at saving the remainder of generations of Osler industry and fortune.

"I decided to kill her. I stormed downstairs, but when I got near enough, she hissed, 'My secret for your secret.'

"That stopped me. No amount of money was as valuable as the Osler name. My few seconds of hesitation gave her time to escape out the front door."

So, Edward was there on the night of the murders, and not only there, but in Marshall's room. I can't speak. I want to believe Edward, I do. And I will.

"Edward, Elena will surely say you did the murders and it'll be her word against yours. Any evidence left in the house burned up in the fire."

What I don't say out loud is that Edward's only chance is a witness who'll support his version. That would be me. I heard it all on the baby monitor.

I'm about to blurt out everything to Edward when there's a peremptory knock at the door. That's a mere formality because Edward's door is locked from the outside.

The door handle rattles, and Clere steps into the room. He halts at the sight of me. "How long have you been here?" Then he notes the messed up bed. He could ask something more personal, but he doesn't.

I dodge behind his back, bang on the inside of the door, and slip out when the ship's guard sticks in his head. Clere's quick though. He's right behind me.

"Be in the cafe in an hour, Mrs. Forsyth," he orders sternly, then steps back into Edward's cabin and the door hisses shut.

My stomach twists. Can he force me to reveal what I know?

THE POINT

35

DECEMBER 28   NOON

At least my interrogation with Clere's in a café and it's lunchtime. On the buffet I see toffee buns, pecan tarts, and several types of bagels, colourful cheeses, chocolate brownies, carrot cake, and chocolate sprinkles for make-your-own sundaes. Maybe I should get a job on a cruise ship.

I pick up my plate, and reach for the first chocolate thing I see, brownies. Is this a trick of the eye? The chocolate looks like dirt. Who wants to eat dirt? I blink rapidly. They look delicious again. I grab two. And then I add a pecan tart, and two toffee buns.

I wander about the room, and then pick a table away from the center. If Clere's terrible to me, I don't want to burst into tears with an audience.

I realize I don't have a main course for my lunch and return to the buffet. I choose a multigrain bagel, two pats of butter, and a scoop of cream cheese. Who needs OA Monica? I can do this on my own. I stroll back to my table, feeling smug.

I set my dessert plate aside, determined to eat the healthy food first. I do note this is out of character for me. I finish half a bagel and cream cheese when Detective Clere slips into the seat opposite me.

"That looks good." He smiles. "My mother says there's nothing like bagels and cream cheese for health." He pauses. "Though it hasn't helped her lately."

Don't tell me he's going all human on me. But I have to ask, to be polite.

"What's the matter with your mother?"

"Multiple Sclerosis. Since before I was born. Now that Dad's gone, I'm her full time caregiver." He shakes his head. "She put herself at risk because she wanted a baby so much. She was alright for a few years because the MS went into one of its mysterious remissions. But then the symptoms flared up big time. And she's been wheelchair bound for 15 years."

He turns his face away and glances out to the deck. "I support her in every way I can. I'm all she has." His expression softens with affection. "She did everything for me then, so now I do for her." But his face shows strain.

"That can't be easy. How does being gay and living at home with your mother in your 40s go over at the police station?"

"No one knows I live with my mother, except you." He narrows his eyes. "Who'll never tell anyone." My mouth goes dry.

He shifts his weight in the chair. "When I first told my father I wanted to be a cop, he said, 'As a gay cop, you won't have as much trouble with the criminals as you will with your fellow officers.' He was right.

"A few years ago when I was reading a book of poetry in the staff cafeteria, as policemen are wont to do—" He winks.

I'm demoralized. A cop who reads poetry, loves his mother and has a sense of humour. You have to like this police officer. How sick is that?

"Anyway, one of the police thugs started to bait me. 'Pussy cops read poetry.' I put my book down on the seat beside me. 'Every cop force needs a few pussy cops to please our queer politicians, eh poetry faggot?'

"I stood up slowly, sauntered over, and smashed his face into the tabletop. So you see, my father was wrong. I don't have trouble with my fellow officers, any more. " The cold stare's back.

Not a man to be toyed with. I've been warned. I'm doubly scared now. The uncomfortable silence stretches taut. I say the only thing I can think of to break the spell.

"Care for a brownie?"

He heaves a deep sigh, grabs one and downs it in a big bite. Then he wolfs down my other brownie. I glare at him.

"Oh, did you want that? Sorry, but I haven't had a minute of R & R since I boarded this ship." He licks a crumb off his lower lip.

He has the most beautifully-shaped mouth I've ever seen. It isn't feminine pretty, it's strong. What a strange combination of male and female he is. I feel safe for a second. Then I remember I have a history with the police and it's not pretty.

"I've always hated cops."

He chokes on the last bit of brownie. "Thanks for sharing that."

"I'm not joking. You can't be trusted. "

He shakes his head quickly. "So, you had a bad experience. What happened to you?"

I don't know why I tell him, but out pours all the trouble I had as a kid because of the police, the constant raids, the shouting voices, the terrifying scenes with big men forcing my beloved father into black cop cars.

He listens earnestly until I'm done. "Did your father do something bad?"

"Some people might think so," I allow. Some people, my eye.

"Did he harm people other than himself, like other family members, neighbours, or friends?"

I'm swamped with bad memories. My father taking grocery money to use for gambling, cashing friends' insurance premiums to bankroll his day at the track. Sweet talking our neighbours into signing onto SunnyCare Life Insurance, as solid as a rock, only to keep their money for himself, leaving them uninsured. And of course, defrauding the company he worked for, which trusted him with the care of its clients. It was all to feed a gambling addiction, to enjoy his addiction.

But, I won't admit this to a cop. I look away from Clere's compassionate face.

He continues his probe. "A police department's mission is to serve the public and protect the vulnerable from abuse. Were the police doing that?"

I have to admit they were. I nod.

Suddenly, he turns all policeman. "Mrs. Forsyth, I need your help to get justice served. As you may know, Ronnie's refusing to answer any questions about Marshall and Edward Osler."

Before I know it, I'm defending him. "Edward didn't do anything to Marshall. They're best of friends. "

He shakes his head. "Mrs. Forsyth, I'm not accusing your lover boy."

I bristle. "Now you listen here, Detective Clere. Edward Osler's a married man, and I am, too, technically, married."

Clere shrugs. "I need Ronnie to talk to me, not you. She says she doesn't know anything, but I know she does. I don't want her to get into trouble, Mrs. Forsyth. She's had a rough go."

His eyes get sad. Where were cops like this when I was a kid? "Ronnie's a sweet woman, and she's suffered a terrible blow, but if she won't tell me what she knows, how can I help her?"

He keeps calling her Ronnie instead of Mrs. Stohl. Since when does a cop call a murder suspect by her first name? Maybe she's not a suspect. Or maybe this guy isn't gay. Or both.

"Ronnie's telling the truth when she says she knows nothing. She and Marshall have been like strangers for the last few years. Marshall was at the office all the time."

I won't tell him the rest. Marshall couldn't give Ronnie the child she was desperate for, and wouldn't adopt for reasons best known to himself, so she punished him by overeating and over shopping. They had stopped spending time together long ago except for public functions. They were on the brink of divorce when he got TB.

Clere sighs. "Sara, please do what you can and let me know when she'll be in a frame of mind to be interviewed. I'll be gentle with her."

He stands up, turns away, then reaches back and snitches the pecan tart off my dessert plate. He winks and glides out of the cafe, humming.

Should he be this happy knee-deep in a murder investigation?

I head back to my cabin, worrying about a Ronnie and Clere mix. She benefitted too much from Marshall's death. But he doesn't know her like I do. If tell Clere what I heard on the baby monitor, it might exonerate Ronnie and Edward or focus on them more. On the other hand, if I do tell Clere and he catches Elena, what she'll do to Edward and his family will be like a mass assassination.

Is it my job to make this decision? Maybe I'll leave Clere to his own devices. Suddenly, I'm too tired to eat any dessert. Good lord, I haven't had sugar for two meals. And it hasn't been hard. Is it that 12-step voodoo? I don't care. I'm elated. Then I'm exhausted.

It's probably lack of chocolate.

THE POINT

36

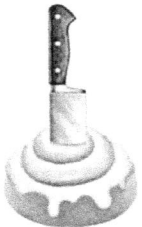

DECEMBER 28   2PM

I slip my key into our cabin door, then glance up the hall at the ship's officer guarding Edward's cabin. He glares at me. I got him in trouble with Clere.

I duck inside our room, and see my freshly-made bed littered with new outfits and a note from Ronnie.

More Treats for my Sweets. I'm with Captain Monet. Try them on. Hugs, Ronnie.

I lie down on her empty bed and fall into a deep sleep. I wake to a thundering on my door then the scratching of a key. Detective Garry Clere pushes inside.

"Where's Edward Osler?" he barks. "The officer guarding his cabin has been stabbed."

I sink back onto the bed. "With a dagger?"

Clere stares hard at me. "What do you know about this, Mrs. Forsyth?"

"Elena has a Hungarian dagger." If only I'd told Clere sooner, this might not have happened. My lips feel thick, frozen. "Will the officer survive?"

Clere takes a sharp breath. "The ship's infirmary's ill-equipped to treat dagger wounds." He eyes me. "But the doctor thinks the officer will survive, yes. The dagger just missed his carotid artery."

I look up at Clere. "Elena Osler did it."

He sits down beside me on the bed. "Tell me everything you know, Sara, if you ever want to see your boyfriend alive again. He's missing, and there are blood stains on his carpet."

I feel cold and clammy. My breath comes fast. The light's dimming. Then my shoulders are hugged.

"Don't faint on me, Sara. Tell me what I need to know to find your Edward."

I tell him about the baby monitor, and I tell him about Elena and Edward's sordid secret. His arm muscles tighten around my shoulders. "Don't leave this cabin, you hear me, Sara?" He bolts out.

I watch as he breaks into a run on the deck. Where's Edward, my friend, my protector? There's a bang on the cabin door. Edward? I run to open it and am shoved back inside.

Elena Osler stands in front of me, a blood-stained dagger in her hand.

"These doors aren't soundproof. You know too much. And you told that policeman much too much. You deserve this!" she snarls.

"No!" I cry, throwing up my arm to ward off the blow. Elena feints up then thrusts down, stabbing me in the abdomen.

I fall to the carpet in shock. The cabin door opens and hisses closed. I see blood oozing out of my stomach.

I lie frozen on the cabin floor while daylight fades, turning afternoon into evening. Most of the passengers will be back from their shore excursions, getting dressed for a lavish dinner.

As my blood drains, my energy drains with it. I want to sleep, but I've seen enough movies to know this is a bad thing.

I attempt to move my left leg, which is under my body. No problem. I try to move my right leg. A pain I've only felt in childbirth rips through my body. Okay, no moving right.

Inch by inch, I roll to my left side. If I can sit up, I can reach the cabin phone and call for help. I push up with my left arm. A searing pain makes me scream. I drop back down. I'm gushing blood from the area now.

The gash is large and the wound is gaping. I peer into it, terrified I'll see my intestines. Instead, I see yellowish muscle, or's that fat? Saved by fat? I snigger, then gasp in pain.

I hear a jostling at the door, and Ronnie bursts in. "Sarie? Why's it so dark in here? Captain Monet says..." Her jaw freezes mid-sentence. "Sarie, why are you on the—oooh, blood," she moans, falling to the carpet beside me in a faint. Nothing new here.

I lie on the floor, staring at the ceiling. My energy's flowing away. If I don't get help soon, I might die. But, that means I'd be leaving my children. I cannot die. I will not.

My energy's less than before, but my determination's more. I push myself up on my left elbow again, shriek from the scalding pain and fall back. I push myself up again. Again the pain forces me down.

The room's getting dark as night falls. The air conditioning's still on and the cold air along the floor chills me. All Stevie and Sally will have's Dale, a father no one should have. He doesn't love them. He wants to use them. I will not leave them. I push myself up once again, and fall in a heap on the bloody carpet.

I pass out.

37

DECEMBER 29   8AM

W hen I open my eyes, I'm lying on a narrow bed with a wool blanket over me. Above me are bright florescent lights. I turn my head. No pictures on the walls, no cabin porthole. I turn my head the other way. Ronnie's asleep in a chair near my bed.

"Pssst," I hiss. "Ronnie, wake up."

Ronnie swallows and opens her eyes. She leaps up and hugs me. I shriek.

"Oh, Sarie. I'm so sorry. Your wound." Ronnie pales at the thought of blood. She takes a deep breath. "But you're going to be alright. The dagger didn't hit an organ because your fat got in the way. Mars Bars are our friends." Ronnie giggles. "You're in the ship's infirmary. They caught that horrible ship guard who did this to you."

I inspect her expression. She doesn't know what really happened. I can't remember much after the attack myself. Was it just last night Elena broke into my cabin?

"What day is it?"

Ronnie purses her lips and looks up at the ceiling. "I think it's December 28. Wait. Yes, it is because we were to get back on the 29th but we left Lahaina a day early for some reason."

"Sarie, I don't know how to tell you this, but Edward Osler's missing, and so's his wife, Elena. I know you're sweet on him, but I think he's gone back to his wife."

It's like a dagger in my stomach all over again. "Ronnie, who told you this?"

She looks scared now, knowing something's going on, but not what. "Captain Monet told me." She sinks onto the chair. "Why?"

"When can I get out of here?"

"You have to stay in bed until we dock. We'll be in Honolulu in a couple of hours. They're going to have an ambulance meet us and everything, just for you. And I get to ride in it." She grins, and then forces a more somber expression.

"Poor Sarie."

There's silence in the room except for the ticking of the wall clock. It looks like the ones at St. Ives School. What will become of Edward's job? His family fortunes are going to disappear into the maw of that blackmailing Lady Macbeth. And if he loses his job, he won't get another in a school, not when the truth about him and his half sister comes out.

Not to mention, it'll destroy his father's political career, and as for the Senator, there's no way he'll survive this. His job's one thing, but his health's another. At 78, how many shocks can he take?

Without the family money or jobs, they're going to be up against it for the first time in generations. They'll have lost their reputation, too. What will they have left?

The doctor bustles in carrying a large orange sleeping bag.

"This will protect you while we transfer you from the ship to the ambulance. "He sets about unzipping it and slipping it over my legs and stomach. "It's just a precaution. Your wound has been stitched and most of the oozing has stopped." Ronnie and I gag in unison. "It shouldn't hurt now since we've dosed you up on Percocet. You're flying back to Canada today."

"Wonderful," I say while Ronnie pouts.

"I want to stay with my captain," she says in a small voice, "but of course I'll go with you, Sarie, because you need me."

The doctor continues, "We'll ask the airline to put you in the bulkhead seats where there's extra legroom. You'll be fine."

I nod. I'll be fine on an eleven-hour flight because at the end of it, I'll see my children.

"An orderly will be along in a minute to help you into a wheelchair and onto the deck to disembark. You'll be the last off. We don't want the other passengers to think it was the food." He chuckles.

Food. It feels like I haven't had anything to eat in hours. I must still be in shock because I'm not hungry. I've got to be beating Ronnie on our weight loss bet.

"Oh," he says, turning back for a moment, "a woman passenger gave me this note for you." He smiles and leaves.

Gingerly, I unfold the paper. There's a phone number on it and OA Monica. She knew I'd lose the other one. Apparently, I'm that obvious.

"What's it?" Ronnie asks, eyebrows raised.

I refold the note. "Put this in my purse, please."

"Can I see it?"

I shake my head. "Not now. You have enough on your plate." I start to laugh, but stop quickly. It hurts.

Detective Garry Clere rushes into the room. His face's haggard as if he hasn't slept all night. He takes my cold hands in his slim warm ones, and says gently, "I can't leave you alone for a minute, can I?"

When this is over, I'm going to be friends with Garry Clere.

"Who did this to you?" he growls.

I glance over at Ronnie. I don't want to scare her or involve her. In the last few days, Elena Osler, the woman who murdered her husband and his nurse, has gone from greedy blackmailer to mass murderer. I was to be number three. And if Elena thinks I told more people, like my closest friend, I know what she'll do to her. I'm keeping Ronnie in the dark on this.

I look at Clere intently, beaming him the name. "I think you know who did it."

Clere nods once. "I have a U.S. police escort meeting you when we dock in Honolulu who will accompany you to the airport. I've arranged for a local constable to accompany you once you land in Toronto. You'll have twenty-four hour protection from this day forward." He looks ferocious. "Until we have arrested the person who did this to you."

Before I can speak, he rushes from the room, accidentally bumping into the orderly pushing in the wheelchair. Clere stops, turns around, and apologizes. The orderly looks at him curiously. Obviously, he's never experienced Canadian manners.

I think he knows who to go after. At least, I hope so. Once on the plane, I'll tell the escorting officer everything, that is, after I get Ronnie out of earshot.

At the bottom on the ship's gangplank, an ambulance is waiting with the police guard, as promised. I've no idea where Detective Clere is, or Edward and Elena Osler.

Are they in this together? Did Edward commit murder with the encouragement of his wife? I know for a fact they colluded to keep the murders of Marshall and Kim Park a secret, each for their own purpose. Maybe Edward's just an accessory. Whether it's before the fact or after the fact I'm not sure since TV detective dramas only teach so much.

I'm hauled up into the ambulance with Ronnie by my side and whisked to the airport. There we're hustled into a private room where they remove me from the wheelchair to do the security check. Once done, they roll me along the corridor to our flight area.

"Sarie, I'm going to pick up a postcard for my captain." She smiles and hurries over to the convenience store.

I glance idly around at the other passengers. Over in a corner, a familiar-looking tall man and woman are arguing with each other, and then they rush away from the passenger waiting area.

It's them! Edward and Elena.

I turn and alert my U.S. police officer, but she doesn't know what I'm talking about. I twist my head to find them again, but they've disappeared in the crowd.

I start to cry. The officer asks worriedly, "Mrs. Forsyth, are you in pain?"

I shake my head no. I'm weeping in relief. Edward is alive.

THE POINT

38

DECEMBER 29   7 PM

O nce we're settled into the roomy bulkhead seats, once again in Business class, I twist as much as I can to see if Garry Clere's with us on board.

Ronnie asks, "Hey, where's that cute Detective Clere?"

"Ronnie, you have to find him right now. Edward and Elena Osler are in the airport!"

Ronnie yawns. "Oh, that's nice. They're getting along better, aren't they?"

Though I'm not sure I can keep lying well enough to fool my close friend, and get what I want, I know I have to try.

"Yes, it's nice, but Detective Clere says he has some important news for us, so can you see if he's aboard the plane?"

Ronnie says, "You know, if I didn't have Captain Monet, I could go for Garry Clere." She wrestles her way through the arriving throng of passengers to the back of the airplane.

My cell phone rings. Who would be calling me? The kids? I reach for my purse under the seat, but have to wait for the flash of pain to stop before I can talk.

"Hello?"

"Where's my grandson?"

"Senator, I have bad news." He says nothing, but I can hear his raspy breathing. "Edward and Elena attacked a ship's officer."

The Senator's voice cracks. "Where's my grandson now?"

"We don't know."

Silence. "Who's we?"

I close my eyes and say, "Detective Garry Clere's here. He's the officer investigating the murder of Marshall Stohl, and his nurse, Kim Park."

Longer silence. The flight attendants are finishing up their preparations for takeoff. I'll have to end this call shortly.

"Why's Edward involved in any of that?"

Poor grandfather. "He was in his cabin when the officer was stabbed. His cabin door was unlocked when it shouldn't have been."

I hold my breath, unwilling to reveal what I know. The Senator may be old, but he's been around wily politicians most of his life. He knows I'm holding something back.

"What else? I can take it. Please, tell me."

"Edward was in the house with Elena the night of those murders."

Senator Osler exhales long and slow. If Edward's put on trial for murder, the Senator's son, Lawrence Osler, can kiss a seat in the House of Commons goodbye. His opponents will never let such a scandal die. In fact, the Senator's own position might not be able to withstand the public censor. In addition to that, Elena has worse plans, which will be the straw that breaks his family's back.

"Where's my granddaughter now?"

"She's with Edward."

He gasps. "That wretched girl!"

A flight attendant walks down the aisle, asking passengers to cooperate with flight procedures. She leans toward me.

"We need you to end your call, please. We're about to take off."

"Keep me posted," the Senator orders, and hangs up.

Ronnie slides back into her seat. "Garry Clere's in the bulkhead seat in Coach." She drops her eyes to her hands, to her wedding ring. Then out of the blue, she says, "Garry Clere's so sweet, don't you think, Sarie?

I have to tell her. "Yes, Ronnie. Garry Clere's a very sweet gay man. "

Ronnie gapes. "How do you know?"

"He told me when I tried to kiss him."

"You kissed…?" Ronnie asks, stunned. Then, curious, "How was it?"

"Painful, in so many ways."

Ronnie says dreamily. "I bet I can turn him."

"Ronnie, what century are you living in?" I ask in disgust.

The gentle noises in the airplane contrast with the pulsating pain of my wounds. I try to ignore it in order to concentrate. Dale will be returning the children to me on New Year's Eve, which gives me less than four days to help Edward out of his cesspool.

Since the officer was stabbed, in all likelihood, Elena did that. I bet she was trying to get into Edward's cabin. And since I'm sure I just saw Edward with Elena at the airport, the stain on his carpet might have been the officer's blood dripping off her dagger.

A few minutes after the plane takes off, I'm startled to look up and see Detective Garry Clere standing in the aisle next to my seat. He taps Ronnie's shoulder and she snaps out of a cozy nap.

"Washroom," he whispers to her.

"I have to go to the washroom," she mumbles, and stumbles from her seat. Clere slips in beside me.

"How are you feeling?"

I bite the corner of my lip. Now that he mentions it, something's oozing down there. That idea brings on instant nausea. "Things have been better."

He places his cupped hands above my bandaged area and wiggles his fingers.

I pull away. "What are you doing?"

"Therapeutic touch. I took a course through Toronto East General Hospital. Took me two years. I use it on my mother to relax her."

I feel warmth emanating from his hand, but surely that's normal heat from any hand.

"I also use it when I get on the scene first and the ambulance's going to take awhile. I don't touch anything, so I never get complaints. How does it feel?"

To my surprise, it feels hot but relaxing.

He exhales. "I'm in an awkward position. I need to be more on top of you."

"Not on your life, you cop," I splutter.

"Sara, you do remember? I'm not hitting on you. This is what works best on my mother." He shifts his body to a higher position and keeps waving his hands in what he calls ruffling.

I don't care what he's doing; the pain's ebbing. His eyes never leave my face.

"Do you have any idea where Edward and his wife are?"

I blurt out, "I saw them in the Honolulu airport just before we boarded."

Clere groans. "They probably took a different flight. They could be home before we are and I'll never catch them. "He makes to rush away. "I have to contact the Hawaiian police to be sure they aren't still there."

"Garry, she said I deserved it when she stabbed me. Maybe I did. I was a bad wife, a neglectful daughter, a fat person."

Clere narrows his gentle eyes. "Sara, you didn't deserve any of this." He flips open his notebook and reads, "'Elena Osler's infatuated and obsessed with herself, cares nothing about anyone else, and is ruthless in her grab for gratification, dominance and ambition.' That's the psychological profile our police psychiatrist drew. She's a narcissist."

Now I'm worried for a different reason. "Is it genetic? I mean, might Edward have these tendencies?"

Garry shrugs. Then a worse thought occurs to me.

"Can this psychiatric diagnosis be used as an excuse for her to avoid legal consequences?"

"I'm a detective not a psychologist or a judge, Sara, but Elena will get the sentence she deserves. You, on the other hand, did not deserve anything she did to you."

It feels like warm honey pouring over my head and down my body, sweet forgiveness.

Ronnie sashays down the aisle. Clere slides out and winks at her as she settles in. She smiles back, and then dreamily watches him return to his seat. Those two are in for a world of hurt.

39

A n hour before the plane lands we're treated to another sumptuous buffet. Ronnie piles my plate high with my favorites. I need energy. I need quick energy, don't I? I've been through a rough time, haven't I? So, I relish the waffles with chocolate sauce and enjoy every morsel. Ah well, Rome wasn't built in a day.

The plane lands without incident. Ronnie and I are last off. I take the wheelchair ride to the baggage claim area to avoid using up what energy reserves I have left. Clere's there waiting for us. He has the relaxed stance of a ballet dancer, lean and graceful, but he's all business.

"Officer Erika Cochran here will drive you home and stand guard at your house. Mrs. Stohl, you'll need to answer a few more questions, I'm afraid. Will you be staying with Mrs. Forsyth?"

Ronnie's face is blank. She stands motionless, a stone statue. She's back in the land where someone murdered her husband and his nurse in her home.

"Of course she'll stay with me," I cut in.

Clere considers this for a moment, then gets behind the wheelchair and pushes me out to the arrivals area. There's a man in a chauffeur uniform holding a sign with my name on it. Next to him stand Lawrence Osler and Senator Davis Osler.

Detective Clere stops in his tracks. "Who are they?" he asks, suspicious, cautious.

"Edward's father and grandfather." I wave at them.

Clere nods and walks over. After a few words from him, the Osler men look at me in alarm.

Clere comes back. "Mr. Osler will drive you to your house. A police escort will follow you."

Ronnie stops stock-still. "Why the police? Captain Monet arrested the ship's officer who stabbed Sara. Why do we need a police escort here?"

Clere casts a furtive look at me. I shake my head. Ronnie's still in the dark about everything.

"Just a precaution, Mrs. Stohl," Clere adlibs smoothly. Are all cops such good liars? In my experience.

Mollified, Ronnie nods. "As long as we get home quickly. I promised Andre I'd check in with him the moment I got back."

Clere nods curtly and stalks away. What on earth's that gay man thinking?

Lawrence Osler helps me into his car, and then says, "We know what happened. Go home and rest and we'll talk later. Senator Osler and I have an important meeting right now, but my chauffeur will make sure you get to your house safely. Good day, Mrs. Forsyth, Mrs. Stohl." He turns abruptly, and flags down a taxi.

"Who's Senator Osler?" Ronnie asks, unclear of the Osler lineage.

"Edward's grandfather."

She gawks. "Edward has a real Senator in his family?" She settles back into the plush seat, hums for a minute, and then out of the blue asks, "Who really stabbed you, Sara?"

I catch my breath. Edward Osler and his deranged wife, Elena, are on the loose. How long can Edward control her and her dagger?

"Oh, Sarie, I'm sorry." She pats me solicitously. "You must be in pain, exhausted. You take a nap during the drive home. I'll wake you when we get there."

I glance behind us and see an unmarked police car following. When we get home, the chauffeur carries our luggage to the front door while Constable Cochran helps me out of the Osler limousine. She's going to sit outside in her police car and protect us.

I search in the depths of my purse for my keys, but I can't find them. Ronnie's dancing up and down beside me.

"Sarie, hurry up. I have to pee."

I'm so tired. My hands slip off my purse and it falls to the concrete porch. Ronnie swoops in to retrieve it while, at the same time, lifting the outdoor mat where I always leave a spare key in case Stevie gets locked out.

"Where's the key, Sarie?"

"I don't know. Oh, maybe Stevie took it when they went to stay with Dale."

Ronnie picks up my purse, digs down and yelps. "Ow! What do you have in here?" She pulls up my metal nail file. "You could kill someone with that thing!" She continues rifling and locates my keys. She unlocks the door and she and Officer Cochran help me into the house.

Officer Cochran then returns outside to sit in her car. I hope she gets relieved soon because it's freezing outside. Of course, I've just come back from lovely Hawaii, so the cold weather's a bigger shock.

Ronnie wanders into the living room. She looks dead on her feet. If anyone has a right to be exhausted, it's her.

"Why don't you take a nap, Miss Lorraine?"

She gives me a wan smile. "Sounds good, Roomie." She drags herself up the stairs to the guestroom without another word.

The house's quiet, disconcerting after all the hubbub on the ship. I look around my living room. There are shots of the kids in various states of dress and costume, at various sports and outings, with Dale in so many of the pictures. We look like the perfect family. Appearances can be deceiving.

212

Once Dale and I were married, his real personality came out. He believed women should ask their husband's permission before they made financial decisions over $100. He had to approve of my friends. And there was to be no career outside of the home.

This came as a shock and a betrayal of all I was taught to expect of a modern marriage. I disconnected from Dale and felt lonely. What was the point of a marriage if there was no emotional connection?

So why did I put up with it? This was the biggest shock. I willingly gave up control of my life for security. And I ate C-foods: cookies, cakes, and candies to stuff my emotions down. I gained weight and went from a seductive Marilyn Monroe pinup to a caricature of her.

When I managed to get pregnant, you could hardly tell at first because I was so heavy already. Once Stevie was born, I didn't lose the weight either. Oh, what's 30 pounds among friends? After Sally, I gained 10 pounds over that. Dale used to like the full Marilyn figure, but I was beyond Marilyn. So he decided to go for a different model, and lo and behold, he found it in Chloe-the-Very-Thin.

There's rustling in the hall. Ronnie must have come down for a drink.

"Ronnie?" No answer. "Ronnie, are you okay?"

"Fine," says Elena Osler. She saunters into my living room. I'm stunned. How did she get past the police guard? Not only that, but what has happened to this once beautiful woman? Her face is grey and gaunt, her beautiful mouth, so like Edward's, is thin and cracked. Her luxuriant black hair's dry and wild, and her shoulders are hunched into her black mink, which hangs about her like a giant's robe.

With the lightning speed of a snake, Elena darts forward and before I can get away, slashes me on the side of my neck. Blood spurts into the air in a rhythmic fountain. It's déjà vu all over again. I know I only have a short time before I pass out.

"Where's Edward?" I demand.

Elena laughs. Even that once-tinkling sound has become metallic, grating. "He's getting rid of Detective Garry Clere as we speak. Or, shall I say, as I watch you die. You deserve it," she taunts. "Because my life's none of your business. You had no right to pass any of it to that police prick. But with you two gone," she breathes in heavily, "I'll finally get what's coming to me. I deserve this! In my mother's name, I'll ruin Lawrence Osler as he ruined her.

"Edward thinks we were after his inheritance, but that's only part of it. We want them to be poor, ruined, social pariahs like my mother and I were."

Elena steps closer and pushes me hard on the shoulder. I collapse to the carpet. Not on carpet again. I want to get Elena out of here before she realizes Ronnie's upstairs, ripe for stabbing.

"Get out," I pant. "I promise I won't survive this time."

"That's the plan." She starts to hum as she wanders over to the hall and peers out the window. "Doesn't that police idiot guarding your front door know you have a back door?"

She whirls around, her coat flying out from her thin body, hairs from the dry leather floating off into the air. "I can simply walk out your back door, through your backyard and to the street behind where I've parked my car."

She snaps, "Once I'm sure you're dead this time." She leans down, and touches my pulse, which is getting fainter by the second. I let my eyelids fall slowly, and hold my breath, pretending to be dead.

Elena's boot nudges me. She laughs quietly, and I can hear her heels make their way into the back hall. The door opens. I'm about to gasp for air when her heels step back into the hall. I sniff tiny breaths through my nose to ease the desperation of my lungs. I hope my chest isn't moving.

I sense Elena staring at me. The animal she has turned into knows something isn't right. I beg my body to remain dead still.

A siren sounds near the house.

Elena hisses, "If you don't die this time, I'll kill the next level." I hear the staccato sound of her high heels receding quickly across the tile floors.

What next level? Of course, my kids.

THE POINT

40

DECEMBER 30   3PM

T his time when I wake, I'm in a hospital, an IV dripping fluid into my arm. A stiff bandage restricts movement on the left side of my neck. Déjà vu all over again except this time there's no Ronnie sleeping in my bedside chair.

The lights in the room are off, but the light through the window illuminates everything I need to see. I'm alone in a hospital room, which's unattended. Edward Osler has already killed Garry Clere if Elena was telling the truth. And I know who's next. Since I didn't die, she's going after Stevie and Sally to keep me quiet as a witness.

I can't risk testifying for Edward or anyone else. I have to protect my children. That's everything. But if she harms one hair on their heads, I'll see her punished.

I position myself on my side. The dagger wound in my neck shrieks in complaint, but I press my lips tight to avoid making a sound.

I rummage inside the drawer in the side table. Surely whoever brought me to the hospital would have put it in here. With a sigh of relief I feel the hard shape of a cell phone. I just have the Senator's old phone, but it will do the job.

I turn on the video and in a harsh whisper record everything I know or think I know. I outline how Edward's being threatened by Joseph Irondale for telling the truth about his rotten, druggy kid. About Elena and Edward being half siblings. About Edward being tricked into marrying her.

I detail how before she died, Beatriz Osler created this blackmailing scheme to ruin Lawrence Osler and his family as revenge. How Beatriz squandered the $300,000 she got in lieu of child support and alimony, and then blamed Lawrence Osler for her poverty.

I tell of the murder of Marshall Stohl in his sick bed, smothered with his own pillow by Elena Osler because he wouldn't undo changes to Edward's inheritance trust. I quote what I heard on the baby monitor, Elena chasing Kim Park down the stairs, stabbing her and letting her fall to the basement because Kim had seen Elena murder Marshall.

I tell about Edward Osler's complicity in hiding who did these murders to save his family's reputation. His attempt to throw Elena overboard, and their escape from his cabin, leaving a ship's officer bleeding in the corridor. I describe my own two stabbings.

Then there's Detective Garry Clere. My heart sinks. Because of his attempt to catch and stop her, he has been murdered by Edward Osler on orders from Elena.

Tears stream down my face as I repeat Elena's threat to get my children if I tell anything. I beg whoever's viewing this video to protect Stevie and Sally. Then the phone slips from my hand, the battery almost dead. I, too, am almost done.

But there's one last thing. I force strength into my hand, pick up my phone, and post everything on YouTube. I've decided who will get the link.

He's the only one distant enough from this to be able to take the evidence to the police, and make something happen. I have to trust him. Surely I can still trust him. He cared about me and the children once. I email the link to Dale Forsyth.

He isn't to open the link unless I die in suspicious circumstances. I fall back onto the pillows and am about to give in to sleep when my cell phone rings. I grope around the bed for it, finding it tucked under my arm.

"Hello," I say groggily.

"Mommy, where have you been? We've been trying to call you all yesterday morning." It's Stevie.

"I'm sorry sweetheart. I didn't hear my phone. Are you having a good time with Daddy?"

"Yah and he wants us to stay for New Year's night. Can we? Chloe says we can stay up as late as we want and try champagne."

That treacherous viper.

"Chocolate, my Mommy," Sally chirps in the background.

"And Sally really wants to stay," he adds, almost as good at manipulation as his father, "because Chloe promised her a chocolate bar for her very own."

I start to cry. They're having a good time without me. They come cheap, too, a bit of laxity and chocolate. The phone voice changes.

"Sara, we're keeping them in Collingwood for New Year's Eve," says a woman who has to be Chloe. I've never spoken to her myself.

"You child thief, and husband stealer," I hiss, feeling impotent rage, unable to stop her rampage through my life.

There's a frozen silence, then her voice continues, this time cold and hard.

"They'll be home New Year's Day." And she can't resist adding, "They'll have more fun with us than being alone with you on New Year's Eve." Bile rises in my throat. "There's night skiing in Collingwood every year and of course, the kids want to go in the outdoor hot tub and on the toboggan ride. So, you'll see them in the New Year," and she hangs up.

I drop the phone on the sheet, its battery finally dead. Everyone I care about is gone. Stevie, Sally, Marshall, Edward, even Garry Clere. I feel the bandage on my neck loosen from the strain of my convulsive crying. Warm blood dribbles down onto the pillow. Then the wound in my stomach starts throbbing.

218

I know the only thing that'll stop this descent into terminal depression's chocolate. A pile of chocolate the size of the CN tower, also chocolate cake, and chocolate biscuits with chocolate icing in between. I twist to my side to ring for the nurse. I don't care that blood's spreading on my pillow or that my sheets are soaked red from my weeping stomach wound. All I want is a little sweetness in my life.

Out of the blue, OA Monica comes to mind. She said just call on God and these food thoughts would stop. But I don't want to call on OA God or anything else that will prevent stuffing my feelings into oblivion with chocolate. A thought intrudes on my food fantasy. Cake, cookies, and chocolate have never relieved my pain for long.

"Oh, God," I moan. "Help me, help me, help me help help help help."

"Nurse!"

My eyes snap open. Detective Clere's staring at me, his knuckles white as he grasps the call button.

"Nurse, Emergency!" he bellows over his shoulder.

"You're alive?" I whisper. "But Elena sent Edward to kill you."

Clere freezes for a moment. "Yes, that was her plan. But in fact, Edward saved me. He knew we were both in danger, so he told Elena he'd dispose of me. That way she let him out of her sight, and he alerted me. Elena's gone over the edge."

Edward's alive? Garry Clere's alive. My kids are okay in Collingwood with their father and his person. Just one more to locate. "Where's Ronnie?"

"She's at your place, taking a nap I believe. Your stabbings are wearing her out."

My world's spinning in a new direction. I asked for help from Monica's God, and this is the result? What a system!

The nurse bustles in, clucks at me as if I'm a naughty child, and efficiently changes my blood-soaked bandages. Then she tugs the bloody sheets out from under me, and gets Clere to shift me while she remakes the bed.

Once she fusses out, I ask Clere, "How did I get to the hospital this time?"

"Ronnie found you, again, and called 911. You lost a lot of blood, so naturally, Ronnie had to be sedated." Clere grins, pleased with his little joke. "A police reporter for the Star heard it all on the police monitor, and posted it in their online paper. It's all over the media now."

I sigh in relief. "Everything's ok now. But where's Elena?"

Clere says, "She's still on the loose, but we think she's in Collingwood."

41

DECEMBER 30   6PM

I pry open my eyes open. I feel groggy. A news reporter's excited voice comes from a TV mounted on the wall.

"The manhunt for Elena Osler goes on after her brutal attack on Sara Forsyth, the second in as many weeks!"

Now I remember why I'm groggy. Detective Clere told me Elena Osler's in Collingwood, near my children. I must have reacted like a maniac.

A young redhead peeks in. "You're awake? That's good because we have a phone call for you. Your cell was dead so he called at the nurses' station. Do you feel up to taking it? It's your husband."

I have to warn him about Elena, to be extra careful with the kids. Dale has no idea who she is or what she's capable of.

I grab the hospital phone from the bedside table.

Dale, sounding agitated, says, "What are you doing in the hospital, for Christ's sake? Can't you take care of yourself for five minutes?"

Awww, he loves me.

"How are the kids, Dale?" There's dead silence. "Where are my children, Dale?"

"Chloe met a lovely woman here...."

"Dale, I don't care about Chloe! Where are...."

He doesn't pause. "Gorgeous, actually, that long black hair, bluest eyes I've ever seen. I didn't let on, of course. No need to get Chloe jealous."

I clap my hand over my mouth. It's Elena.

"...and we wanted a little together time, Chloe and I, and the woman, Chloe would know her name, the woman said she'd be glad to take them for hot chocolate, and a toboggan ride, but we can't seem to find ...." his voice trails off.

I hang up. Elena Osler has Stevie and Sally.

The phone rings again. I grab it. "Dale, if she hurts one hair on their heads, I'll hunt you down and I will kill you."

There's a soft snicker. "He's a loser, isn't he?" says Elena Osler. "Someone here wants to say hi to Mumsie." There's a pause, then Stevie's voice comes on, tight and scared.

"Mommy, where's Daddy?" He yelps. "That hurt!"

Elena hisses, "Shut up."

I can hear Sally sobbing in the background. "Point, point, point...." She needs me because she's terrified.

I sit up so fast I rip the IV out of my arm. "You touch one hair and I'll kill you!" I shout. "You and your whole insane family!"

Elena snickers. "Oh, Sara, even Edward, your lover boy, but my husband? Now, listen to me you fat cow. I'm Chloe's new best friend. She hates your kids, by the way. Happy to let me take them for a toboggan ride so she and her sugar daddy could have some alone time. You get it, Sara? Nobody loves your children except you, and I have them."

"If you touch—"

"You mean like this?" There's a squeal from Stevie.

"Stevie! Sally!" I scream. But the phone line is dead.

The redheaded nurse rushes into the room. "You're screaming, Mrs. Forsyth. That's not good for your stitches." She scoots over to look at my bandages. "And look what you've done to your IV." I shoot her such a murderous look she stumbles. "I'll just put in a call to your doctor for another sedative." She scuttles out of the room.

My hospital phone rings again. I snatch it up. "Mommy," howls Stevie, "we're hungry. Oww, you're mean."

Elena's raspy voice comes on the phone. "Sara, your children are hungry. Are they allowed to eat cigarettes?"

Bile rises in my throat. "What do you want?"

"I want you to tell the police I stabbed you in self-defense."

"Self…?"

"Don't you remember? You came after me with a dagger in a jealous rage over Edward? You attacked me and were going to stab me. I grabbed the dagger from you and in self defense, I accidentally cut you."

My heart's pounding so hard it hurts. But, I ignore it because my children's lives depend on it.

"I stabbed you twice, is that what you want me to say?" I can't help it. I add, "You are a lunatic!"

"I told you to die when I stabbed you, Sara, but no, you wouldn't. So, now it'll have to be one of these brats."

Sally yelps.

"No!" I cry, shaking my head from side to side in helpless impotence. Suddenly, a warm stickiness oozes down the side of my neck. I've reopened the wound, the Elena cut. My breath comes in short gasps. "Leave the kids alone, Elena. Okay? What do you want me to say to the police?"

"I already told you, you stupid pig. Say I cut you in self-defense. There were no witnesses, so it's your word against mine, anyway. If we tell the same story, what can they do to the clever Elena?"

She's talking about herself in the third person. Isn't that what psychotics do? What else do psychotics do? The children are silent. What has she done to them?

"Elena, of course I'll say it. But surely you know the police won't buy it."

"Maybe not at first. They'll put us both in jail until they believe it. "

I shudder. If Elena tells that story, I'll be charged until they clear my name. That means a police record. How will that play out in a custody battle against Dale?

There's a scuffle and Elena snarls, "Stop pushing me, you little brats!"

My children are fighting back. There's a slap. Sally howls in terror. No one has ever hit her.

"Ow! You little brat, I'm going to bite you back." A howl from Stevie. My children are fighting against an adult monster.

"Elena, Elena!" I shout to distract her from them.

She shrieks, "Stop that, you little monster!" Another hard slap. Stevie howls louder. She huffs into the phone, "Are you hearing this, Sara?"

"I hear it," I whisper, frozen in despair. She has killed two people and tried to kill me. What will she do to little children?

"Now you listen before I silence these brats of yours for good. You tell the police you'll never testify against me. You'll say nothing about Marshall and that little nurse. You got it?"

I'm breathing hard, trying to ignore the searing pain in my body. "Yes, I'll do that."

"You'd better if you hope to get your squalling brats back, in one piece. You understand? Your silence is for life, just as their lives are in my hands for life. You get that? "

Threats and blackmail: Elena Osler's stock and trade. But these aren't empty threats. If she got my kids this time, she can do it again.

"I get it. I'll never testify against you for Marshall Stohl or Kim Park's murders, or your attacks on me. And my children will live as long as I keep your secrets."

Marshall and Kim must be turning over in their graves. And I'll have to live with her shadow over my head for the rest of my life, or for as long as Elena Osler remains alive.

As quick as the idea appears, it draws me in. Her death would benefit so many people. How can I arrange it? But as soon as the thought appears, I'm shocked at myself. Her wickedness has infected me. It'll grow if I let it. Isn't that what happened to Elena, fed by a foul mother's revenge? I don't want to go that route.

"Let me talk to Stevie." But there's no answer. The phone's dead. I start to tremble. Where are my children?

The nurse presses herself against the door as Garry Clere strides into the room. "What's going on? Who was on the phone?"

I look into his beautiful, worried face, close my eyes and say nothing. The nurse helps me lie back down, and starts to remove the blood-soaked bandages from my neck and stomach.

Clere keeps up his questions, but I never open my eyes, I never open my mouth, and I never will. Clere knows I won't answer him now. What he doesn't know is I'll never answer his questions about Elena Osler, or Edward Osler, or his entire dysfunctional family.

Wait, that's wrong. There's only one dysfunctional member of that family, and she has a cruel hold over me.

Clere interrupts my thoughts. "I'm on my way to Collingwood to find Elena Osler. You have to help us get her, Sara. She's a maniac." He hurries out.

I lurch over the side of my bed and retch on the black and white tile floor. When I stop, Clere's gone, and Ronnie's leaning over me.

"Geez, Sara, you're throwing your whole guts up." She sinks beside me on the bed, grabbing my cold hands. "I've a mind not to give you the doughnuts I brought us."

I don't speak. I'm praying under my breath, "Don't let her hurt them don't let her hurt them don't let her hurt them..."

"Did you hear me, Sarie? Coconut doughnuts, your faaaavorite," she sings. But I ignore her. I must pray. "Sara, what's the matter with you? You're scaring me."

I think of that OA God who has been working lately, and I have nowhere else to turn. "OA God OAGod OA God, don't let her hurt them don't let her hurt them don't let her hurt them...."

Something's shoved under my nose. I smell coconut. I push it away, sticky icing clinging to my fingers.

Ronnie knows me. Only one thing can be affecting me like this. We lock eyes. "Sarie, where are the children?"

226

I have to concentrate. "Help help help help OA God OAGod OA God don't let her hurt them don't let her hurt them don't let her hurt them...."

"Sara, are you praying?" Her voice's a mixture of shock and terror. She's never seen me pray. She pushes her fingers against my lips to stop me. I grab her hand and squeeze hard, like I'm in childbirth. Ronnie squawks, tries to yank it away, and then stops trying.

She whimpers. "Sarie, where are our children?"

I moan.

Ronnie closes her eyes and though she doesn't know who I'm addressing or why, she starts to chant with me, "Don't let her hurt them don't let her hurt them don't let her hurt them...."

42

DECEMBER 31   10AM

In the morning, Constable Cochran rolls a wheelchair into my room. The police think it best for me and the security of the hospital if I recuperate at home under police protection.

Ronnie looks like death warmed over, having slept once again in a chair by my bedside all night. She dozily packs up my things, following us in her car.

Detective Clere's sitting in my living room when we arrive. How am I going to lie to him given he saw me after each Elena attack? The likelihood of his letting go of the woman who did this is nil. Momma's boy or not, he's as tenacious as any police officer I've encountered.

But, he'll have to take my changed story that she cut me in self-defense because I'll never admit to the truth again.

"We combed Collingwood, but we couldn't find a trace of Elena Osler. Do you know where she is, Sara?"

He calls me by my first name these days, as if we're friends. I do like the man, but he doesn't realize he's my enemy now.

My mantra must be: Elena Osler stabbed me in self-defense. That will bring my children home safe. I must believe, past evidence to the contrary, that Elena Osler will keep her word.

He settles gingerly on the couch beside me. Ronnie whips open a new box of doughnuts. She must have detoured to get those. I would have, too, in the old days.

Clere takes one, but I'm as shocked as Ronnie to hear me say timidly, "Can I have tea and whole-grain toast instead?"

Surely this miracle will beget another miracle, and my children will be coming home safe. If this God thing can make food disappear before my eyes, what's bringing home a couple of small children?

Her red curls quivering outrage, Ronnie disappears into the kitchen to make a traitor's snack. I lean closer to Clere and whisper, "Where are my children?"

"We found your kids in Collingwood with your ex-husband and his, um…"

I blubber, "Oh my God, oh my God." I bend to hug Garry, but gasp in pain. He catches my hands in his strong ones.

"They were there all this time, Sara, just as your husband said. What did you think?"

Have I given myself away already? I shiver. "Oh, silly me. Of course they were. Just a normal, worrying mother." I stretch my lips to form what I think is a smile.

Clere nods thoughtfully. "Well, we still need to talk to your kids when they get home in a couple of days, in case they had an interaction with Elena Osler."

I gasp. "No. The kids cannot be interviewed!"

"Why not?" He leans forward, "What do you know about their activities in Collingwood, Sara?"

OA God, give me the words. I feel that warmth melt over me again. "I wasn't there, Garry, but I know the kids will be tired from the trip, and not ready to do much more than have a nice bath. Can it wait?"

Clere narrows his eyes. I'm afraid. I say the first thing that enters my head. "Dale plans to relocate to B.C., and sue for sole custody. I have to make my claim first, and forcefully. This business with Collingwood, and all that, will make my case stronger. Do you know a lawyer who does custody cases?" I ask.

He pounces. "What business in Collingwood?"

I should have prayed before I spoke. I press my lips together. Clere knows something's wrong and, given his record for persistence, he won't give up.

Ronnie arrives bearing a wooden tray of fragrant Earl Grey tea, crisp toast, and the few remaining doughnuts she didn't eat in the kitchen. When was the last time I had solid food? It hasn't even crossed my mind till now. Maybe I'll lose weight over all this? What a trivial silver lining that will be. I wolf down the toast and tea, ignoring the rest.

Ronnie devours the last of the doughnuts, washed down by black coffee. Clere refuses any more. We stare at him. "My mother and I have a weight loss contest going. She's put on a lot of weight, being in that wheelchair all day. So I challenged her to weight off."

We look Garry Clere up and down. The man doesn't have an inch of fat on him. He'll vanish if he loses a pound.

Ronnie pushes next to Garry on the couch. "You've been taking care of an ailing family member for a long time?" This is something she can identify with.

The front door bangs open and Stevie and Sally tear into the room, throwing themselves on me. The pain from the dagger wounds surges against every nerve, but my rush of joy over seeing them outweighs everything. They're home early. The Elena incident must have scared them homesick.

"Mommy, we skated, and skied. Sally fell a lot."

"My Mommy, I fell in big snow." Sally raises her snow-suited arms high above her head.

"And Daddy made a snowman with us." I look up to see Dale standing in the doorway, alone, a bulging paper bag in his hand. He's watching me steadily.

"And Daddy bought sups." Sally reaches up and pats the bottom of his paper bag.

Stevie translates, "Submarine sandwiches, Mommy."

Dale steps back. "But I didn't know you had company. I brought lunch. I thought we could all eat together, and talk."

Clere stands up, approaches Dale, and puts out his hand. "Detective Garry Clere, Toronto Police."

Dale frowns. He hisses at me, "Sara, why are the police here? What have you done now?"

Awww, my caring husband's back.

Ronnie fumes, "Get lost, Dale!"

"No," Clere says, in command. "Mr. Forsyth, I need you to answer a few questions—before I show you out of the house." Clere prods an irritated Dale into the kitchen.

Once they're out of the room, Ronnie whispers, "That Garry Clere's so attractive."

Good Lord. The woman has the memory of a goldfish.

"Ronnie, Garry Clere is…"

"Captain Monet was attractive, too, but he's not over his wife. Plus, he's totally disinterested in having kids." She muses for a moment. "I bet Garry Clere would make a good father, though. He's so sweet himself."

"Yes, he's very sweet, Ronnie because remember…."

Stevie interrupts: "He's not a real policeman. He doesn't have brass buttons."

"He's a detective, dear," I say, thrilling him.

Ronnie chimes in, "It's lunchtime, kids. Where's that bag of subs?"

I indicate the end table.

"Beat you into the dining room." She races off. The kids untangle themselves from me, and tumble after her.

In the kitchen, I hear Clere's voice rise and fall, then Dale's rise and stay that way. He storms out of the kitchen, glares at me, and bangs the door on his way out.

Clere saunters back into the living room and sits in the green-flowered armchair opposite me. He shakes his head. "He's gone, but he's up to no good regarding you, and especially your kids."

Don't I know it? We sit in silence as I chew on this for a while. Even now, I would have taken him back to recreate a family circle, anything to give the kids a happy home. Didn't I send the YouTube link to him? But how long will I fool myself?

What was his response when he called the hospital to talk to me? He didn't utter one word of concern for my condition. What's his reason for wanting his children? To use them as pawns to further his business interests. How did he react when he discovered a policeman in our living room? He accused me of having done something wrong. And of course there's Chloe-the-Very-Thin. Maybe it won't last, but once she's gone, given he's done it once, it's likely there will be another Very Thin.

Like OA Monica said, why would you stay where you're not loved? No matter how pretty the picture of a Mommy and a Daddy and a little boy and girl, no matter how easy it would be in some respects, I stay only when I'm treated with love.

I don't want to be with the man he is. He has bad character.

"Dale wants the kids to move with him to B.C. for his business image."

Clere clears his throat. "Maybe that's not such a bad idea, Sara. Your kids might be safer in B.C. Far away from all this."

He's right. In B.C., they'll be far away from Elena Osler. Maybe I'll move there, too. I can reinvent the B&B. The kids can live with Dale and Herself, which avoids the B&B dangers he's so sure are there.

But can I recreate my life? Ronnie won't come with me, will she? What about Edward? He isn't mine. And Edward's an unknown. I can't run my life and the safety of my children on that hope.

I'm scared and angry at everyone. Why hasn't Elena Osler been caught, ending my misery?

Clere smiles sadly. "I hate to see a family break up, especially when there are kids involved."

"What would you know about it?" I snap. "You don't have children."

Clere looks away. "I'd give anything to have that opportunity."

Why's it easy to see solutions for other people's lives? "Garry, other gay men have figured it out. Use a surrogate mother, or find a woman who wants to have a child but doesn't want a full time partner. You could arrange joint custody. "

I've never seen a light bulb going off over someone's head. His face lights up. His stands up and looks towards the diningroom.

"Maybe I should help Ronnie with lunch. Are you hungry?"

"No, tension has curbed my appetite."

He whirls around. "You mean Elena Osler?"

I clamp my lips tight and stare straight ahead.

"That was her who called you in the hospital, wasn't it, to threaten your kids if you, what, do something or don't do something for her?"

He steps back towards me, willing me to speak to him. I want him to catch Elena Osler because with her in jail, the kids and I'll be free of danger. But what if Clere can't catch her, and she finds out I talked?

Clere urges, "Sara, tell me. I'll help you. I'm your best bet."

He's pleading with me, tempting me, but I learned all about betting from my father. It's a loser's game. My only chance to save my children is to avoid telling him anything.

I need strength to resist him, though, so I begin to pray, "Helpme helpme helpme ...."

Clere's phone rings abruptly. He grabs it out of his pocket, listens for a few seconds, and then leaves the room to talk in private.

Well, that was helpful.

43

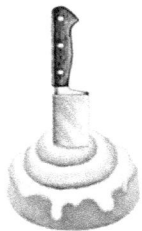

DECEMBER 31   2PM

R onnie saunters back into the living room after putting the kids
down for a nap.

"They're whacked out by that trip."

Clere grins at her. "You'd make a great mother.

Ronnie says, "I love kids."

"Hey, I know what you mean. I'd like to spend some more time
with your kids, Sara."

I look up in alarm. "Don't go trying to get close to my kids.
You just want to worm information out of them."

Ronnie blanches. "Sara, that was rude." Though I glare at her,
Ronnie says, "We want Detective Clere here for protection," she
adds sweetly, "and companionship. Detective, won't you like
dessert? We have," she winks at me, "Sara's homemade chocolate
macarons."

Clere looks puzzled. "I enjoy coconut macaroons. Why do you
pronounce it differently? Are these special somehow?"

Ronnie shakes her head in amazement at someone who hasn't
experienced French macarons. "These are meringue shells filled with

chocolate butter cream. The French prefer lavender or pistachio filling, but we prefer the Canadian way, don't we, Sarie?"

"I don't care for them anymore myself."

Ronnie jolts as if burned by a match. "You don't…? You made five dozen and ate them just days ago. You pushed me out of the way when I tried to get just one."

"Tea time," sings Detective Clere, slipping Ronnie's angry hand into his, and leading her to the kitchen.

Their conversation drifts back to me in the living room, light and girlish from Ronnie, deep and resonant from Garry Clere, but muffled, like I heard on the baby monitor. Where is Edward Osler?

Clere saunters back into the living room carrying a tray of pastries.

"Ronnie's making the tea."

He sets the tray on the coffee table, unfurls a large cloth napkin and ties it around my neck. Then he unties it, and does it again, ensuring it's just so. "This is what I do for my mother." He flashes a quick grin. "Now, you eat, I'll talk."

I lay my head on the back of the couch and close my eyes. "I'm not hungry."

"Well, then I'll eat and you can talk." I hear him lifting a plate. "First of all, your kids need…."

My eyes snap open. "You can't talk to my kids."

He stops mid-bite in a macaron. "Ever?"

Ronnie waltzes into the room pushing the tea trolley. "Oh, Garry, would you mind getting the tea mugs from the counter?"

He looks intently at me for some seconds, then leaves. Ronnie watches him walk away, and then whispers, "Sarie isn't Detective Clere the cutest man you've ever seen?"

"Are you out of your mind? In the last week you've lost your husband, had a fling with a sea captain, and now you're after a cop. Has your brain melted?

She smiles like the Cheshire cat.

"Ronnie, Detective Garry Clere's a gay man. Do you understand? He's a homosexual. He dates m…"

"But, he wants children." She grabs two macarons and shoves them into her mouth. "We have so much in common."

She waves the plate in my direction. My children are under threat by a crazy woman and I'm sworn to lie for her for the rest of my life. In a knee-jerk reaction, I reach for a meringue.

But my sane mind fights back. I want to do what OA Monica said to stop compulsive eating, but I can't recall. A chocolate macaron's in my fingers when I remember: *You don't have to eat over it.* I put the cookie back on the plate.

Ronnie gapes at me. "Help us all!"

Clere hollers from the kitchen at a crash of pottery. Ronnie runs out of the room, taking the plate of macarons with her.

The hall phone rings. There's such a ruckus going on in the kitchen, they don't hear it. I press my fists into the couch to help me get up, but fall back at the pain. The phone keeps ringing. Rocking so the cushion pops under me, I manage to stand up and hobble over to the phone.

"Where's Clere?" It's Edward.

"Where are *you*?"

"My grandfather's missing. Let me talk to Clere."

The phone flies out of my hand. "This is Clere. Edward? Geez, I thought …. Yes, I can be there in 10 minutes." He drops the phone on the table. A cold wind whips in the house as he pauses at the open door. "I should have tapped these phone days ago. You're going to get that man killed." And he's gone.

"Edward, I need to talk to you. Edward?"

"Yes?"

"Do you know who has your grandfather? "

"I didn't say he was kidnapped, Sara. I said he was missing." His voice is low and unsettling. "What do you know about this, Sara?"

I know a lot more about this than anyone else with the exception of Elena Osler. I can't tell him anything, but I can give him a hint.

"Maybe it has something to do with Elena."

"Why hasn't that fool Clere caught her? Do we have to wait until everyone in my family's dead?"

236

The thought of Edward dead brings tears to my eyes. "But Elena needs your family alive to give her the blackmail money. If you're dead, no more money."

Edward's voice is ragged with strain. "Unless she can get it all now." He hangs up.

I stumble back to the couch. When is all this going to end?

44

DECEMBER 31   3 PM

S ally's sleepy cries echo downstairs through the baby monitor. Ronnie hears her and dashes upstairs before I can stand up. Who's the mother here anyway?

I turn to look despondently out the window. A yellow and black car pulls into the driveway. It's a taxi. A middle-aged woman bends to say something to the driver, then turns uncertainly, spots me in the living room window and waves. It's OA Monica.

"I hope this isn't a bad time, Sara." Monica flashes a warm smile at me. "I was in town on business and I'm on my way to the airport. But I have your phone number, looked you up in the reverse directory, and here I am."

I step aside to let her in. I'm at a loss for how to be a good hostess. Am I allowed to offer her food, a drink, anything?

Monica's eyes bore into me. "Sara, I don't remember you looking this pale on the cruise. Are you ill?"

To my horror, I burst into tears. Then I do the unthinkable. I tell her everything, every single thing, the blackmail of the Osler men, my stabbings, and to the threats on my children's lives if I don't lie about Elena.

I've no idea what I expected Monica to say after hearing such stories. But, I don't expect her to clutch my hands, close her eyes, and begin to pray:

"God, we ask for Your guidance. 'Step 1, We admitted we're powerless over Dale Forsyth, and the Osler family situation, and our lives have become unmanageable.' Is your life unmanageable, Sara?"

"My life unmanageable?" I splutter. "That's the understatement of the decade."

"Okay, Step 2. 'Came to believe that a Power greater than ourselves can restore us to sanity.' That means you can be restored to emotional, mental, physical and spiritual balance, and see the whole truth. What's the whole truth here, Sara?"

I have no idea what Monica's talking about. Haven't I just spilled out the whole truth?

"May I take a run at it?" she asks. I nod. "The whole truth, it sounds like to me, Sara," Monica pauses, "is that most of this is none of your business."

I want to slap her across the face. Monica must have read my face because she sits back.

"Now, listen to me for just a second. You heard two murders on the baby monitor. Elena Osler has threatened to harm your children if you don't lie about this. Everything else about Edward and his family, and Elena and her half brother's none of your business." She rushes on as I blush. "Also, you didn't cause it, did you?"

I have to admit that I didn't cause the tawdry affair between Lawrence Osler and Beatriz Magyar. I didn't cause the blackmail she and Elena cooked up. Nor did I cause Edward and Elena's deal to hide the truth about her murdering Marshall Stohl and Kim Park.

"No, I didn't cause any of it."

"You can't control any of the people involved either, can you?"

I look away. "No."

"And, here's a news flash, sweetie, you can't cure the situation. Not really. You can't sail in on superwoman wings and be the hero. It isn't your life. Your life involves calling in expert help, that's the

Detective, Clere, is it? Let him in on the details. That guy's working his buns off trying to solve this hideous crime," she pauses, "and prevent future crimes."

I pale at the implied threat to my children.

"Your only job's to be rigorously honest about what you've seen. Once Clere knows everything, what's-her-name will be in jail in a second, and your kids will be safe. And once you've told what you know, you'll have done your part."

I sigh so deeply I think my heart will slide out of my mouth. No more threat to Stevie and Sally.

"You with me so far?"

"I am. And I'm starting to feel better by the minute."

"Okay, now, Step 3. 'Made a decision to turn our lives and our will over to the care of God, as we understand God.' That means you turn your thoughts and your actions over to the care, the loving care of any God you like. I personally like God as a name, but it's up to you. Do you call your god God?

I smile faintly. "Lately I say OA God."

"Nice one." Monica chuckles. "Now, all you have to do's your part. Be rigorously honest about Elena, and leave the results up to OA God. He'll take care of you and your children. Does OA God have a good track record with you lately?"

That Guy has been in my corner constantly these days. I feel warmth like honey once again pouring over my head and down my shoulders. I can't speak, only smile.

"Good, excellent. But, there's one thing you need to stop. You're too busy sticking your nose into other people's business." My eyes narrow, insulted again, but she ignores me.

"You aren't doing enough about your own life. For example," she points at the stain of blood seeping through my abdomen bandage, "Are you getting all the medical help you need?"

I am so peeved by her calling me nosey I refuse to answer. How mature.

She inhales deeply. "What about your life? Your family? Your dreams? You need to pay attention to that. "

I blurt out, "All I want to do is run my bed and breakfast so I can be a stay-at- home Mom."

"And what about your own dreams, not those of your children?"

I honestly don't know. They've been my only focus for years. Monica looks down the hall and her eyes light on the kitchen. "That's one professional-looking oven you've got there."

I redden. "I bake a lot, as must be obvious."

She looks at my face, not my body, her eyes are soft with compassion. "So, that's your goal in life, to create delicious desserts?"

I shift uncomfortably. "Maybe. But that's not all."

"What else? Because what you want, what your dreams are, this is how your Higher Power communicates with you."

"Okay, I want to do more than bake award-winning caramel brownies. I want to help people with my baking, somehow."

Monica sits still, listening, waiting. "So, what's the problem?"

"I can't do anything like that until I have my home situation resolved. If I don't put in a partition to separate the B&B bedrooms from the family sleeping quarters, Dale will get the courts to give him custody of the kids when we divorce. But I don't have the money to do it. "

"Once you're divorced, won't you get a settlement?"

I groan. "No. He's got the child support locked up in a trust till the kids are each 18 so I can't touch it. A judge actually believed his lawyer that I was a danger to their financial well-being. I'll get the house only if I buy him out which means taking on a higher mortgage. If the B&B keeps up its present success, I'll be able to afford that, but I need the money now to put in the partition. Without it, Dale might get the kids. "

Monica takes my shaking hands into her calm ones. "So, you're also powerless over money for the partition."

I bark a laugh. "Powerless is an understatement. Food, too."

"I beg your pardon?"

I blush, but if this entity can help me with Elena Osler and money, surely it can help me control a little bingeing. "I have an overeating problem."

She laughs. "Sara, did you not hear the name of the program I go to? Overeaters Anonymous. I can assure you, God can handle your food problems, too, if you ask for help. Try it."

I know what she's asking me to do, but suddenly I think it's ridiculous. Why would a god care about a trivial thing like what I eat for dinner? I say nothing.

She sighs. "Well, first things first. You have an urgent money situation. So, what would an emotionally balanced, sane Sara do in this money situation?"

"I'd go over all my stuff."

"Excellent. Do you have any assets besides this house, like stocks, bonds, jewelry?"

With a flash, I remember my safe deposit box. There's my grandmother's engagement ring worth $25,000 last estimate. Though I want to keep it for Sally, selling it would pay for the renovation. In my state of panic, I hadn't thought of this before now.

"I can sell my grandmother's diamond engagement ring. That will be enough."

She screws up her face. "So, why don't you look happy?"

"Because it's the only family heirloom I have. I wanted to pass it on to Sally."

"Ok, let's try a God minute."

I look at her quizzically. She closes her eyes and murmurs, "God, please guide us to right thinking and right action. We align our wills with Yours." Then she stops talking.

I sit beside her on the couch, trying to keep my eyes closed but more interested in seeing what she's doing. I peek. She's just sitting there. So, I close my eyes again and wait in the silence.

After a minute or so, Monica whispers, "Time."

I open my eyes and look around. I feel refreshed, like I've had a nap. Monica's bright-eyed.

"I got an intuitive thought during that meditation." That was meditation? "You can get the money, and keep the ring at the same time."

This sounds too reminiscent of my father's scams. I stir uneasily.

"I bet the bank will give you a secured loan on a ring like that. Not for the whole value of the ring, but probably enough to get your partition done. You'll have to pay the loan back, but as it's for a business, you'll be able to deduct the loan interest on your income taxes. If you get a tax refund, you can use it to help pay off the loan. That way, the ring will still be there for your daughter."

I feel hot tears in my eyes. "What a remarkable solution."

Monica says, "Ask for a miracle and watch God show off. God has done for you what you could not do for yourself."

I'm not convinced OA God did this. I'm pretty sure OA Monica did it.

Monica says, "I have to catch my flight back to Vancouver, now but you have my phone number, right?"

I nod, though I've no idea where it is. Fortunately, Monica pulls out a business card.

"Why don't you call me tomorrow, and we can talk about how your day went, and where you can find an OA meeting. We suggest you attend six meetings to see if OA's right for you. And you can keep me in the loop on what's happening with your new life plan. Would you like that?"

What I'd like's for Monica to move into my house and be my on-call guru. I give her a kiss on the cheek, which she returns. And I feel peaceful.

She stands up, brushes nothing off her slim hips, and heads to the front door.

"Don't forget. Call me. If I'm not home, I'll get back to you within a day, I promise. But you're never alone. If you're uncertain about the next right step to take, or the next right thing to say, take a God minute, like we did. And use the Help prayer, remember it?"

Oh mammy, that's the one thing I do remember. The taxi's still in the driveway. We hug gently at the door. As the cab backs out of the driveway, my phone rings.

"Sira! How's the cow? I'm calling all d'way from Brinch, Newfinland. Do you remember me, Andy Nash?"

Oh I remember, and how. That kiss he gave his wife still lingers in my fantasies.

"I hiv a fivour to ask ya."

I smile. "If there's hug that goes along with it, I'm all yours."

He bellows a laugh. "D'at's wot I means. Yir me best. Me brudders 'nd woives saw Nora's goodies from Torono, now they wants to come d'ere. Do you hiv d'space?"

"When would they like to come?"

"End of the minth, Januery if you cin mange it. T'ree rooms."

I shake my head in wonder. All three rooms rented at the slowest time of the B&B year?

"Yes, of course. I'll book the space for you. How long will they be staying?"

"D'ey'll be siven nights last week of Januery. Good?"

I'm gob smacked. I'll be able to pay all the bills and more to the end of January now.

"Very good! What are their names?"

"Oh, sorry, Sira. Nash, all Nashes. Me brudders. Bot, then Nora's sisters will be there start of Febery for five nights, ya knows, and d'eir partners. Two Butlers and one Carruders."

I sit down.

"So, t'ree Nashes in Januery, last week, and then two Butlers and a Carruders in Febery, first week. What a wicked kitchen party that'll be!"

I now have enough business to pay all my expenses until Easter. After that, there's a convention in town and the summer, which is always busy.

I'm home free, and OA Monica hasn't been out the door five minutes. I can't deny it. This is a miracle.

When I hang up the phone, Ronnie's standing in the hall, staring out the window after the receding taxi, a wistful look on her face.

"If I go to OA, whatever that is, can I get to look like that woman?"

"Ronnie, I thought Captain Monet liked your body size."

244

"Sara, there's no more Captain Monet, I told you. Not only is he still in love with his dead wife, but he told me he never wants children. Now, Garry and I…"

"Ronnie, come on, you must know you're barking up the wrong tree."

She snaps, "Step 1: mind your own business."

45

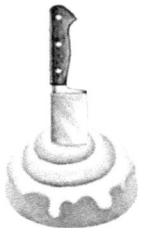

DECEMBER 31   5PM

I now have this God thing on my side, obviously. So, what am I doing? I'm sitting here like a slump on a log, marinating in Percocet and stress.

Edward's grandfather is missing. That dear old man. And I bet it's Elena. Ronnie saunters into the living room.

"The kids want Chalet Chicken."

My mouth gets slick at the thought of those French fries.

"Ronnie, you know I don't like them to eat that stuff."

"It's once, it's chicken, and it's a treat. I'll pay."

"Deal."

"What do you want for a side dish, as if I didn't know." She mimes dipping fries into that special sauce.

"Make mine a salad."

Ronnie totters off to call in the order as if she's a zombie, intoning, "Who stole my friend? Where's my friend? "

Stevie runs into the living room. "Mommy, Thomas the Train's on now. Can we please watch TV a little longer?" He raises his eyes and makes them big. "We've been through so much."

246

I snort. The little beggar. But, he's right. They've been through too much. I hug him tight.

"Mom," he pants, "you're killing me." I fling my arms open.

When's Elena Osler going to be put in jail? How hard can it be for Clere to find a tall, black-haired woman? Alright, it's hard.

I wonder why she kidnapped the old man? He's a good man, a Senator. What has she ever done in this world but make it darker.

But what can I do, especially in my present physical condition and drug stupor? My body isn't functioning and my brain isn't functioning. Big help I'd be.

Maybe I should just let the police handle things. Why not? Garry Clere's exceptional for a policeman, and helpful in many ways. I reach for my phone and call him. He doesn't pick up. Am I that unimportant to him, or might he be a little busy? I leave an urgent message on his voicemail.

I try again to force my turgid brain to work. If I get involved, I could be putting myself in danger. If I don't get involved, what, an old man may lose his life.

I turn to the best place I've gotten help lately, my new friend OA God. I settle myself, close my eyes, and take a God minute. As soon as I do, I get an image of my cell phone.

Of course! Senator Osler has my phone since he gave me his to use for long distance calls on the cruise. I can call him and ask him if he's alright.

My fingers tremble as I punch in my cell number. It rings once, twice, three times then goes to my voice mail. I'll leave a message and mark it urgent.

"Senator, where are you? It's Sara Forsyth. Remember? You asked me to keep tabs on Edward during the cruise. Can you call me back? Don't forget I have your cell phone, so call your own phone number and I'll answer."

I sit there for a minute. Now what? I decide to consult my oracle again. OA God, that was a good start. What's next?

Immediately, a thought pops into my head. Track My Phone. I set it up when I first traded with the Senator. The phones can locate each other. If he has my phone with him, I can find him.

And, I realize, I'd better find him because if the police find my phone at the scene of Elena's crime, whatever she did to him will implicate me. There'll be another police encounter, another black mark which Dale will use against me.

I punch Settings and press Find My Phone. The spokes of the small circle begin to twirl. A map appears. I tap the phone icon. A pulsing blue circle beams out the phone's general location.

I widen the map. The street's Lakeshore Boulevard. But, that's in downtown Toronto. The icon keeps turning and turning, and finally the blue dot settles on a brown rectangle. It looks like a hotel, no, motel. There's a park on one side of it and a children's playground on the other. It's only 40 minutes from here. I can easily get there.

I enlarge the image to see what else's in the area to help identify the motel. Lake Ontario spreads out right at its front door. The motel's actually on the lake shore, just as the street name promises.

I google Lakeshore Boulevard motels, and am thrilled to see there's only one hit, the Beach Motel. Now I know where Senator Davis Osler is, but is he in danger? I decide to call Edward. After all, it's his grandfather. I punch in his number but voice mail clicks in.

"Edward, I know where your grandfather is." I mark the message urgent. Then I text him. I wait a few minutes. No response. What if Elena really does have the old guy? She's killed two people, attempted to murder me, and if she has Senator Osler, there's little doubt what she'll do.

I text Clere, wait a few minutes, but no response. So, it's up to me. I'm the only one who knows where the Senator is, and given Elena, it can't wait.

I begin the prayer, "Helpme help me, helpme." Gingerly, I push myself into a standing position. Nothing hurts. I walk to the coat closet, at a slower pace than usual, but acceptable.

I know there's a constable watching the front door, but it's not Cochrane anymore. The new cop doesn't know me or Ronnie. And I don't think he can force me to stay in the house. Clere thinks I'm still in danger, but I know I'm not. My assailant won't harm one hair on my head. We have an ironclad deal. But, to avoid any debate, I slip on Ronnie's red winter coat and fuzzy white hat.

I step onto the front walk and the police officer opens his cruiser window.

"Going somewhere, Mrs....?"

"Stohl, Ronnie Stohl."

"Good evening, Mrs. Stohl. I'm Officer Sean Dudley, here to keep on eye on things for you."

"Yes, I know you, Officer, and I appreciate your help. The thing is, Officer, Sara's little children want dinner from Chicken Chalet and they've been through so much, how can we refuse them, even if it's junk food?" I chuckle, mustering every ounce of Ronnie charm I can muster.

"But, wouldn't it be easier for you just to call for delivery?" he asks genially, though his eyes are sharp.

"Yes, it certainly would be easier to get delivery, but the food's never hot enough when it gets here, so we reheat it and it dries out and the kids won't eat it. It's better in the long run if I make the short drive to pick it up."

His face remains impassive. I try a different tack.

"Officer, you must be freezing out here. Why don't you go inside for a few minutes to warm up? That way you can keep an eye on things in the house until I get back. I'll even bring you a piece of chicken."

He grins. "I just like the fries." Okay, so he's not dumb.

But he shakes his head. "I'm warm enough in my heavy clothes. And look at these." He pulls off his gloves and on his palms are hot packs. "They're life savers."

What's this? Another human cop? He takes a deep breath, and nods. "Better get their dinner then."

I walk as quickly as I can manage to my car before he changes his mind. Miracle of miracles, it's clear of snow. I set my GPS for the Beach Motel.

I back hastily out of the driveway, keeping an eye on the cop who's keeping an eye on me.

46

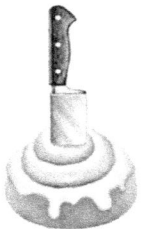

DECEMBER 31   7PM

T he Beach Motel's located in front of Sunnyside Beach. We used to go there in the hot weather when I was a kid since it was free, but I don't take my kids here now. The summer beach sand's littered with dead fish from Lake Ontario's contaminated waters.

No one's walking on the waterfront as far as I can see, too dark and too cold. The wind's whipping mounds of snow into the air. They've been there so long this winter, they're turning blue, like in that painting of Alaska.

I scan the dimly lit motel parking lot. There's only one car parked in the guest area. The building has a main storey and a thin metal staircase along the outside wall leading to a second storey. I check my Find My Phone setting. It's showing my phone on the upper level.

At the front of the building a light shines from what must be the front office. I park out of sight in the back and mount the rusting stairs as quietly as I can. I watch my phone screen as I walk along the metal balcony until the icon shimmers. It points to exactly where my phone is, Room 14.

I'm about to try the door when it dawns on me I don't have a weapon and Elena Osler always has that lethal dagger. Maybe I should call for the police again. But what if she's gone and they arrest me? I'd better check things out alone, first.

The curtains over the window are drawn. I lean my head against the door and hear a woman's voice snarling, "Shut up, you old liar!"

It's Elena. It's strange how through the door I recognize it as easily as the one I heard on the baby monitor.

A hoarse man's voice protests, "But, you don't know the whole story." That's Senator Osler. She does have him. And he doesn't sound good.

"You mean your family's lies about my mother, you scum?"

"You need to know the facts, Elena. Your father, my son Lawrence, gave your mother a lump sum of $300,000 instead of monthly child support and alimony."

"Which she never got."

"Your mother has been feeding you that lie all your life, but it's not true, it's not true. I'm your grandfather. I wouldn't lie to you."

"And my mother would? A naïve immigrant who your son seduced, impregnated, and then dumped. Dumped me! Left us to starve. Left us to die. She's dead, just as you've all wished. She died of poverty and neglect and a broken heart. But she left me to finish the job.

"And I'm going to finish off the rich Osler family. You'll wallow in poverty and disgrace as we did while I laugh all the way to the bank."

Elena says, "Give me your wrists. Now!" There's a ripping sound. What's she doing? "That'll keep you fastened to this chair, and this'll keep you quiet." I hear a sickening blow.

The motel door handle rattles. I scuttle to the other end of the metal landing where I turn my back, pretending to open a room door. High heel footsteps clatter in the other direction. A moment later, the car in the parking lot skids away.

I hurry back and try to open the Senator's door but it's locked. "Senator? Can you hear me? It's Sara Forsyth, Edward's friend? Can you let me in?"

If he doesn't open the door, there's no way I can break it down. The last thing I need's for my wounds to open. I hear nothing but silence. I need the key.

I stumbled down the rickety stairs to the front office. A neatly groomed young man perched on a stool looks up from a book and smiles.

I'm momentarily surprised. "You aren't the motel clerk, are you? "

He laughs. "I get that reaction a lot. I'm a medical student paying my way through school. How can I help you?"

I tell him my grandfather's in one of the motel rooms and may be ill. He leaps to his feet like Super Doctor man.

"I can help him."

"No!" I shout. "Call an ambulance. And the police. And give me the key to Room 14."

He twists around, locates the key, and throws it neatly to me as he grabs the phone. What a multi-tasker.

I steel myself to mount those stairs again. I'm afraid of what I might see behind that door. I turn the key in the lock and hear a feeble voice.

"Don't hurt me again. Please."

"Senator," I hiss, "It's Sara Forsyth. I've come to save you."

The Senator's eyes open slowly. He stares at me. "I'm in some danger," he croaks. "She told me she was coming back to kill me."

I'm shocked to see him. His wrists are tightly taped down onto the chair's arms. His face is slack face and there are two gaping cuts on his temple. Blood is flowing down his cheek. He's deathly pale.

"Don't talk now, Senator. We need a doctor to see you. I've called an ambulance."

He raises a shaking hand to touch his temple. "She hit me with her fist with that beautiful engagement ring Edward gave her. That ring was my wife's their grandmother." His eyes close.

Maybe I should have brought that medical student upstairs. Where's that ambulance?

"Listen to me," he says in an exhausted voice. "Write this down, in case…"

I dive into my purse for a piece of paper and a pen, but I yelp. I hit something jagged. I pull out my metal nail file. Perfect. I press my phone to record his account while I use my nail file to saw off the tape binding his shaking wrists to the chair arms.

"Elena called me earlier today. She said, 'Grandfather, it's your dear granddaughter.' She only contacts me when she wants something. Terrible girl, terrible."

I'm making progress loosening the tape. I pull it off one wrist gently, but he yelps as it rips out several grey hairs, leaving a red welt. I debate whether or not to remove the last bit of tape and decide to let the doctors deal with it.

"She ordered me to meet her here, alone, if I hoped to save the Osler family. What choice did I have? I called a taxi and took my cell phone so I could call a taxi for the return journey."

He's been talking with his eyes closed, but now he looks straight at me, his lips trembling with a small smile.

"It's not every Senator of my age who carries a cell phone, you know."

I nod my head in respect. The old guy's still a going concern. I want to hear the rest of his story, but I'm edgy. What if Elena returns before the police?

At that moment, I hear footsteps coming up the metal stairs. Is it Elena or the cops? Better safe than sorry.

"Senator," I whisper, "pretend to be asleep. I'm going to hide inside the bathroom. But, I'll be watching. I won't let her hurt you."

I dip behind the bathroom door leaving it open a crack just as a key grates in the lock. I see her enter the room and freeze.

"How did you get that tape off, old man?" She raises her fist with that huge diamond ring and aims it at his face.

I leap out of the bathroom. She reels back in surprise, then fury.

"You!" she spits. "How many times do I have to kill you?" Dagger forward, she lunges at me just as Detective Garry Clere bursts into the room.

"Toronto Police!"

She whirls around and shrieks, "She's attacking the Senator. Shoot her!"

Officers Erika Cochran and Michael DeBraie, my former protectors, barge into the small motel room, their guns aimed directly at Elena. And behind them stands Edward Osler.

Clere says, "Mrs. Elena Osler, you're under arrest for the murders of Marshall Stohl and Kim Park, and the attempted murder of Sara Forsyth. We have been looking for you for a long time. These officers will read you your rights as they drive you to the station."

He nods and Cochran and DeBraie handcuff a resisting Elena Osler, and force her, struggling all the way, down the stairs.

Clere turns to the rigid Senator Osler. "Sir, we have an ambulance parked in the back. Would you like them to come up and carry you down?"

The Senator bristles. "I'm a member of a venerable Canadian family, and a Senator." Edward moves quickly to help him up. But the Senator isn't done. "She told me if I didn't persuade Edward to release the funds of his final inheritance to her, I might get very hungry, like she and her mother were when she was a child and my son Lawrence left them to die.

"All those same lies and drama. I couldn't stand it anymore. I stood up to leave the motel room, but I'm old. She easily pushed me back into the chair. I hit my elbow wrong on the edge of the wooden arm. The pain made me cry out. Arthritis, you know. It comes to all of us. You should see my knees. Edward knows. I have an operation scheduled. I'm willing for them to do both knees at once, but they say..."

I whisper to Clere, "I think he's going into shock. We need to get him to the hospital."

He nods at one of the policemen who slips outside.

"She called me a dried up old fool. Then she whipped out a roll of tape and tied my wrists to the chair arms. I figured if I appeared terrified, she'd go easy on me. So, I made my eyes big, even managed tears. 'Don't hurt me. Please. I won't make a sound. Please, I'm old,' I whimpered.

"She yelled, 'Shut up or I'll gag you, too.'"

The Senator smiles. "I kept acting scared. You might not know this Edward, but I did Shakespeare in my university Curtain Club. It was good training because as a Senator, sometimes you need to playact.

"But Elena isn't stupid. She sneered, 'How convincing. Like, your check's in the mail. Except you never sent it.'

"'Elena, you're my granddaughter,' I said. 'I'm telling you the truth. Your mother drank, gambled, and wasted the money on crazy schemes, and…men.'

"That's when she hit me the first time. I felt woozy, but she shook me by the shoulder.

"'There'll be time enough after you talk to Edward, old man. Just a few little details to attend to first, then I'll be back and be rich, and head off to, well, never you mind where I'll be going.' She did that maniacal laugh that crazy people do.

"'You'll be hiding in your mortgaged mansion with hungry reporters clamoring for more details of your abuse of two innocent women, and,' she mocked, 'sibling incest.'"

He stops. Then he says, tears in his eyes, "This is how easily lies can ruin even an honourable family."

Edward finally interrupts. "Your Lordship, Grandfather, that's enough for now. Here are the ambulance attendants with a stretcher."

The old man bristles once again. "I am an Osler, and a Canadian Senator in the House of Lords. I'll walk under my own power." He smiles gently. "But I would appreciate it if you would take my arm, Edward."

Once they're out of the room, Clere turns to me. "I'm going to nominate you for a Civilian Citation. In the face of great personal danger, you helped the police in the performance of their duties."

I did help the police. I don't know whether to be ashamed or proud.

47

JANUARY 1   10 AM

I'm curled on the couch when Ronnie answers the doorbell. It's Dale. His shoulders are sagging, his coat's missing a button, and he's wearing a smarmy grin.

"How are you feeling, dear?"

My antennae go on high alert. Dale hasn't used an affectionate endearment for me in years.

"I'm doing as well as can be expected. Why?"

He oozes into the room and perches on the flowered chair opposite me. "How are the kids?"

My stomach drops. "What're you doing here, Dale?"

"Can't a husband come and visit his wife and kids?"

"Chloe dumped you."

He ducks his head, and then forces a tight smile. "Well, who dumped who's not important." I can't help it. I smile. "The important thing," he rushes on, "is that I didn't make a horrible mistake. Did you know, Sara, Chloe didn't actually like the children?"

"What are you up to, Dale?"

256

He scoots to the edge of the chair. "Sara, I was wrong, very wrong in what I did." He drops his head, but watches me through narrowed eyes. "I should never have left you for another woman. Why, you're twice the woman Chloe is." He snickers.

I move to stand up and show him the door, but he waves his hands frantically.

"No, wait, it was a joke, a silly joke." He clears his throat. "Can you forgive me, Sara?"

I'm speechless. The man wants to come back? I've fished my one-time wish, the millionaire's family again, with the older boy, the younger girl, and Mommy and Daddy bears. I have to admit it. For a second, that rosy picture fills my vision. But the fantasy fades quickly enough when I remember Dale's a snake. Nothing indicates that has changed. In fact, it's the opposite. He's still who he is. I'm spared giving him the boot when my cell rings. It's my divorce lawyer. Providential intervention?

"Dale, I have to take this. Why don't you go into the kitchen and make us some tea?"

"Tea? Who drinks tea?"

"I do. And I always have."

He scuttles out of the room.

"Louise, it's good to hear from you."

"Sara, you won't believe the good news I have for you. I appealed Marshall and Dale's judgment to put the kids' support payments into a trust fund, and the higher court overturned it!"

I'm having a red-letter day here.

"The judge acknowledged that Dale had contravened the first child support order by not giving you any money for two years. In order to avoid a repeat of that, the judge ordered his new lawyer to have Dale pay you a one-time lump sum in lieu of monthly child support."

That rings a bell. Where have I...?

Louise's still talking. "The figure's based on monthly amounts for two children from the time you separated until each is 18. Dale has to pay you $500,000. Right now." She chortles. "Oh, I'd love to see his face when he hears this."

"I think he's already heard it. He's here."

"Dale is at your house? I bet he's begging for reconciliation."

"Louise, when would I get the money?"

"Well, apparently, Dale has recently sold his business. He begged the judge to change the payments back to monthly because he wants to start some new thing out west. But the judge chided him. 'I have trouble believing your word you'll make those payments given your bad track record, Mr. Forsyth.' I loved it!"

"So, Louise, are you saying Dale has that money now?"

"Yes, and you'd better get your hands on it fast if you don't want him to tie it up in another business from which it'll take years to extricate it. I'll also be sending him my legal bills, all of them, even from the first go round, and so you're in for a refund there, too."

Dale walks back in the room with a tray of teacups, and a plate of my seven-layer cookies. So, he knew where I hid them all along.

"Keep in touch, Louise." I hang up the phone and glare at Dale. "Still moving out west?"

He places the tray carefully in the middle of the coffee table. He sighs deeply. "I've run into a little snag, Sara, and I was hoping you could, would help me out."

It's still all about him no matter who else will be hurt, even his children.

He clears his throat. "The thing is, Chloe has moved back in with her family who have a thriving Amway distributorship. They added Chloe as an additional applicant to transition the business over to her, Chloe being the next generation. She had agreed to add me as an additional applicant before the uh, change in our status. She's still willing to add me so we can work the business together, you know, sans benefits." He sighs.

"But now she wants a fee to do it, a big fee. She says I'm buying into a successful business, which of course I am, I know that. " He smiles weakly. "I sold my real estate business, so I thought I had the funds." He looks at me with big, sad eyes, which look so much like Stevie's, I almost weaken. He spots it. He can detect weakness at a 100 paces.

"I know I haven't been the model of the Dad the kids deserve." He bows his head. My stomach roils.

"What do you want, Dale?"

He looks closely at me. "Sara, have I asked for anything? You have become so aggressive."

"We call it assertive these days, Dale, you know, in the new millennium."

His face gets red. But when he speaks again, his voice's sugary sweet. "Sara, I want to give you something, not get something. I'd like to start making monthly child support payments to you right now." He pulls out a checkbook. "I'll even include the last two years." He starts to write on the check.

I can't help it. I laugh. He thinks I don't know the judgment against him, and he's trying to put one over on me, to buy their eighteen-year support payments at a two year rate. Then stop paying us as soon as he moves away.

"So, let me get this straight, Dale. You have a big business deal with the family of the woman who dumped you." He squirms but says nothing. "And you also want to make good on your legal obligation to your children." He nods with the phoniest smile yet. "But, you can't do this unless I ask the judge to reverse his decision to make you pay me the huge lump sum he's awarded us."

His expression changes like lightning. "You knew about the judgment all along, but you let me make a fool of myself?"

"No, Dale, you did that on your own. So, if I read this right, you no longer have a girlfriend, you no longer have a real estate business, and you no longer have the money to buy a new business in the garden province of Canada."

I hear the doorbell and voices in the foyer. Dale stands up and covers the ground between up rapidly. He leans over me, and threatens, "You'd better change that arrangement, Sara, or you'll see what I do to…"

Garry Clere and Edward Osler step into the living room. Clere grabs Dale. Between tight lips he hisses, "Are you uttering threats against Sara, Mr. Forsyth? That's against the law. Could mean jail time. Are we clear about that?"

Dale shrinks back. "I wasn't, she's, we were taking, that's all. Sara, tell this…"

"Detective Clere, Dale Forsyth not only threatened me, as you heard, but he was also trying to scam me into letting him change the child support process ordered by a provincial judge."

Clere's eyes snap onto Dale. "Now you are in trouble, Mr. Forsyth. Please sit in that chair while I make arrangements to interview you more closely at the station."

Dale shouts, "No! She's lying."

Edward says quietly, "Mr. Forsyth, I was in the room when you threatened Sara, and I'll be a witness for her if it comes to that."

I watch the drama unfolding before me, a triumph of good over evil. Except, I'm sorry it's come to this point. A husband and a father revealing the blackness of his character, selfish, callous, and unloving.

I'm glad I live in a society where this behavior isn't tolerated. I'm glad I have protectors, even if from unexpected places. And I'm glad I've finally accepted the whole truth. There is no point in self delusion.

48

JANUARY 1   1 PM

C lere grins. "Ding dong, the witch is dead, Sara. Elena Osler's behind bars and likely to remain so for many years."

Edward smiles at me. "And Grandfather's resting safely at home, thanks to you, sweetheart."

I note that 'sweetheart.' And I realize I've been holding my breath for years to hear it."

Edward turns to Garry with a warm smile. "Plus the help of our fine police department."

Garry Clere's eyes light up. Is it with appreciation or affection?

Clere says, "Listen, Edward, I need to confer with Ronnie about a personal matter. Will you fill Sara in on the rest? And by the way, Sara, I've handed in my commendation for your heroic actions. And I'm officially offering to mentor you should you ever decide to join the Toronto Police Service. It would be my honour."

The man actually thinks I'd join a police force? But then a thought pops in my head. If I were a member of a police force, I'd get to carry a gun and know how to use it. I'd have a cadre of armed buddies who'd run to my side when a released Elena Osler or one of her henchmen comes after me or mine.

On the other hand, I'd rather be a chef.

Edward's watching Clere's retreating back. He turns to me. "Clere told me he wants to discuss something unorthodox with Ronnie. Is she an unorthodox woman?"

I guffaw. "That's putting it mildly."

Taking my cold hands tight in his, he says, "Sara, it's all going to come out now. I married my half sister, my family tried to hush it up by paying blackmail. Unless I give her an alibi saying I was with her all evening, so she can't have been near Marshall and Kim Park, Clere told me she's going to implicate me in their murders."

"No! How can she do that?"

"Because you know and I know you know, I was there. " My hands begin to tremble. He says, quietly, "All you have to do is testify to what you heard, however you heard it. And what Elena said when she attacked you. It'll create sufficient reasonable doubt of my involvement to exonerate me. After all, they only have Elena's say so, and she's hardly a credible witness."

OA Monica said all I have to do's be honest, and OA God will take care of me and my children. But, what if Elena Osler has a long reach? She's already kidnapped my kids once. She could arrange to get them again. It's easy to trust God around cookies, but something else again to believe He'll save my children from a vengeful Elena Osler.

"I need you to back me up, Sara." I drop my eyes. Edward takes a shaky breath. "Well, whatever you do, we're letting it all come out anyway. My father will never get elected as an MP now. The Conservative Party has already rescinded his nomination. Our family tradition of public service, to give something back to the country that has treated us so well's over, another casualty of Beatriz and Elena.

Edward rubs his hand over his grim face. "Grandfather's not involved in any of this except in name. But his name's going to take a beating. He can't face the scorn of his peers, so he's retiring from the Senate.

"And Joseph Irondale will now have all the ammunition he needs to force me out of St. Ives. But first, he'll report me to the College of Teachers. My teaching license will be toast."

A family in tatters. No matter what I decide, their lives are never going to be the same. And what's my life going to be like now? After being threatened, and almost dying, twice, how do I proceed?

"One good thing from all of this is I can file for divorce, which I've wanted to do for years. It'll take time, but I'll be a free man." Edward single? I can't help it. I smile. "Without Elena draining my Trust Fund, I have the money to restart my inner city school. I don't need a teaching credential to be an administrator. The silver lining, if there's one, is this experience has changed my family's perspective on what's important. Grandfather has agreed to be the head of the School Board. His status should help override any gossip, not that those kids would care.

"And Dad will act as our legal counsel and fundraiser. Ronnie's going to help with the uniforms and classroom designs."

"My Ronnie?" I stammer. My worlds are colliding.

"If she's not too pregnant." He winks. "Ronnie and Clere are hooking up as partners, his body part and hers together at last."

I laugh. "So much for her manly man ideal." Then I add, "Yet Garry Clere's as manly as they come if you count character, heart, and courage. They'll make a great baby."

He rubs my cold hands. "But, I still need an executive chef to plan healthy but tasty breakfasts and lunches. Do you know anyone who might like to help disadvantaged, vulnerable kids? It's part time." He puts his arm around me.

"Assuming, of course, I don't get put in jail first as an accessory to murder."

All I have to do is be honest, testify to what I heard. Monica as good as promised OA God would protect me, but do I have the courage to believe it?

I have to because how I cannot let a man like Edward Osler go to jail for something he didn't do.

"I'm getting a divorce," Edward interrupts my thoughts.

264

I can't help it. I smile. "Maybe you and I can use the same lawyer and get a volume discount. "

Then he leans closer and whispers into my neck, "I'll have to work very closely with this executive chef in executive meetings long into the night."

My heart thuds, hard, too hard. Not a heart attack at this time of all times. The emotional high jinks of the past few days and two dagger wounds have done their worst. I feel myself slump against Edward, and I'm out.

49

JANUARY 1   6PM

I wake up to the smell of greasy fried chicken. Stevie and Sally are standing beside my bed, proffering a plate with a chicken leg and a pile of salad.

"Play horsey!" Sally beams.

"Not you, Mom," Stevie corrects. "Edward. He played horsey and we both got on his back and he galloped."

"Fall down!" Sally's eyes sparkle.

"Sally fell off him about 11 times."

Sally giggles, clearly none the worse for wear. Stevie plops the plate of food on my chest. "Edward made this for you. He said he'd sleep over so he can hug us in the morning."

"Good job, my Edward," Sally crows as they run out of the bedroom.

Edward, once again, is the hero in my life: cook, horsey, protector. I fall back into a deep, peaceful sleep.

It's still dark when I awaken, starving. A shriveled chicken leg and wilted salad are splayed across my duvet. I scrape it all into the garbage. I want something delicious.

Didn't Ronnie say something about chocolate macarons? I notice OA Monica's card on the bedside table near the phone. I pick it up and turn it over in my hand. But the thought of chocolate macarons is what gives me the momentum to get out of bed. I've eaten almost nothing in the last two days. I must be down a ton of weight. Anyway, I deserve a reward for what I've gone through.

I creep along the dark hall, lit only by a star-shaped nightlight. In the living room, on the couch is a large person covered by a quilt, snoring softly. Edward's still here. My heart leaps, then my stomach growls. I head for the refrigerator and open it. I see leftover chicken, and the box of macarons.

I've had a bad time. I need a little sweetness in my life. My hand reaches for the delicate chocolate cookies, then stops. Still in my other hand is OA Monica's card. Healthy food, in healthy amounts, at healthy times. The devil and the angel, which will win? I'm unable to choose.

Then a thought occurs to me. I almost lost my life. Am I willing to give it up now for a food whim, a bad choice? For my sake and for the kids, I want a healthy life, one worth living. I'll start the New Year right.I push the cookie box aside and take out the chicken. Healthy food in healthy amounts at healthy times. Of course, midnight's not a healthy time to eat, but two out of three ain't bad. To start.

That's the point; I have to start doing what's good for me. I glance towards the living room and realize what's good for me, and it has nothing to do with food.

I replace the chicken in the refrigerator, and walk into the living room. Snuggled into the back of the wide couch is Edward Osler. All I want to do is to lie down beside the man who has stood by me so many times and who I've loved for years.

Careful not to disturb him, I lift the patchwork quilt made of the children's outgrown clothes, and slide in beside him. He gives a heavy sigh, rolls over, and clutches me to him. This is it, the food I want. The Beatles got it right---All we need is love.

Suddenly, I hear a squeak on the baby monitor. My heart skips a beat. Not again! But it's only a mother's sweet voice hushing her baby back to sleep.

First thing tomorrow, no matter what the cost, I'm buying a new baby monitor.

The End

THE POINT

A line Strong is the author of the non-fiction book, *Live Well Within Your Means* published in 2014.

She also has binders full of poetry, plays, short stories, children's books and other novels, all best left to be discovered and marvelled at posthumously.

Her wonderful children are Michael Strong and his wife, Laura Howson, and Erika Strong. She lives in Richmond Hill, Ontario with her extraordinary husband, Davis Strong.

Point to the one who you love best.

www.ingramcontent.com/pod-product-compliance
Lightning Source LLC
Chambersburg PA
CBHW070324260626

47160CB00003B/945